YOUNGER

DANI LAMIA

WITH CLARE DEAN

Published by:
Level 4 Press, Inc.
14702 Haven Way
Jamul, CA 91935
www.level4press.com

Library of Congress Control Number: 2019943918

ISBN: 978-1-64630-767-8

Printed in the United States of America

Other books by
DANI LAMIA

Scavenger Hunt
The Raven
666 Gable Way

PROLOGUE

Lord Marryat heaves in a wheezy breath. The dust in the library is as thick as fog, brought about by the shedding of too much skin, too quickly. Oil lamps attempt to light the book-lined room, and in the dimness, the volumes appear as scales might on some sea monster. The mirror stands in the center of the room, ringed with a frame of brass gargoyles impaled together with thorns.

There is no comfort in this room, in this house, anymore. Only threat, only maleficence. Even the portraits of Lord Marryat and his wife when first married bring him no pleasure, no joyful recall, as they once did. They only underline the evil that has taken place here. They are reminders of the natural order that has been brutally disrupted.

The old man writes with aching fingers. He seeks solace in the journal, its truth his only remaining comfort. "*I pray that tonight we shall excise the daemon. But if we fail, I shall take her life and my own. There is no alternative.*" He reads the sentences back and splutters a scoff at their seeming absurdity, wishing they were fiction.

"Reverends Donohue, and Baker, and Deshon, my lord," Mr. Hartley announces, his once-clear voice now tired and worn. Lord Marryat struggles to his feet and reaches for his cane as his butler is followed by the clergymen.

"Reverends," Lord Marryat manages as he wobbles forwards. "I am in your debt. I am so grateful for your service." The old man hangs his head in respect, something he has rarely had to do in his life. Or perhaps he hangs it in shame. He has become the kind of man who pleads with the church for his wife to be exorcised. He doesn't recognize himself.

The church men are dressed formally, their garb transforming them into exotic birds, each draped with a purple stole. Reverend Donohue carries a small urn Lord Marryat supposes must be holy water. The thought of its sacredness brings a little relief, despite himself.

"Is everything ready?" the clergyman asks with a solemnity befitting the occasion.

"Of course." Lord Marryat gestures to the mirror at the center of the room, draped with an altar cloth embroidered with scenes from the twelve stations of the cross. The cloth is pulled to the sides, like stage curtains, held open by two gold chains and exposing the mirror itself. Across from the mirror there is a small table with lit candelabra, and on this table the religious men lay their urn, bible, crucifix, and rosary beads. Lord Marryat is unfamiliar with such objects. He is a man of science, not of silly religious fables. But still, the things he once dismissed as futile have bewilderingly become his last hope.

"Your wife?" Reverend Deshon asks.

Emotion catches in Lord Marryat's throat when he tries to reply, so he simply nods. Mr. Hartley takes his cue and leaves the room for a few moments. Wails echo from the hallway beyond, followed by a guttural scream, becoming louder as it approaches the room. Lord Marryat winces, trauma bending his diminutive frame into a defeated hunch. He stifles a sob as the door opens. The groundskeepers appear, burly and stony-faced, their strong arms pushing a large wrought iron cage as they wheel it through the door. Perhaps they already know what proximity will do to them. It's possible they already feel the effects of her.

The gnashing and snarling from the young woman within are purely animal. She pulls at the bars and tears at her clothes. Her corset loosens, revealing a full, round breast. Rather than making her appear vulnerable, she looks even more vicious, offensive. Lord Marryat can do nothing but hang his head, looking away in shame.

The groundskeepers don't react and deposit the cage in the center of the room as directed by Mr. Hartley before leaving, their heads lowered unquestioningly.

"Please. Extinguish the lamps," Reverend Deshon requests of Mr. Hartley, who complies as the young woman's screams reach an unbearable pitch. Donohue lifts the urn and sprinkles the holy water in a circle around the cage. The screaming intensifies, tearing feverishly at the air, and the woman clings harder to the iron bars, their sharp edges snagging her skin so that blood smears her fingers.

"Oh, dear lord!" Lord Marryat exclaims at the sight of his wife, almost unrecognizable in her current state.

Deshon and Donohue chant as Reverend Baker raises the heavy ornate crucifix high over the cage. With the steady light from the oil lamps extinguished, the flickering from the candelabra makes dancing shadows of the figures in the room.

Florence Marryat stabs her limbs through the cage bars, willing her escape. Her creamy, youthful skin is bruised and scratched as though she's been attacked by an animal. Lord Marryat sinks into a chair, holding his head in his hands. It is too unbearable, this contorted version of his wife, her nubile body twisted around an evil core.

Florence collapses in the cage, then looks up, apparently confused. "Francis?" she asks her husband, with a tremble. "Why am I in here? Don't you love me? How can you be so cruel to me?"

Lord Marryat turns away, with difficulty.

Florence seems to notice her torn corset for the first time. She begins to slowly unbutton it. "Francis, I need you. We need each other." She fully exposes both breasts. "We can leave, spend an entire weekend in bed."

Lord Marryat turns to the clergymen. "Reverend Donohue, shall we begin? Where do you want me?"

Florence snarls and resumes her inhuman screaming.

Donohue leads Marryat to stand in front of the mirror, whispering instructions and handing him something to hold behind his back. As he steps away, he warns, "Remember, you will be the only one of us who is unprotected. Timing is critical."

The exorcism seems to last for hours, though Lord Marryat suspects less than a half-hour actually passes. He should understand the Latin, but the men of God speak fast, often with all three of them shouting at the same time, and he catches only a word or two of the meaning. But the impact on Florence is clear, and it's painful for him to watch.

At last, her screams rise to an impossibly high pitch, and her back suddenly arches at such a dramatic angle Lord Marryat thinks it must be broken. Her head is flung back so far it almost touches the ground behind her. Her mouth's "O" enlarges into a terrifying gash, and a shape emerges, dark and shadowy, the vapor forming an erratically moving figure. The sight of it strengthens the clergymen's resolve. The crucifix is raised higher, the chanting becomes louder. The air hums furiously, the dust motes disturbed, fearful, forming clouds and smearing the space between them.

Florence is reduced to a trembling, huddled mass on the cage floor, her screams replaced by the thing's tarry, unknowable snarl. Lord Marryat watches, stunned and horrified, as the tall, spiky black figure tries to move past the clergymen, its movements erratic, furious. An animal, cornered. Each way it turns it is met with a resolute man of the cloth, one with a bible, another with a cross, a third with holy water, and it recoils as if pummeled, this way and that, dangerous and roiling. Then, with a feral, inhuman, soul-rattling roar, the figure tears directly at Lord Marryat.

Marryat jerks the crucifix from behind his back, almost dropping it as he stumbles to the side, exposing the glass. With a final scream of rage, the creature leaps into the shadows of the waiting mirror.

Reverend Donohue shouts, "Quickly! For God's sake, man, quickly!"

Recovering, Marryat fumbles the altar cloth closed in front of the mirror, pulls together the clasps of the chains, thrusts the crucifix through the hasp, and drops to his knees.

The sudden silence is painful, desolate. The air continues to vibrate with its trauma. It is done. The thing has gone. Trapped, dormant.

Lord Marryat crawls to the cage. Hartley hands him a key, and he unlocks the door with shaking fingers, swings it open, and scoops his wife into his arms to cradle her, no longer an animal but the woman he loves, restored. A fragile, broken bird.

"Oh, my love! My love!" He sobs, desperately kissing her dark hair.

The young woman stirs and caresses his wet cheek. She ages rapidly, and is once again Florence Marryat, the woman he loves, the woman he grew old with, the wife he recognizes. She looks at him, and in little more than a whisper, tells him, "I love you."

Lord Marryat is elated in this moment, this half-moment, before his world crashes down one final time.

Her face loses color first, becoming white, then tinged with grey, as her skin droops like melted candle wax. Her hair falls out in clumps until only wispy strands remain, and her body thickens, slackens, bends, stiffens.

"Oh!" Lord Marryat exclaims again as he searches her desperate, mournful eyes. The whites yellow before her irises cloud. Her skin is now papery . . . Now feather-thin . . . Now tearing.

She has died, but Florence Marryat's decimation continues. Her flesh disintegrates, her muscles sliding away, until Lord Marryat is left cradling nothing but her skeleton.

"No!" he screams, grasping the bones only to find they, too, crumble in his old arthritic hands and fall away into dust.

1

I stretch my aching fingers as I look around the room, waiting for my turn. The walls of Marryat Manor vibrate with the wheezing and rattling of fifty-two, no, fifty-one—Emily went last night—pairs of lungs.

The elderlies sit in a semicircle of armchairs around the roaring fireplace even though it is a warm September day. Even the tiniest whisper of breeze makes them flock like cats to the nearest heat source, zombies trying to prove they're still alive. The chairs are positioned so close to the fireplace that I'll be surprised if the residents' rheumy eyeballs aren't scorched by the flames. They're all bones and protruding false teeth too big for their shrunken gums, white hair spun up into pale puffs of candy floss, emerging from hunched, brittle shoulders. Their necks have long ago disappeared.

I still have a neck. I used to be praised for my neck, elegant and swan-like. People used to travel for miles to see my neck. It may not be swan-like now, more—what—ostrich-like? No. Ostrich necks are too thin and long and hairy. Or am I thinking of an emu? It doesn't matter. The point is that at least I have a neck.

My hand hovers at my throat to find the diamond and sapphire pendant I wore for decades and discovers wrinkled folds of flesh instead. But before disgust envelops me, Margaret speaks. I'd forgotten she was here.

"'And silent was the flock in woolly fold.'" She nods towards the elderlies. I harrumph inwardly. Or maybe even outwardly, I don't care. Margaret is always quoting things I don't know. "*The Eve of St. Agnes.* John Keats," she murmurs, then prompts, "Your turn, dear."

"Oh! Sorry." The game. Scrabble. I've been distracted by the corpse circle by the fire. I angle my head to see Margaret's last word—trollop. She wears a teasing smile.

"You bitch!" I half-snarl, half-laugh.

"You hussy!" she replies with mock seriousness before laughing herself.

"Now then, ladies, I hope you're behaving yourselves. How are we today?" Melissa, whose hair is pink today, appears at the glass door of the game nook. I've never understood why the orderlies insist on treating us—each a paying resident—like schoolchildren.

"Thank you, dear, yes we're doing very well," Margaret replies, nodding and smiling warmly.

"You two are always causing trouble," Pink Hair claims as she whisks away our teacups.

"I give up!" I tell Margaret, pushing away the board, half-filled with tiles. I'm losing, as I always do when playing Margaret. I mean, she was a professor of literature, for heaven's sake! My best word today was "post." Hers, "croquet." I'm keen to get away from the game nook, this afterthought of a room barnacled onto the main living room, lined with the expansive but unremarkable butterfly collection of some relative of Florence Marryat's. Margaret calls it "the winged mausoleum." She's such a show-off with her words. I have always hated pinned butterflies. They make me think of that John Fowles novel *The Collector* in which that butterfly collector captures a woman he's obsessed with and keeps her in the basement until she dies, as though she's pinned too. At least, like the butterflies, she was beautiful in death.

As the mid-morning sky squeezes itself of the remaining fog and the sun appears, I head for the Manor grounds while Margaret is absorbed with something dully studious in the library. I can still walk properly, at least a couple of miles at a time, unlike the elderlies who shuffle in bent-over pairs around a two-hundred-square-foot patch of lawn, like grazing cows. My spine is not as stoker straight as it was. Is it "stoker?" Stoker straight? Or poker straight? I can't remember. Are pokers straight? Isn't poker a game? Or no, a dance! It must be "stoker" then. No matter. The point is I always had excellent posture but seem to have lost a couple of inches in height in recent years. Still, I do not stoop. I am more or less vertical. Not bent like a shepherd's crook. Do shepherds still use crooks? I haven't seen a shepherd in years.

The grounds are admittedly as grand, though not as elegant, as those of my own property—well, my own before I was forced by my belligerent son-in-law into selling it. Mine was a classical English landscape garden, with several excellently maintained lawns edged with perennials and groves of well-behaved and thriving oaks. Serene and respectable.

The gardens closest to Marryat Manor are Renaissance-inspired and overly symmetrical, with neat patterns of shrubbery and flowers—the latter deflating as summer nears its end—interspersed with slightly overgrown topiaries, their shapes blurred. They remind me that I need to schedule my next beautician's appointment for my own trimmings.

Further from the house is a rather imposing and overly complicated maze. A maze! At a residential home? Absurd. Fortunately, it is ignored by the residents, and only the visiting children are tempted to try it. Not my own granddaughter, of course, who is unfortunately a bit of a lump and not prone to voluntary exercise. Incongruously, diseased-looking trees spear the surrounding land in a tangle, reminding me of the thicket of thorns surrounding Sleeping Beauty's palace. Or was it Rapunzel's tower? I rarely walk as far as the trees. It is a Marryat Manor rule that we can only go where we can be easily seen and helped if needed.

As I'm walking past the maze I see an Adonis blue butterfly—the rarest of blue butterflies in England—a tiny, beautiful thing. I gasp as, unexpectedly, it lands on my lapel in exactly the position as the blue enamel butterfly brooch my late husband gave to me for our first Christmas together after we were married. I'd been secretly disappointed with it at the time. I'd hoped for something grander—diamonds, perhaps—that my friends would be envious of. But I grew to love it. It matched my eyes. The reason, William claimed, for his giving it to me. And now, this real butterfly. If I were religious like Dr. Phillips and believed in the afterlife, I may think this was a sign from William from beyond the grave. But to say what? Just that he's here?

The butterfly flutters off as soon as I take a step forwards, disappearing into nothing, as if it was never there, and suddenly I don't want to be in the garden anymore. I don't want to be alone here, where yellow-grey clouds roll in. It must take me longer than usual to reach the house again, as when I do, it is starting to rain, and time for tea. I decide not to mention the butterfly to Margaret, though I'm not sure why.

Nobody notices me as I reenter the living room. It's something I've had to get used to, being treated as just one of the flock, unseen. I was once thought of as remarkable. A glorious first course that everyone wanted to get a piece of. Now it's more like I've gone off and crusted over slightly on an ignored buffet table. A flaccid tarte Tatin? A slightly stale prawn vol-au-vent? What would Margaret be? Something sophisticated and slightly surprising. Asparagus, steamed, with a jug of melted butter, the way the Germans eat it. I glance over at her. She's forgotten to brush her hair again today, and the sunlight catches the fine down of her face. Perhaps the butter would start to solidify again, and the asparagus would be damp and soggy.

It's all so depressing—this place. I can't bear the thought that I've been brought here to die. Like a hospice. Or an abattoir. As retirement homes go, it's the best that money can buy. Expensively decorated. Nothing too modern. Full tea service—real loose tea, no teabags—and proper china. No common mugs with "world's greatest nan" plastered over the front of them. Attentive staff. A prize-winning chef. An excellent doctor. Yet sometimes it feels too comfortable. It reminds me of the time we had to put down our Great Dane, Christopher, and I held his head in my lap, stroking him as he drifted away.

The Wedgewood teacup I'm holding rattles slightly against the saucer as I lower it.

"How's your arthritis today?" the eagle-eyed Margaret enquires.

"Fine, thank you," I lie, nibbling on the edge of what I know to be a Fortnum and Mason ginger biscuit.

"You seem a little . . . deflated since earlier," she remarks, and I briefly think of the butterfly. "Is it your crushing Scrabble defeat?"

"I'm perfectly fine, thank you," I respond curtly. I never welcome remarks on my mood, particularly not when referring to my mental well-being and especially in reference to my losing something. Margaret knows this and is trying to provoke a reaction out of me for her own entertainment.

"You have a very long chin whisker," I tell her, looking her in the eye. Margaret does not care to de-fuzz as I do.

"Oh, I don't mind," she answers with an irritating smile. It's impossible to rankle Margaret. Impossible to offend her. After a moment, she nods. "Ah yes, flocculent."

I don't know the word and stay quiet.

"'There was an Old Man with a beard,'" she begins. "'Who said, "It is just as I feared! Two Owls and a Hen, four Larks and a Wren have all built their nests in my beard."'" Margaret beams, noting, "Edward Lear."

"You, sir, are a scholar and a gentleman," I quip, my mood suddenly improved, and she laughs hard, resulting in a coughing fit so severe she's sent to Dr. Phillips to be checked over.

"Ralph!" I exclaim delightedly as Margaret's son makes his way across the living room to the game nook where I'm currently paying his mother an extortionate amount of rent for landing on Mayfair. It is the afternoon, and the sun has reemerged, beaming into the creamy living room, lighting Ralph up, making him look almost ethereal.

"Hello Harriet, you're looking lovely as usual." Ralph grins at me, displaying straight, unstained teeth, as he bends to hug his mother from behind. I'm wearing a plum and fuchsia floral dress. Highstreet. Not my favorite. A gift from my daughter. I wish I'd changed.

"Hello, Mum." He plants a loud kiss on Margaret's cheek before settling himself in the chair between us and bending over the board. "Harriet wiping the floor with you again, is she?" he asks cheekily, knowing full well that it's very rare for anyone to win a game against his mother.

"She's a real shark," Margaret agrees kindly, which is more aggravating than if she had corrected him. It makes me feel like a child being indulged.

"She's got Mayflower again," I tell him.

"May*fair*, dear," Margaret corrects, and I flush.

"Mayfair, maypole, what does it matter?" I say irritably, before remembering to adjust my features back into a more agreeable assemblage for our guest, saying brightly, "A surprise visit, Ralph! On a Friday afternoon too. I thought you had work?"

His grin slips a fraction. "Well, not as many clients this month. I can afford to take a little time off to visit my favorite ladies."

Ralph is not an Oxbridge sort like Margaret. He's something called a "web designer" and has his own freelance business, although he seems to spend just as much time looking after his wife's son by a previous marriage. The poor man is nanny-less, despite his wife being a solicitor and them being well-off. That woman really takes advantage of his kindness. And she has an annoying, squashed-looking kind of a face. A face for radio, as they say. I don't know what he sees in her.

"Well, it's always so nice to see you!" I coo, a little over-effusively. "Margaret, you have such a handsome son!" I direct the comment directly towards Ralph, flirting without shame. It tips another beguiling grin from him.

"Could you tell my wife that, please? She thinks I'm just a handyman these days. I need to get myself a Harriet!"

I flush delightedly. *Get himself a Harriet!*

Despite his smile, I notice something different about him today—a world-weary slumping at the shoulders, shadows under his eyes. His dark hair flecked with only a smattering of greys is styled but has grown longer than usual. I may not be an academic like Margaret, but I am astute. It occurs to me that something might be wrong, that he might want to talk to his mother alone.

"Well, this Harriet's going to ask for a pot of tea." I tip forwards to stand from my chair and stumble slightly, catching myself on the table and upsetting the board. The houses and hotels rattle off their properties.

"Earthquake!" Margaret cries jovially. "Unusual, for Surrey."

"Are you okay there, Harriet?" Ralph stands to help me.

"Perfectly fine, thank you. It's just these blasted shoes, a little sticky on the sole," I say, embarrassed, running a hand through my hair before leaving to find somebody to make a fresh pot of tea.

"Poor Ralph," Margaret says.

It's supper now, the remainder of the afternoon disappeared. Baked salmon, boiled potatoes, leeks, dill cream sauce. All easy on the gums and digestion. No doubt something spongy with custard for pudding, something traditionally British, which I'll refuse. I had a biscuit earlier. Or did I? Was that yesterday?

"Why poor Ralph?" I ask.

"Trouble with Lisa," she replies, concern crumpling her forehead.

It's not yet dusk, and the dining room is east facing and lit softly with lamps in the evening. Despite her scowl, the light makes Margaret look younger, smoother. I wonder, not for the first time, if it has the same effect on me. Wouldn't it be nice if Ralph could stay for dinner one evening? To dine with his mother and her friend? I could wear my diamonds.

"Trouble?" I ask. Lisa is such a common name. Or no, it's *nearly* a common name. Not a Sharon or a Tracy or a Danielle. But it's a hairdresser's name. An estate agent, maybe. Not worthy of a Ralph.

Margaret has barely eaten anything from her plate, which is unusual for her. A sign of real worry. I've nearly cleared my own. "They're not getting on well at the moment."

"Why not?"

"According to Ralph, she's not interested in him enough and doesn't make time for him. He seems a little restless, a little bored. I think . . ." She pauses.

"Yes?" I prompt.

"Well, I think he's a little bit spoilt. I love my son, but I think sometimes he is a little too needy, a little immature. Lisa's busy. She has a full-time job, a son, a house. Ralph has never liked it when he doesn't feel adored enough. He needs to be the center of attention. It would be challenging for any woman, I think. He's a lot to handle."

I sigh loudly in protest as Margaret smooths her hand over the white tablecloth, thoughtful and upset.

"Your son is a wonderful man," I tell her sternly, cutting into the over-boiled vegetables aggressively so the knife finds the plate too quickly and makes an audible clank. "She's very lucky to have him and needs to be more appreciative."

What I wouldn't give to have a man notice me again. How I would appreciate the attention!

"I half-suspect he has a somewhat wandering eye," Margaret murmurs, and, absurdly, her comment stirs me a little. A wandering eye? For whom? It obviously can't be me. I'm far too old. Although, I don't look as old as I feel. I dress nicely, always in bright colors. I refuse to go grey or get fat. Hence the lack of pudding.

"A wandering eye?" I probe. William didn't dare to let his eye wander.

"Well, Ralph's a natural flirt," she starts.

"He's charming," I correct.

Margaret pauses, thinking, then finally slides a few flakes of fish into her mouth. "I think what I'm trying to say is it wouldn't surprise me if he were to find himself in a situation . . . well, bluntly, if he were to have an affair."

"Don't be ridiculous!" I scoff, chewing quickly in time with my racing thoughts and swallowing down unwanted fluttering.

"You must have seen how he ogles Alyson and Imani?"

Two members of staff. Both young and moderately attractive, I suppose, but unrefined. Not special. Alyson is a passable name, but whoever heard of an Imani? Pleasant enough girl, of course, despite being from some ghastly city in the North.

"I don't think Ralph ogles anyone. He's a gentleman," I insist, and she replies only with a "hmmm."

"Some people rely too much on other people for their fulfillment," she continues after a while. "He has no . . . inner life. No natural curiosity. He barely reads at all."

I, myself, am no great reader and bristle. "I don't think you can conflate the two. I'm sure he has a deep inner life. Not reading has nothing to do with it. Some people just don't have the patience for it. Perhaps he's too busy *having* an inner life to accommodate the thoughts of random authors too."

"When is Judith coming to see you next?" Margaret asks, changing the subject from her offspring to mine.

"I have no idea," I dismiss, more aggressively than I intend. "You know Judith. She only pops up when she has an appointment to discuss me with Dr. Phillips." I feel myself tightening at the thought of her. Drippy, unremarkable Judith, exerting control over every aspect of my life.

"Oh, Harriet, she's a lovely lady, you know that. She's very kind to you."

There are so many things wrong with this assertion that I don't bother to tackle it at all. *Lovely lady?*

"You've barely eaten anything, Margaret." I motion to her plate, the salmon fillet retaining its perfectly rectangular shape. She smiles weakly.

"I'll have no option but to tell Dr. Phillips," I threaten jokingly. "He'll have to punish you. Extra fish oil tablets."

Margaret attempts a laugh, as if trying to put her concerns for her son to one side.

But I believe I understand Ralph more than his mother. I, too, was restless in my forties. I had spent the previous two decades deftly dismissing the attentions of other men. Scores of them, and even the occasional woman, who attempted affairs. Then suddenly, the attention waned, and I tried harder, became an even larger presence, flirted more. Truth be told, I gave in a couple of times, gave in to far lesser men I'd have rejected in my twenties and thirties, just so I could feel wanted again. Those dalliances were disappointing. Flabby and awkward. The men didn't enjoy sex itself as much as they wanted to stoke their egos with seducing Harriet, the un-seducible.

I think again of the blue butterfly that visited me earlier. I'm glad William never thought me invisible, even when the rest of the world had stopped seeing me. There is still no more powerful currency for a woman than youth, than allure. Now, I disappear more every day. Everything creasing, folding, spotting, sprouting, swelling. Every day I become a little less significant. A little more of an afterthought. I hadn't understood that there would be this—*descension*. And I have no idea how to bear it.

2

I can't walk. I can only claw and pull my way across the landing on my front. It's dark, and at first I don't notice that the wood-paneled walls are moving—inwards, outwards, side to side, twisting up, up, up like a corkscrew. A blue illuminated butterfly flits in front of me, guiding me forwards. Dimly, I hear the elderlies wail from their rooms as I finally reach the stairs and find a queue of cloaked figures descending. I join the line, now somehow upright, but as I take each step I'm going nowhere because of the twisting of the walls, like walking down the upwards escalator. I can't escape. The blue butterfly has disappeared, and the staircase is even darker. I'm lost.

The cloaked figure in front of me turns towards me, its face a dark hole of nothingness.

"No elderlies!" it hisses and lunges as if to push me back.

I wake, hot and panting, reassured to find the walls are as I left them.

The old oak floor mocks me today, echoing the stammer of my footsteps as I emerge from my bed. I cough to dislodge the morning's phlegm into a tissue and wince at the taste, sighing as I make my way to the bathroom, still stooped. It takes me longer to fully unfurl into a straighter shape. This is my "new normal" as the young people like to say. The tremors of age rattle through the day, dragging at its edges.

I try to shake out the remains of my nightmare as I perform my ablutions. I never had nightmares before I came here. In fact, I rarely dreamt, or at least I rarely remembered dreams. Now, suddenly, these nightmares bear in on me. It doesn't feel fair that I must deal with them on top of everything else. That this house should dare to impose them on me. Margaret claims people who experience nightmares when they move to a new place are sensing the presence of malevolent ghosts. She has speculated, unhelpfully, that I must be sleeping in a particularly haunted room.

Today is . . . Thursday? Saturday? Days tend to blend together in this place. No matter how well it's dressed up, it's still the place we have gone to die. To make death more comfortable, plumping up the pillow of our final years. A place where nobody is expected to do, achieve, or be recognized for anything. Each day passes disconnected from the last. A new pot of tea, a new game, a visitor. Like that ghastly American film—what is it? *Hog Day? Hog-Roast Day?* The same day, over and over, with slight variations depending on my choices. At least my comfort is the intention.

It's foggy again. A deep, warning kind of gloom. Appealing to a child who wants to try walking through a cloud. A density you could get lost in.

"Harriet, what are you doing?" Pink Hair—Melissa—asks. I look down to see I'm wearing my walking boots and raincoat. But I'm standing in the drawing room. I must have intended to go outside. I don't know why I'm here.

"What does it look like I'm doing?" I snap at her, immediately unsure why I'm so sharp. "I'm going for a walk."

"It's Monday, Harriet. Monday." Her voice is raised and she's talking slowly like I'm a simpleton, although it is well known that being hard of hearing is *not* among my many ailments. "On Mondays, you see Dr. Phillips at nine."

"Oh!" I knew that. How stupid of me. Only, I had no idea it

was Monday. Somebody moved Sunday. They're changing the days around again. Nobody will ever leave anything alone. "Well. Yes, I had better . . ."

I return to the cloakroom to change out of my outdoor gear, uncomfortably flushed with embarrassment. I didn't expect Melissa to follow me, help me off with my jacket, escort me to the doctor's office. I feel like a child going to see the headteacher after being caught out for misbehaving. Like the time when I was six and hadn't known showing the boys my knickers was unacceptable.

"Harriet! My favorite patient!" Dr. Phillips greets me with the same over-the-top benevolence with which he greets all the residents. He's standing, and so tall he's silhouetted in front of the overhead light. His doctor's coat is fit to the length of his arms rather than his girth, so it flaps about his trim frame as a cloak might when he raises his arms. The whole effect is half owlish, half vampiric. His tone is a fraction condescending and, though kindly meant, off-putting from a young man of thirty-five regardless of his professional status.

"I hear we got a little confused about the day today." He grins at me.

"Clearly 'we' did not. 'I' may have done," I concede churlishly. My bad temper does not affect his relentless cheer.

"Easily done, easily done." Dr. Phillips's toothy smile rankles. "How are we today then, Harriet?" He leans forwards on his stool as I try to disguise my puff of relief at finally sitting down in a chair. He misinterprets the puff and holds up his hands. "Sorry! Sorry, not we, you. How are *you* today?"

"Creaky," I tell him, and he motions for me to expand. "It's the . . . you know . . ." I can't find the word I know perfectly well. "The . . . Oh, for heaven's sake!" I motion to my knees and wave my hands a little. He's not helping. "The . . . elephant?" No.

"Elephant?" Dr. Phillips looks surprised, attentive, pretending he doesn't know I've found the wrong word.

"The thing with the joints. Not elephant," I clarify and continue to search for the word. "Envelope," I try, then dismiss it. Not envelope. Envelopes are for letters. Letters. I haven't had a letter for a while. Why did people stop sending letters? I had hoped my granddaughter would write to me. It's good practice to write to one's relatives. But of course, it wouldn't occur to Judith to encourage Molly to do something so considerate.

"Harriet?" Dr. Phillips says. I look up at him. "I think you wandered off there for a moment. You were telling me about your arthritis."

Arthritis! That's the word.

"Yes. It's particularly bad today. The fog, probably."

"How are those new pills I gave you, Harriet? They're not helping?"

"I've noticed absolutely no difference, Dr. Phillips. I think they must be . . ." I search again for the word I knew perfectly well the moment prior, then give up, settling for, "broken."

Dr. Phillips nods thoughtfully. I wonder if he knows how shiny his head around his widow's peak is. The light bouncing off it accentuates his every movement. I'm always glad I'm a woman when I see a balding man, particularly one so young.

"We'll see if we can make some adjustments. I'll speak to Judith." The man seems to think he has to clear everything with my daughter, which is utterly demeaning. He writes something down on his pad before looking back up to me, his tone turning softer, sympathetic, as though I've recently suffered some great bereavement. "And how are you otherwise, Harriet?"

"Perfectly fine, thank you," I tell him curtly.

"You don't seem . . . relaxed today. You seem a little anxious."

Anxious? Yes, I suppose I could be anxious. From that dream. My hands are tightened, not into fists—that would be too painful—but more like tense claws, and my stomach feels strange, despite my settling breakfast of toast and soft-boiled eggs.

"I think I'm just a little flustered," I tell him, pleased with myself that I found "flustered." "Forgetting the appointment, mixing up my days."

"Do you often mix up your days?" His tone is still sympathetic, but he's leaned back slightly, widening the space between us.

"No." I don't expect my response to be so clipped.

"Do you get mixed up with anything else, Harriet?" He's writing something down again.

"Only the things you'd expect for a person of my age." My voice crackles, and I clear my throat.

"Like what?"

I can't stifle my huff of irritation, but he doesn't withdraw the question. "Oh, occasionally words," I concede, given he's already seen evidence of it.

"People?" he asks. "Or the past and present? Do you get those mixed up too?"

"Good lord, no!" I protest, insulted. I know what's past and present. "Before you ask, it is October twenty-sixth. My husband William has been gone these past eight years. I have a daughter, Judith, and a granddaughter, Molly. And this is Marryat Manor."

I don't like Dr. Phillips's beam. It's too congratulatory.

"Excellent, Harriet. Anything else bothering you? Anything you need?"

"Not unless you have the elixir of life on hand," I quip, and he laughs, too loudly.

"I do, in a way." He smiles gently and I catch sight of the crucifix resting on the fireplace mantle behind him. He knows I'm not a Christian though. His comment was unprofessional.

"Ah, the afterlife. What a pretty myth," I say meanly, but he is not offended, as is common with these Christians when you attempt to undermine their faith. They are too bestowed with "grace" to be offended by your lack of belief.

"I know you're not a believer, Harriet, but you are loved. Whether or not you believe in God's love, you are loved by people on this earth. Remember that they care about you."

I am silenced for a moment, not knowing how to react to this unexpected reminder that I have friends and family, that I'm not alone. And yet I feel . . . *so* alone. It dawns on me that love feels unwarranted because in my diminished, aging state, I am not myself. It feels like a betrayal of the real Harriet to consider that someone might love the pathetic shadow I've become.

"I miss my house," I mutter without thinking, surprising myself. My house. Haywood Hall. As magnificent as Marryat Manor but softer somehow, its light brighter, its shadows rounded. A buoyant, supple place, eager to please, like one of my Great Danes.

"Of course, you do, Harriet. It must be so difficult."

"I feel like a boarder here," I admit, thinking back to my school days. "And I was always a day girl."

Perhaps that's why I feel so imprisoned.

"Hello! Fancy seeing you here!" Margaret says as I leave Dr. Phillips's office.

"Good morning," I greet her vaguely, distracted by thoughts of home.

"Good morning, Margaret." Dr. Phillips directs his beam at her, my own issues clearly forgotten.

"Dr. Phillips! I nearly missed my appointment!" she says, and I sigh. This again.

"Why, Margaret? Were you in bed with your lover?" he asks, not expecting a reply, and they laugh at the ongoing joke that isn't remotely funny and is beneath them both.

"Come now, Harriet," Dr. Phillips says, noticing my grimace. "We don't want to deny Margaret here her sexual freedoms now, do we?"

"I wouldn't dream of it," I tell him humorlessly, and head back to the drawing room to recover from my appointment.

I have no appetite for lunch. Although I have eaten this quiche many times before and know it to be quite delicious, it is unappetizing today. Possibly, it's the thick bands of overly flabby bacon straddling the glistening cheese topping. When Judith was a small baby, I inadvertently became a vegetarian. Our nanny had taken ill, so I spent more time with little Judith than people usually did back then. Holding her so much, feeling her soft flesh on mine for such a large portion of the day, put me off eating meat on some base instinctive level. It felt cannibalistic, as though I were eating my own daughter, or at least somebody's child. It was temporary, thankfully. The lack of iron soon drove me back to eating meat.

"Not hungry, dear?" Margaret asks, snapping me from my thoughts of baby Judith.

"No, not really," I reply flatly.

"You seem a little out of sorts today." Her gentleness is unsettling, as if there's some legitimate reason for being careful with me, as though I'm made of glass.

"No, no. I just—" It occurs to me to tell Margaret of my dream. It's the kind of thing that would interest her. So I describe it, as best as I can, in that looping, nonsensical way people always use to relay their dreams.

"Well, no wonder you're out of sorts," Margaret says after I've finished. "A truly horrible dream."

"Yes." I nod glumly and wait for her to tell me again my room must be haunted, but instead, her voice brightens, and she sits a little straighter.

"But as Robert Frost once said, 'It's not the quiche's fault.'" She motions at my plate with her fork, encouraging me to eat.

"Did he really say that?" I ask.

"Of course not, you dunce!" She chuckles, and I roll my eyes, feeling very tired.

"Ralph!" Margaret exclaims and my head snaps up. He's pulling out a chair at our table.

"Ladies!" he greets, his smile a crescent moon. I'm disorientated by his being here. It's usually days between his visits.

"Not hungry, Harriet?" he asks, looking at my full plate.

"No . . . How are you here, Ralph?" I ask. "You were here only yesterday."

His eyes skid over to his mother's briefly before he answers. "You must be thinking of some other handsome man, Harriet. I was last here on Friday."

"Yes," I agree, disorientated.

"And today is Monday. We've had a whole weekend in between."

A weekend. I don't remember a weekend. A whole Saturday, and a whole Sunday, disappeared into a sinkhole, accosted by daemons. The cloaked daemons descending the stairs. They made off with Saturday and Sunday.

"Do I have reason to be jealous, Harriet?" Ralph asks with a flash of teeth, and I manage a small laugh alongside Margaret's heartier one, his flirtation thawing my confusion a fraction. It's a characteristic Margaret finds exasperating. I find it endearing. The younger generation don't usually bother to extend their liveliness to those of us with advanced years.

"I don't think you could be mixed up with anyone, dear." Margaret places a hand over her son's, and Ralph turns his hand over to hold hers. "You're one in a million, coming to visit me so often."

From the side, I notice that the skin over Ralph's jaw is taut, firm and smooth. His hair is still thick and has barely started receding. By forty-eight, William's had started thinning considerably, though he barely mentioned it. He wasn't a vain man. Not like some of the others.

Ralph is wearing a violet shirt, crumpled slightly at the cuffs. Ironed, but not particularly well, as though he did it himself when unused to ironing. He's wearing silver cuff links in the shape of airplanes. The kind a pilot might wear. He's a web designer, though, so aren't the planes a little misleading? I suppose he has the confident look of a pilot. I met men like him in the days when I entertained William's clients. Charm covering substance.

"That's a very becoming color on you, Harriet." His phrasing is old-fashioned, not something he's likely to say outside the Manor. I look down to see the cornflower blue blouse I usually only wear in the summer. It is too light for October, and I'm cold. "It matches your stunning eyes."

I feel a giddy lightness in my stomach, but before I can return the compliment, Margaret cuts in. "Oh, for heaven's sake, Ralph! Leave poor Harriet alone. Honestly, you can't even be trusted in an old folk's home."

"Retirement community," he corrects her sternly, and now it's Margaret's turn to roll her eyes and tut. Always shutting him down. Why doesn't she realize he's in his element when joking with and complimenting others—lighting them up with his hundreds of tiny kindnesses.

"Have you eaten, Ralph?" I ask him, offering my untouched meal.

"I have, I have. Thank you, Harriet. Protein shake."

"A what?" Protein is meat, surely?

"A kind of milkshake drink that's mainly protein. A meal replacement."

"God lord!" Margaret grimaces. "What in heaven's name are you drinking that stuff for? There's nothing wrong with you!"

Ralph's smile drops slightly.

"Whatever it takes to catch the attention of my wife," he says, tipping back slightly in his chair and glancing around the room. His gaze seems to land on Alyson, who's talking with Tom at another table.

"Oh, Ralph," Margaret sighs. "You know, Lisa really is a good woman. She's very busy."

His shoulders lower an inch. "I know, Mum. But what's the point of being married if she's too busy to be in the relationship?"

I think back to the times when William was at his busiest. My social calendar never dwindled. In fact, if anything, it picked up. There were so many contacts of his to win over through parties, shoots, charitable events. But I remember that same feeling of neglect, how one burns to be admired and recognized as something special, something more than a business colleague, domestically or otherwise. People like me, people like Ralph—the special people, the sparklers—we need to adore others and feel our adoration returned as much as we need oxygen. Without it, we disappear.

It's not often that I nap in the afternoon. Usually, I find myself watching Margaret doze off in an armchair around three and distract myself with a crossword or book for half an hour until she wakes up and is ready for tea.

But today I feel unusually drowsy in the warm sitting room, despite my lack of exercise. Having been thrown between confusions all day, I drift away, a couple of steps towards unconsciousness, a step back into wakefulness, a couple of steps more towards sleep, a step back, until I face a complicated half-daydream, half-dream.

The walls of the drawing room are perfectly still as you might expect, but the furniture is sliding around as though we're on a ship in the middle of a storm. The other residents seem unconcerned in their swaying chairs, bothered only by the flapping pages of their books and magazines, as though they're caught in high winds. Only I am frightened and see the room's behavior as alarming, as though this is another "new normal" I have forgotten.

"Margaret? What's happening?" I call out to her.

"Don't worry, dear. As Robert Frost writes, 'We are but the playthings of a ginger cake.'"

"A what?" I ask, confusion twisting into my terror.

"A ginger cake. Oh, Harriet, you don't know?" She laughs then. A horrible, condescending, non-Margaret kind of laugh, and there are suddenly others—elderlies and staff—all laughing along with her. "Ignore her. She's an ignoramus!" Margaret bellows.

"Harriet?" Margaret's tone is different now. "Harriet. Harriet?"

I snap awake. Margaret is leaning over me.

"Would you like some ginger cake, dear?" she asks. "I'm sorry for waking you, but it's getting towards the end of the tea service, and we'll miss it if we don't ask for some now."

"Oh!" I sit up, fuzzy headed. My mouth is dry. The end of the tea service? How long have I been asleep?

"Er, yes, ginger cake," I reply, without properly registering what I've been asked or what I want. "I just had . . . a dream."

"I thought you might have done, dear." She nods. "You were saying some quite peculiar things. Let me ask for that cake."

Margaret disappears to find a member of staff, and I use the time to collect myself. Robert Frost hadn't said anything about ginger cake any more than he had about quiche, at least as far as I know. The room is not sliding around. There are no high winds. Everything is as it usually is. Still, comfortable. A rousing chatter from the elderlies, post-nap and fueled with tea and cake.

As usual, I feel dragged down after napping, as though a chunk of me remains sleeping.

Is this how it feels to have a stroke?

Margaret sees my lingering grogginess and ushers us to the television room following afternoon tea, where I'm subjected to watching the peculiar antique-selling competition programmes that appear to delight my fellow residents. Worse, every advert seems directed towards me specifically. Skin cream designed to firm creping skin. Discrete incontinence pads. Denture cream. Panic buttons. All featuring glamorous people at least a decade younger than anyone who would need to use any of those items. All of them smiling and drinking tea. A dozen reminders that I'm old, destined only to decline. That I will only look more haggard, more withered. That my bodily functions will one day cease functioning, without warning, and days will continue to abscond.

Turning to dust even before my death. Falling into a chaotically hostile whirlwind, overly ready to spit me out towards the deathly precipice, as though I am a rotten fruit, an off nut.

And yet, everyone around me seems quite accepting of their decline, as though it hasn't occurred to them to mind. They do not feel as I do, unmoored and betrayed by time. I cannot resign myself to this fate. It is too hideous. Too final. I am not finished with beauty, even though it has shrugged me off without a thought.

I am not finished with dignity.

3

I am told it is Wednesday, although what Monday and Tuesday did with themselves, I can't imagine. I am eating marmalade on toast, trying to force the acid back down my bile-scorched throat. Another dream, dense with terror, has branded me with darkness.

I dreamt I awoke in my room at Marryat Manor to the smell of smoke, the sound of crackling, and the glow of fire appearing from the gap beneath the door. Immediately, I started to panic—how was I going to get out?—before being suddenly assaulted by the deafening screams of my fifty fellow residents, each perishing horribly in their rooms. Was I the only one not yet on fire? Could I save myself and get help? Why weren't the fire alarms ringing? Was anyone able to call 999? I tried to get out of my bed, but my legs wouldn't move, as though they were made from concrete or nailed down. As I managed to sit up, the screams of agony became even louder, as if people were screaming directly into my ears with no space between us.

Panting, I caught sight of myself in the mirror fastened to the wall opposite the bed, and the breath left my body. I didn't look like me. It wasn't *me* staring back, but something blackly charred and monstrously glowing, as though it were made from cooling lava with a magma center. It couldn't be me. And yet when I moved my hand, so did the—creature, daemon?

It *was* me.

Horrified, I noticed something in the hand of the daemon and, upon closer inspection, saw it was a box of matches. *I* was responsible for the fire.

It was then, as my soul folded in on itself, that I woke, hot and aching, with acid racing around my chest and into my throat. Was I having a heart attack? No, it was panic. Just simple panic.

Margaret peers at me curiously from behind her teacup. "You're not yourself today."

"No," I agree. "Another dream."

Her smile is sympathetic. "Your buttons are done up wrongly."

I look down to see she's right, I skipped a buttonhole. Hastily, I start to re-button and notice I selected a wild combination of colors today—an orchid-pink blouse and scarlet skirt, together with my old daffodil court shoes I usually only bring out in the summer. It's late October. A wet, mud-clogging day, drained of all color. I must stand out rather. Look a little clownish.

"Judith and Molly are here, Harriet," Alyson tells me brightly as she approaches the table. She has a bit of a soft spot for Molly, although she has no children of her own. "Judith's been chatting with Dr. Phillips, but she's popping over to see you now." Oh, good, another time she's made the trip to see him, discuss me as though I weren't here, and eventually grace me with her presence. The very cheek of it.

"Do I have time to change?" I ask, but see that no, they're following Alyson directly into the breakfast room.

"Hello, Mummy!" Judith sings brightly, as though she were pleased to see me, as though she were fond of me and hadn't made me sell my house, depositing me in this haunted, harrowed place and experimenting on me as a lab rat with Dr. Phillips and his latest concoctions.

"Hello, Granny," Molly parrots from beside her.

"Hello, darlings," I reply, noticing an uncharacteristic crack in my voice. I gather myself as the two exchange greetings with Margaret and sit at our table.

"Oh, lovely, thank you," Judith accepts the offer of tea from Alyson. "I could murder a cuppa."

I close my eyes for a moment to let the commonness of the expression, which is beneath her, wash over me. She notices. Judith is, unfortunately, what the young people call "basic." Ashamed of her privilege, she insists on using these silly working-class expressions, even with her still plummy Surrey accent.

"How are you feeling, Mummy?" Judith places a hand on mine, an over-lipsticked smile plastered on her face.

"Perfectly fine, thank you." I nod, my voice neutral, taking care to edge out my confusion and upset from last night's dream. I am self-conscious about my odd outfit, but as I take in what Judith is wearing, care less. A bright, ill-fitting, off-the-rack Kelly-green sweater, black and white polka-dot trousers, and mud-smeared white ankle boots. An oversized plastic necklace. As though she's walked straight out of the Boden catalogue. As though she's a cheerful office manager somewhere in one of those ghastly industrial parks, offering "cuppas" to a clump of unwashed people wearing headsets. Little Molly looks equally Highstreet, in a red corduroy dress that is probably meant to disguise her overly rounded mid-section—it doesn't—and stripy tights. She offers me a drawing she brought with her. I slip on my glasses to see it properly. I think it's supposed to be a monster—an odd drawing to bring to a grandmother—and I'm about to comment on it when she says, "It's you."

"Me?"

Molly nods.

"Of course, it is." I look up to see Margaret stifling a giggle.

"Granny, can we play hide and seek?" Molly asks shyly.

"Hide and seek?" I ask, appalled. "I should think not! This isn't a playground."

She shrinks back as much as her pudgy body will allow. I think she's a little scared of me, though I can't imagine why.

They've only been here a few minutes, but I can understand she must be bored, with Judith dribbling on inanely about their recent middle-class activities. Molly has just joined the Brownies. They're going to a cheese and wine evening at the school. Something about a cat. She hasn't even bothered to tell me what she and Dr. Phillips discussed, even though *I* was the subject matter.

"Come now, Harriet, don't you think it might be rather fun?" Margaret asks.

Judith beams at her, probably wishing Margaret were her mother rather than me.

"No, I do not. The staff will think we're half-mad!" I think I sound authoritative enough to put an end to the idea, but apparently not.

"Then I'll play with you, Molly dear." Margaret smiles at the child and pushes to her feet, the child skipping ahead of her merrily.

I roll my eyes, but decide to take advantage of being alone with my daughter. "Judith," I start, increasing the severity of my tone. "I don't think this is the right place for me."

"Oh, Mummy—" she cuts in, but I hold up a hand.

"Really, Judith. You dump me in this place, forcing me to sell my beautiful house, treating me as though I'm about ninety when I'm only—"

"Mummy," she interrupts again. "You know how long the waiting list is for Marryat Manor. When a spot opened, we had to take it. That house was too much for you, too big for you. Here there's staff, friends." She motions towards the door Margaret had left through with Molly. "And doctors on hand in case you need anything. In case you get a little forgetful."

"I am not forgetful!" I respond vehemently, swallowing down the lie. The days of the week would object. "And look at the other people here, Judith. They're not like me. They're elderly. I'm not elderly."

"I know, Mummy," she placates with a sympathetic tone. *Mummy!* She really is a drip. "But it's lovely here. The best kind of place for you. I wish I could stay! Playing games all day in this lovely house, being brought tea and delicious meals, waited on hand and foot! It sounds marvelous!"

I'm not sure when Judith started talking to me as though I were a child, as though I were Molly. It is the worst kind of irritation. I can't tell her what effect this house is having on my mind. I can't tell her that it's trying to confuse me, that it's playing with my fears at night. I can't explain that it isn't what it seems on the surface. She won't understand. It will seem like an excuse, a ploy to get out of here.

"Mummy!" Molly squeals and runs into the room and into her mother, her face bright pink and soaked with tears.

"What happened?" I ask Margaret, who walks in slowly behind the little girl, her face a picture of confusion. She holds up her hands in a shrug.

"I don't know, I think she frightened herself. She has a vivid imagination." As Judith is busy consoling her daughter, Margaret sits down and leans over to explain. "We were playing hide and seek, and the girl somehow found herself in the basement."

"The basement? Well, no wonder—"

"That's not it," Margaret interrupts.

"Mummy!" Molly wails again. "It was horrible!"

Judith's face is as stricken as her daughter's. I don't often get to see my granddaughter, but this reaction does seem rather out of character.

"What is it, darling? What happened?" Judith's voice wobbles.

"She said she was trying to find a really good place to hide and found her way all the way to the back of the basement, some place under the kitchen I don't think anyone ever goes," Margaret said.

"There was a cage there!" Molly whimpers. "Do you think people were kept in it?"

"People?" Judith looks to Margaret for more details.

"I think it must have been an animal cage of some kind," Margaret fills in.

"There were scratch marks on it!" Molly cries. "Scratch marks like something or someone was trying to get out!"

"A dog crate?" I try to help.

Margaret smiles sympathetically at my granddaughter, who howls into her mother.

"My word," I continue. "I don't know what films that child has been watching, but that's quite . . . creative."

"But then . . . but . . . that's not it." Molly sniffles now. "I was scared when I saw the cage, and I jumped and bumped into something." Not hard given her largeness, I think before chastising myself. Not a charitable thought when the poor girl is in such a state. "There was a mirror. A big mirror like Mummy has in her bedroom, but even bigger and very old." Molly looks between Judith and I to make sure we're paying attention. "There was a cloth hanging over it. I lifted it up to see what was underneath . . . and when I looked in it . . ." Molly gulps and Judith rubs her shoulder encouragingly.

"What did you see, Molly?" I ask.

"It was so horrible. It wasn't me. It was like a monster version of me."

"A monster version? My word!" Acid surges up my throat again as I think of last night's dream. A premonition? "How terrifying!"

"It was just dirty, darling, or one of those mirrors they used to have at old fairgrounds. What was it? A hall of mirrors?" Judith looks at Margaret and I meaningfully.

"Oh, yes, one of those joke mirrors supposed to scare people." Margaret nods along. "Or even just a very dirty mirror. The light down there is terrible."

"It wasn't a joke mirror!" Molly sounds adamant. "The thing in there was giant and black!" She turns to Judith. "And it moved, even when I didn't!"

A short silence ensues, and Judith's face becomes a shade paler, if that's possible.

"I think we better go." Judith stands, carrying Molly, which is amazing since the girl is ten and not small. Molly's traumatized face is still buried in her mother's sweater.

"Yes, it sounds like she had a bit of a fright. This isn't the kind of house to play in," I tell Molly as gently as I can.

"Poor little thing," Margaret murmurs as they leave, then retreats to her room for a long nap, noting that her time with Molly tired her out.

For the rest of the day, I find myself doing very little, unable to concentrate. I linger at the windows, unthinkingly examining the drab, uninviting views—a dirge of a day that doesn't deserve to be looked at. But my mind won't detach itself from the events of the morning. The uncanny symmetry of Molly's experience to my own dream has deeply unsettled me. A monster version of her. A dreamt monster version of me. Mirrors. My chest aches from the acid that continues to gurgle. It's a coincidence, I tell myself. How could it be anything else? I start to wonder if my granddaughter is telepathic, if she somehow sensed the shape of my dream.

I am quite alone, lost in my thoughts and vacantly scanning the library shelves, when a familiar voice calls, "Harriet!"

I turn in shock to find Ralph standing there. "Oh, my dear, Ralph, you made me jump!" I tell him, hand to my thudding chest.

"Sorry! Sorry," he says, and it occurs to me this is the only time we've been alone together. But given the events of the shadowy day, I'm unable to enjoy it. He seems out of place, walking into a bad dream expecting a party. "You're looking lovely today, Harriet."

Usually, this kind of comment thrills me, but today it seems hollow. He says the exact same thing every time I see him. I feel anything other than lovely.

"Oh, thank you, Ralph." I smile self-consciously, plastering over my desolation. "Are you in search of Margaret?"

"I am, indeed."

"She's taking a nap, I believe."

"Ah. No nap for you, then? Too vibrant for afternoon naps?" Ralph senses my need for cheering, and flattery is the only way he knows how to do it.

"Naps don't sit well with me. Too much to do, to think about." The comment seems thin. What do I have to do? I twist the topic. "Like you, I should imagine. You're a busy man, with your business, your family, *and* visiting your mother so regularly."

"I am indeed." He nods dramatically. "But nothing would stop me from visiting my favorite ladies." His flirting has an inauthentic tenor, either because we're alone or because I seem unable to return it from beneath the shadows of the day.

Alyson appears in the doorway, looking no less fresh and pretty at 3 p.m. than she did at 7 a.m.

"Harriet. Ralph. What are you doing standing here in the dark?" she asks in her pleasing Scottish accent. "We have lights, you know."

I realize she's right, we're barely lit in this east-facing room, the scant daylight falling through the window lethargically, casting us with a depressive purple-grey mere suggestion of light.

"Alyson. How lovely to see you." Ralph moves towards her as she turns on the crystal chandelier overhead, and the library is suddenly golden and warm. He follows her from the room without another glance at me. I'm trying not to think badly of Alyson. It's not her fault she's young and pretty—but I can't help thinking that she's rather beneath Ralph. She works in a retirement home, after all, and she's rather . . . insubstantial, intellectually, I think. She watches reality television, for goodness' sake.

"Flirting with Harriet again, are we?" I hear Alyson tease as they leave, her voice lowered.

"Are you calling me a granny-chaser?" he replies, and they laugh.

They probably think I can't hear.

I fall into a chair and, absurdly, feel tears slide down my aged cheeks where they pool at the hollow above my jowls. I remember when tears shot their way down my face with alacrity from over higher cheekbones.

I am forgotten. Invisible. Again.

"You're still here?" It's Margaret, without Ralph. "They said you were, but that was hours ago."

I look up and register where I am. The library. That's odd, I'm not often in the library. Am I looking for something? I vaguely remember searching for something important.

It's dark outside, so it must be nearly dinner.

"I am . . . still here," I confirm, unable to think of anything else to say.

"I'm glad," Margaret says, more animatedly, seeming to take in my confusion and forcing the concern from her brow. "I've been thinking about these dreams you've been having and poor Molly's experience this morning. I know I've teased you about the house being haunted, but we really don't know anything about the place. I thought we should find out more about the history of it."

The history of the Manor?

"I ran into Dr. Phillips earlier," she continues. "You know he took over as medical director here at the Manor when the old Marryat family physician retired, so he knows a little something about the family history. He mentioned in passing that there was a secret about a woman who used to live in this house, generations ago." Margaret waves her hand to indicate the passing of time. "He was frustratingly vague, but you know me. I love a mystery. Thought I might find out a little more about the place we've apparently committed ourselves to live and die in!"

Margaret takes off her regular glasses and swaps them for her matronly reading glasses before scanning the shelves of the vast history wall. She's practically the only person who uses the library. The books are too old and the print too small for most Marryat residents. Exhausted, I stay in my ancient leather armchair and watch her examine the rows of books silently. To look at this slightly stooped old lady, you would never know Margaret has such a curious and brilliant mind. I wonder what she'll discover, and my thoughts wander back to poor Molly's experience this morning, to how badly she frightened herself. Aren't mirrors linked to the occult in some way? A gateway to the other side? I think I saw it in a film once. Perhaps one I watched with William. I vaguely remember his remarks about belief in the occult being for the feeble-minded. *Did* he say that? Or am I misremembering?

It's cold. The temperature drops on this side of the house quite dramatically when the sun goes down.

The dark room is lit only by candles.

I thought we were forbidden to light candles without staff authorization.

I am part of a circle of elderlies. Everyone's eyes are closed, and our hands are touching. The others are murmuring, chanting. I am, too, although I have no comprehension of my utterings. I'm aware of the rattle of phlegm as I growl out the nonsensical words. I feel stifled, claustrophobic, burning hot then blisteringly cold, as though we're traveling through a perilous landscape towards danger with no ability to stop. Descending a mountain on a steam locomotive and it's impossible to get off.

A mirror appears in front of me. I resist looking into it until some unknown force compels me to do so. My eyes hook into a hollowed-out face made up of only negative space. I see only what's around it. It's me. Myself. The absence of everything. As I would be in death.

If terror had a sound, I hear it—an abstract, undiscernible noise, deafening and all consuming—a cyclone lifting me up and spinning me around until I land with a thump, like Dorothy's house in *The Wizard of Oz,* in the silence.

"Are you okay, my dear?" Margaret asks. "You were making a very peculiar sound."

A sound. Where am I? The library.

"What happened?" I sit up. The chandelier still casts its brilliance over the room, and it's no longer cold. Someone started a fire. I must have been dreaming again. The . . . séance. It didn't really happen.

"Another nightmare?" Margaret scans a page of the oversized book in front of her.

"I think—well, yes," I stammer, in a bewildered, lethargic daze.

Margaret nods. "Did you know . . . this library has a *sizable* section on spirituality and the occult?" It's a rhetorical question. "It's quite curious. There must be about fifty books on séances alone."

I'm jolted fully awake. "Séances?" The word emerges as a growl. "That's odd. I was just dreaming . . ." I stop myself, as the details of my dream reemerge.

Margaret peers at me over the top of her glasses, then continues as though I hadn't interrupted. "I mean, some of these books are well over a hundred years old. It's fascinating, what people used to believe. I suppose some still do. I'm half-wondering if that strange woman who used to live here—the one Dr. Phillips mentioned—if they were hers . . ." She trails off, reabsorbed by the book.

How is it possible that Margaret discovered these séance books just as I was dreaming about a séance? I suppose she could have told me, not knowing I was dozing. I could have incorporated her observation into my dream. In fact, one of the older ladies fell asleep in front of the television the other day and told me she had a long dream about a person who'd turned into a vacuum cleaner before she woke to find an infomercial for Vac's Back cleaners still running.

"Séances are very silly, of course, but I've always thought the idea of them is also rather fun," Margaret comments as she turns another page.

"What's the time?" I ask.

Margaret turns her watch towards the light and peers at its face. "Six thirty. Dinner in half an hour."

"Good. I think I need a drink. Something strong. Whisky." Anything to alter my state, maneuver me out of the remnants of this dream.

"Are you okay, Harriet?" Margaret turns her attention to me again. "You look out of sorts."

I feel scuttled.

"I'm not quite myself. But then . . . I don't think I really have been in a rather long time. Perhaps I've been possessed," I joke, uncharacteristically, but instead of lightening my mood it sinks me back deeper into the gnarled atmosphere of my dream, where I saw myself as other, as absence itself.

4

"The staff are concerned about you, Harriet. So is Judith," Dr. Phillips tells me. Somehow, it's Monday again. A wet sneeze of a day outside. November's bluster had distracted me, and again, I'd forgotten my appointment.

"Concerned?"

"That you've been more forgetful lately. Forgetful and a little lost."

I clear my throat of irritation. "Lost? I know my way around perfectly well, thank you."

He offers me an infuriatingly sympathetic and conciliatory smile, as though we're sharing a secret. "I think you know what kind of 'lost' they mean, Harriet. And it's not easy, I know. It's not easy to remember, not easy to—"

"There's nothing wrong with my mind, Dr. Phillips," I interrupt him and hold up a hand to signal I don't wish for him to continue with this line of questioning. "Nothing other than this house, which I swear is out to get me. Every single night I dream it's coming to kill me. It's rotten, I tell you. Some core part of this dreadful place is rotten, and dark, and my . . . mind . . . is picking up on it."

"Margaret mentioned something about that. Your nightmares. Something about séances?" Dr. Phillips's sympathetic tone deepens, and I wonder what else Margaret has been telling the doctor about me. It seems that everyone is talking about me as if I wasn't here. Scheming behind my back. "Nightmares can be an indication of a confused or depressed state of mind."

"I'm more concerned about the state of my body," I tell him. "My arthritis, for one. The fact it's getting harder for me to climb the stairs, and before you say it, no, I don't want to use that wretched stairlift."

"It's for your safety, Harriet."

I'm about to counter his point but don't. I deflate suddenly under the weight of the air around me. It all feels so heavy. "I hate this. I hate getting old. I can't—" I wave my hand in the air to signal my inability to find the words.

Dr. Phillips allows a short silence, letting me breathe. "You know," he says after a while, "there are worse things than getting old."

I think of the "nothing" face in my séance dreams. "You can say that. You believe in an afterlife," I remind him. Also, he's almost fifty years my junior. I don't think he has the right to an opinion.

"Even so. You're at a different time of life. But it's still a time of life, Harriet. Albeit a slower one. A time for reflection. Comfort. The company of good friends."

This sounds like a line he has said verbatim to many elderly patients. What does he know of reflection and comfort? Can he not understand what's happening to me? Clearly, I've become invisible to him as well. A shriveled-down raisin of the woman I used to be, barely there. A ghost. But a ghost who must still face herself, her nothingness. A ghost who must still face the daemon in the mirror.

"You know what I find comforting?" Dr. Phillips asks.

"Jesus?" I answer flatly.

He splutters out a short laugh. "Well, yes, Jesus. But other than Him, I have interests. I like to sing—"

I stop him before he can demonstrate. "I'm sure you do, Dr. Phillips. Singing has never been my forte."

"Not singing, then, but something. Something to occupy the mind." He's smiling kindly again.

"Good plan." I wearily push to my feet. "Distract the patients from their impending doom with hobbies. Give them a toy to play with to distract from the tantrum." He laughs again. A genuine one this time. I like him a little more. "I think I'll choose—" And the word has vanished. "Building," I manage.

"A building? Like this one?"

"No, a small one, with small people inside. Tiny furniture." I don't attempt to hide my scowl of frustration, to smooth out these giant creases of temper. I mean the thing that was my most favorite toy as a child.

"A doll's house?" Dr. Phillips offers.

"As I said, a doll's house," I tell him as I leave his office, with apparently no new medication today.

I think of a doll's house version of my dreams. I wish I could squash the nightmares down inside a miniature replica of my life, letting them play out there, contained. A horror movie inside a diorama.

There! I can think of "diorama" but not "doll's house"?

"Hello, Harriet!" June sails by me without stopping. A "power walker," I think they call her. She's a fellow resident but a good few years younger than me and considerably fitter. She's startled me, and by the time I think to reply, she's too far ahead.

I'm too late. Too slow.

I'm outside, unsure of how I got here. My back is stiff, and my joints ache. I can't imagine why I thought it was a good idea to walk, or hobble, the grounds today. More so, why am I at the back of the property where I never go? I've always disliked graveyards and tend to prefer to ignore the existence of the small chapel and burial grounds here that I believe Judith will shove me into one day. They present a rather awful kind of foreboding.

The tearful yellow-grey sky suggests it might snow, but disappointing fat droplets of rain splash down obstinately instead. It's the kind of day that should be spent having coffees and lunches with friends in town, followed by cocktails with William by the fire. An old-fashioned. Not shuffling around the muddy grounds of a haunted retirement home, miserable in my crookedness, in my torment, exhausted after weeks of terror-disrupted sleep.

Absurdly, the sun breaks through the thick coven of clouds for only a second or two. In that cough of time, I see my shadow silhouetted on the path in front of me. A hunched, hobbling thing. Like a gobble. Is that right? A gobble? Those evil little men in fairy tales?

I wonder if I resemble the old women in the stories I used to read to Judith when she was young. Those women who were always ugly, witchy, and resentful of the beautiful. Like Dolly's—Dolly? Holly? No, Molly—Molly's monstrous portrait of me. Am I the wicked witch now, the one who's trying to take down Snow White, Cinderella, Hansel and Gretel, and the one with the wooden circle? The thing that spun around. She hurt her finger and fell asleep. What was it? Margaret would know. A circle. A spinning circle? Like the circle in my dreams, the one I spun out of. The séance.

My thoughts keep looping back to séances.

I've never been particularly interested in spiritualism, nor have I clamored to connect with anyone who has died. I think of the blue butterfly that landed on my lapel a while ago. The simple beauty of it. Apparently, the dead find a way to visit you.

Is that what these dreams are? Someone from the other side trying to tell me something? Tell me what? That I'm old, and I'm going to die? I'm aware. Too aware.

"While you were in with Dr. Phillips, I spent a little more time in the library. I found something *very* interesting."

It is lunchtime, and Margaret is lit with excitement.

"Oh?" I say, surprised to find myself eager to hear what she's learned.

"Yes, you'll be interested in this. Not a book, but a diary. From a long time ago."

"A diary?" An old diary is infinitely more interesting than an old book. Full of truths and scandals. "Whose?"

"The original mistress of Marryat Manor, no less. And she was quite something."

"In what way?"

Margaret glances around her to make sure there are no staff nearby, before reaching into her handbag and retrieving a leather-bound book. She swaps her glasses again, perhaps the only person here not using bifocals.

"Is that from the library?" I whisper. "You're not supposed to take them out of the room."

She waves away my concern. "Yes, I know. Firstly, before we dive into the diary, you must know spiritualism was becoming increasingly popular in all kinds of circles in Victorian England. Particularly with women. That this lady might have believed such things was not unusual. Elizabeth Barrett Browning herself was much taken with spiritualism. This is likely why there are so many books on spiritualism in the library. I think they belonged to the original Lady Marryat."

I nod my understanding. Before now, I've never been interested in such things. William always dismissed them as "tosh."

"The industrial revolution was partly to blame. The technological and scientific advances were so rapid that the lines between the real world and the 'magical' became quite blurred. With the rise of sectarian religion and freer thinking emerging, but with obvious roots embedded in Christianity, spiritualism was an inevitable product. And it's stuck around because people are so beguiled by the paranormal."

I stifle a sigh. Margaret sometimes forgets she is not in a lecture theatre.

Margaret lowers her voice as she drops the book discreetly into her lap, so the diary is half-hidden by the tablecloth. "There is, quite frankly, an inordinate amount of rubbish about dinner menus and sauces and writing letters and such things that mistresses were plagued with in those days. But then there's a shift. And this must be what Dr. Phillips meant about the history of the house."

She glances around again before she reads from the diary. "*If anyone were to read this, they would think that I've gone quite mad, and that I should be locked up in an asylum. But I have discovered something quite miraculous. Indeed, were it not for the method of my discovery, I would have thought I'd been visited by angels, that my prayers had been answered, and God had bestowed me with His grace and granted me with my heart's desire. But no, I have happened upon something extraordinary through quite another method. A clarity of mind, a freshness, a vigor in my body. An arousal of spirit. And all resulting from a séance.*'"

"A séance?" I interrupt. "Clarity of mind, arousal of spirit through a séance? That sounds wonderful. How is that possible?"

"I have no idea. It isn't, I shouldn't have thought. I mean, it's nonsense," Margaret says dismissively before adding, "but very interesting nonsense, I admit."

Margaret scans the page silently until she comes across another passage she thinks is worth relaying. "Listen to this: '*The spiritualists have quite underestimated the power of the séance. Upon the written instruction of an anonymous elder that I found buried in a book, several friends and I gathered in the library. With a crucifix and rosary beside me, I sat in front of the old mirror, my friends circled around me, we chanted. Morte magis metuenda senectus. Visibilia ex invisibilius.*'"

"Good lord. I hate Latin." I roll my eyes.

"Yes. Jamming those two phrases together like this is a non sequitur." Margaret grins as though she just said something witty.

"What do they mean?"

"'Old age should be feared rather than death.' And then, 'The visible comes from the invisible.' Quite strange really."

Old age should be feared rather than death. It's as though this is meant for me. But what is meant by *The visible comes from the invisible?*

"Then she says: '*After some time, I was aware of something happening. The next thing I knew, I was waking up in my bed, revived with smelling salts with my physician close by. I had taken a funny turn, I am told, a fit, followed by a loss of consciousness. The physician was quite concerned about me. But the remarkable thing is that I woke feeling better than I have in years. I feel well, vital, and a good deal younger than before the séance. Not reborn, exactly, but revitalized. Occupying space again. As though yesterday I were a feeble watercolor, and today I'm painted in oil. Present and opaque.*'" Margaret closes the book, and finally picks up her sandwich. "Can you believe it?"

I'm not sure what to reply. *Well, vital, younger, revitalized. Occupying space again.* This is everything I long for. To stop falling, declining, to claw my way up a little so I can unfurl into someone significant. Someone unwithered who catches attention. To be seen again.

I think of the blue butterfly for a moment before Margaret continues. "What a remarkable coincidence. This lady having such an experience related to feeling younger, when the Manor eventually became a retirement home!"

"And my dreams, when such an extraordinary event occurred here . . ."

"Another super coincidence." Margaret smiles. "Oooh! We should have a séance! You could play Florence Marryat!"

She's fascinated, of course, but only intellectually. This is not affecting her as it is me. To her, it's not personal. She hasn't been singled out to take notice.

"Séances are not plays, Margaret."

She shrugs. "They might as well be."

I dream of the séance again, but this time as the late mistress of the Manor described it.

A throng of women in black Victorian dress, holding hands and chanting. Flickering light. Tension in the cold air. An older woman sits in front of a mirror, her eyes locked on her reflection as she gazes intensely into it. But then *I* am the reflection. It's my eyes she's staring into, and for a moment I think we—the mistress and I—are being spun in the center of the room until I realize it's actually the room itself spinning, slowly at first then faster, dizzying, tornado-like speed, a blur. A terrific roar builds, as if from a storm, punctuated by several terrified, sustained screams, off key and discordant. The mistress, still looking me in the eye, growls, "*Sum quod eris.*"

I don't know what it means, but I'm terrified as I wake.

At first, I think one of my previous dreams has become a reality, and the retirement home is on fire. But then I realize the intense orange glow filling the room is not flickering. I turn in my bed to regard the brilliant and hopeful sunrise, as bold and pinkly orange as a grapefruit, filling my window and throwing itself onto me. I must have forgotten to close the curtains last night.

Sum quod eris. What does that mean?

Despite the aggression of its delivery, it could be something significant. Something instructive.

I can't forget it.

At breakfast, I ask Margaret. "What does *sum quod eris* mean? I dreamt about it. The original Marryat woman said it to me."

"It's what they write on gravestones," she tells me between bites of toast. "I am what you will be."

"How horrible!" I shudder. "A dead woman is telling me I'll be dead too? It's like a threat."

"Well, firstly"—Margaret's tone is matter of fact—"everyone dies. Therefore, it's not really a threat, more a foretelling. Secondly, it's just a dream, Harriet. I don't think anyone's telling you anything."

"But I didn't know that phrase, *sum quod eris.* Never heard it before in my life! Why did I dream about it if it wasn't a . . . message?"

Margaret looks at me and pauses. "Perhaps you read it on a gravestone, or heard it somewhere, then completely forgot about it. Or buried it somewhere in your subconscious."

It can't be that simple.

"I think, Harriet, that we're living small, contained lives. It's easy to make connections between the things in front of us when there are so few of them. It's easy to think there are hidden messages, particularly when we're confused, when we're trying to make sense of things."

"I'm not confused!" I protest. "Well, I am confused, but not in the way you think I am. I'm confused about what this house wants from me!"

Margaret doesn't answer for a while, letting my burst of anxiety diffuse.

"I am very certain that what this house wants from you," she says gravely, and I lean forwards slightly, waiting for my wise friend's profundity to organize my messy thoughts, "is to play Monopoly."

She grins, infuriatingly, and I slump back in my seat, defeated.

"And later, for us to hold a séance," she adds with a mysterious twinkle in her eye. "What do you say?"

I don't know how to answer her. I'm quite stuck. Vitality. Youth. Revitalization. What was it? *A clarity of mind.* My bones ache for these things. I ache. It's surely rubbish. How could a silly séance result in such things? Yet in these unlikely dreams, I have a real sense of inevitability, of being dragged towards something. Is the séance worth trying, even for the smallest chance it might result in something positive?

"Well, I hadn't thought about it. But it might stop these nightmares."

Margaret smiles. "You know, it might! Get them out of your system. Really, it might be rather fun. Oh! I could wear my old festal robes. I still have my gown hanging in the wardrobe. Couldn't bear to part with it. I knew a club of widows who partook in séances regularly, straight after their book group. Just in case their husbands had something to say. I don't think they were hoping for anything profound, just useful, like when should the radiators be bled, when was the right time to dig up the potatoes, that kind of thing." Margaret chuckles. "Different kind of séance, but perhaps we can get some of the others involved too." She nods towards the throng of elderlies dozing in front of the fire. "Shake things up a bit. They could use a little revitalization too."

5

argaret convinced Melissa to bring some chairs into the library and arrange them in a semicircle in front of the unlit fireplace. The chandelier is on, and Melissa placed candles around the room where they're least likely to be knocked over.

Naturally, Margaret is hosting our strange little event, proud and upright in the scarlet festal robes that swamp her. Her head looks too small, too withered poking out from all that fabric, as though she were being devoured by something bilious. Some dreadful plant, like in that ghastly novel, *Day of the . . . Gizzards? Griffiths?* No . . .

I'm not expecting the nervous titters from the other residents as they file slowly into the room. They seem too flippant, discordant with my own darker worries.

"I went to a séance once." It's Tom, one of the oldest elderlies, shaped like a tipped-over barrel on legs and inclined to offer opinions with an overly weighty delivery as though they were great profundities, regardless of topic. "Quite enlightening. Are we going to be speaking to our loved ones? I'm hoping my wife will make an appearance. She could tell me where she put those—"

"No, no, Tom," Margaret cuts in. "Different kind of séance. This one's about connecting with the house and its history."

She winks at me, having decided to appear to take the whole thing seriously so everyone gets in the right mood and doesn't think of the exercise as a joke. She hasn't told anyone about the outcome of the original mistress's séance we're trying to replicate, or that it's about me. "We're not trying to win hearts and minds here, Harriet, we just need warm bodies," she'd explained to me as she recruited the eight fellow residents to join us for "a fun little experiment."

"This is all quite peculiar, Margaret," Elizabeth—the eldest of us all—comments, her voice wobbling, not from emotion but from the exhaustion of having lived more than ninety years. "Wherever did you get the idea?"

"I've been reading about the history of the house."

Elizabeth looks back at her, head tilted and brows creased.

"The history of the house!" Margaret repeats, louder, and the older lady nods a vague understanding, underscoring the reason we're all here.

If this works, I wonder if we'll all feel more energized or if it will only be me.

I glance around at my fellow residents, and suddenly everything feels wrong. Too real, too dimensional, these familiar objects, familiar people. There's no ambiance, despite the antique grandeur of the room—its high ceilings, walls dark with thousands of leather-bound volumes—and the wisdom it contains, the learning it's produced. It's all very much of this world. Very three-dimensional. No sense of the mystical, the magical, the *other*. And as much as I've felt my mind wandering over the past several weeks, right now I feel very much in the present.

"We still need the mirror from the basement," Margaret exclaims. "The big free-standing one Harriet's granddaughter found. That's what started this whole thing. Let me see what's keeping the men."

She disappears, leaving me, the deputy host, in charge of the group. Without her presence, the room feels colder.

"I'm not sure I want the dead to contact me," Elizabeth's voice shimmies out from within the thicket of elderlies. "What if it's someone I didn't like?"

"Apparently not that sort of séance," June informs her.

"Ah. Then what are we trying to do?"

"Margaret's got it all under control." I raise my voice, conscious of my cut-glass accent—everyone here comes from wealth, but they're not all from the home counties. Some are middle class. Ordinarily, it wouldn't bother me, but now, when they're here upon our request, I'm aware of how condescending I can sound to others. How it marks a distinction between us, makes people feel less than, or worse, that you think they're beneath you. "It's about the history of the house, I think." I try to introduce a warmth into my voice I do not feel, softening the truth, polishing the edges. "It's a reenactment of a séance the original mistress conducted."

"Here we are!" Margaret calls a moment later from the hallway. Two of the male staff—a caretaker and someone from the kitchen—stagger under the weight of the mirror, draped with a cloth and held on its side horizontally between them. Margaret beams excitedly, like a schoolgirl finding props for a play.

As they edge it through the doorway, the men groaning and sweating under the mirror's heft, I see it more clearly. Large, with a thick, ornately decorated brass frame. The kind of quality that only comes with unique, handmade items. The kind of object that seems significant, knowing. It makes me think of the magic mirror in that fairy tale—the one with the dwarfs—though perhaps more maleficent. Or less? Was it the mirror itself that carried ill will?

One of the men loses his grip, and the mirror tilts to one end. The room gasps as he catches it on his knee with a stiff groan, something falls to the floor, and the drape falls from the mirror, tangling around the man's knees. As the mirror tilts, the other man steps forwards so the frame can rest on his knee, too, but something crunches underneath his foot.

"Oh!" Margaret exclaims, and once the men are through the door, she picks up the fallen item—a crucifix, broken in half right through the middle of Jesus.

Someone gasps, and I see Elizabeth making the sign of the cross. I didn't know she was Catholic. I don't suppose I've ever asked.

"Oh, good lord!" Margaret utters. "Well, that can't be a good sign."

"Where do you want it?" the one who lost his grip asks.

Margaret points to the center of the circle of chairs. "In the front, by the mantel, please."

Arms shaking with exertion, the men tip the mirror upwards.

"Sorry about that, madam." The burlier of the two men glances to Margaret then comically skyward, as if appeasing a deity, but Margaret waves the apology away and instead helps them position the mirror to her liking. The mirror's longer and thinner than I expected, the glass forming a giant screaming "O." The surface is murky with age and decades of accumulated dirt, the frame tarnished with soot and grime collecting in its grooves.

"That thing's seen better days," Tom considers, and others agree, with comments like "it needs a jolly good clean."

Despite the babble, the atmosphere shifts again, the presence of the mirror and the ominous breakage darkening the space. The mirror is a good foot taller than any of us and towers over us like a scowl. Margaret lights incense, though I'm not sure it's necessary, its sweet and musky stench wafting through the library. It reminds me of black cherries, earth, and acrid smoke, with the tiniest hint of decay, changing the structure of the air. It reaches into the sinuses, pulls at the temples, and tugs at the brow, so you can't help but submit.

I realize I'm hurting myself, clenching my wretched arthritic fingers into claws, and I unfurl them painfully, making myself take deep, rattling breaths that make me slightly light-headed.

Margaret indicates everyone should take their seats, and they slowly comply.

"Harriet?" She nods to me. "The lights."

The staff have all left now.

I walk to the entrance of the room and close the door and switch off the chandelier. When I turn back towards the semicircle, everything looks very different. My breath catches at the scene, transformed by the darkness, by the arrangement of the residents, neat and still around the mirror, the effect the candlelight has on their wrinkled faces, casting deeper shadows beneath their eyes, cheekbones, and necks, light catching only the lenses of their glasses, and by the gentle serpentine smoke swirling from the incense burner.

Margaret does not seem as surprised by the alteration as I am. This was what she'd intended, how she'd imagined it. She nods again, and I walk towards the group. In the silence, my footsteps echo on the old oak floor. They sound deliberate, a progression towards some kind of unknowable inevitability, and I'm suddenly unsure of myself. I long for William. For his logical assurance and bright-blue spirit. The loss of him washes over me, and by the time I've taken my seat at the center of the semicircle, I'm drawn deeper down inside myself, barely present.

I stare at my reflection in the murky surface of the mirror and hardly recognize the old sunken woman gazing back at me, looking vaguely bewildered. I'm not sure how I found myself here.

Something skitters across my vision, there, then gone. I startle, my voice too loud as I ask, "What was that?"

Nine elderly heads turn in my direction, then look around themselves, their concerned murmurs filling the air.

"I saw a shadow," I say. "In the mirror. It looked like a figure."

Only Margaret offers an explanation. "A silhouette of one of us from the flickering candles. Our shadows are moving all over the place."

I want to tell her she's wrong, that what I saw wasn't the wavering shadow of a hunched resident but something still and erect, with a different kind of shape. Something hooded or cloaked. Something or someone *ominous*.

Yet it seems so contrived, and I'm already questioning myself. Did I actually see something? Or was it my nerves affecting me, making me see things that aren't there?

The room quiets again. I stare at my reflection, directly into my eyes, ignoring the elderlies around me.

"*Morte magis metuenda senectus,*" Margaret begins chanting softly. "*Visibilia ex invisibilius.*"

After she repeats it a few times, the others join in, tentatively at first, then with more confidence. The repetition has an almost hypnotic effect on me, and I can't tear my eyes away from the mirror, even if I wanted to. My only thought is *sum quod eris*. The words the original mistress spoke to me in my dream. I am stuck, transfixed. Immovable in body and mind . . .

My body is no longer my own and I am no longer in it. I am looking into my eyes. Not at my reflection, but at my own, physical eyes. From above. I see myself, my head pushed backwards with neck-breaking force, my body contorted into a tense, spiky-limbed shape. My mouth is wide open—wide as the scream of the mirror's "O"—a black, gaping hole.

Then I see it again—the shadowy figure from before. It stands at the front of the mirror regarding my body for a moment before bursting through the glass without breaking it, out towards my body and flooding into my rigid mouth! Only the whites of my eyes are visible as they roll back into my head.

Floating above, I'm transfixed with terror, sure I am witnessing my own death.

More and more of the shadow shape disappears into my body—fluid but solid.

How can it not be choking me? How am I not suffocating?

Perhaps I am. I'm *being* suffocated. Briefly I think of the blue butterfly, of William. His was a very different death. A peaceful death. A slipping, rather than a throttling. Is he here with me? Can he help me, wherever I'm suspended?

My physical body is snatched up into the air, so close now I'm nose-to-nose with myself. It hovers there for too many moments, then it falls. I fall with it, back down into myself, crashing to the floor.

* * *

I'm only aware of the screaming. So much screaming. No chanting, just the audible terror of the other residents. Then light. Beautiful, shimmering crystal-perfect light. The kind that beguiles children when they see a chandelier for the first time. In fact, very much like a chandelier. Maybe it *is* a chandelier. The one in the library? Am I in the library? If so, then why am I lying down? I feel as though I've been dropped from a great height, but at the same time, my body is numb. Am I paralyzed? Perhaps I've broken my neck. Fallen off a ladder. I could be dead. If so, then the light's a good sign. It's a still, white kind of light, nothing fiery. Like the lights on a Christmas tree.

The screaming dies down into a general clamor of upset, and a cloudy-haired head is silhouetted above me. "Harriet? Harriet? Can you hear me?"

I know the voice.

Margaret's words splinter with concern. "Are you okay, dear? Can you hear me?"

"Yes," I manage. I'm not sure how to form other words. Maybe I've had a stroke. It would be just like me to have one in the middle of a séance designed to make me feel rejuvenated.

That's right. A séance. We were having a séance. And now I'm on the floor with the lights on.

"Harriet? This is Dr. Phillips." A second head joins the first, looming above me. "Are you okay?"

"I think so," I say. So I *can* speak. My voice sounds unusually clear, and oddly calm. In fact, I *feel* calm.

"She's in shock," Margaret says, though I don't feel like I'm in shock. But then, that's what shock is. An unreal feeling.

"Can you move your toes for me?" Dr. Phillips sounds more serious than usual as he examines me, gently feeling my head and neck, my limbs.

I wiggle my toes, then rotate my feet before I even think to move them.

"Good, good," Dr. Phillips says. "How about sitting up? Do you think you can, Harriet?"

I inhale deeply and slowly push myself up, without even registering the difficulty of it.

"Excellent." Dr. Phillips takes a deep breath, his shoulders visibly relaxing.

"Oh, thank God!" Margaret holds a hand to her chest, the lead singer among a chorus of relieved sighs and murmurs.

"Okay, let's get everyone out of here," Dr. Phillips says. "She's okay, everyone! She's okay. Time to go back to your rooms."

"I'm getting a stiff drink!" I hear someone say under their breath followed by sounds of assent.

"What happened?" Dr. Phillips demands of Margaret once everyone else has gone.

"We were having a séance," she offers feebly, looking both guilty and bewildered. "It was just a bit of fun. I thought it would help Harriet with her nightmares. Get it out of her system."

"And what went wrong?" he asks.

"Well . . ." Margaret sounds uncertain. "It's all very strange. I can't really explain it. Harriet sat in front of the mirror, and then she went stiff, with her head back, and . . . well, it looked like she floated in the air a moment before she fell to the floor. I . . ." Poor Margaret looks wretched as her voice trails off. "I just can't explain it."

"It sounds like a dramatic fall, possibly during a neurological incident of some kind," Dr. Phillips says. "We'll need to have Harriet checked."

"Stop talking about me as if I weren't directly in front of you," I snap, hating the return of my invisibility. "There's nothing wrong with me. Look." I climb to my feet, finding it easier than usual. Perhaps shock can energize a person. Or maybe the fall stunned my muscles into loosening.

"I'm so sorry, my dear." Margaret looks unusually upset and unsure of herself.

"And are *you* okay?" Dr. Phillips softens, turning his attention to Margaret now.

"Me? Well, yes, I . . . it was all just a bit distressing. I thought I'd broken her!" She offers a pathetic little laugh.

"Harriet's all right, Margaret," Dr. Phillips reassures her, placing his hand on her thin shoulder. "Not that I approve of any of this. You should have checked with me first, especially since you roped in several of your fellow residents—many of whom have heart conditions."

"You're right, doctor. I should have thought. But in all honesty . . ." Margaret's hand hovers at her throat. "I didn't think anything would happen. Anything at all."

"And where did you find that mirror?" Dr. Phillips stares at it. In the light of the chandelier, it seems diminished, out of place, like the debris of a party the morning after.

"The basement," Margaret explains.

"And this?" He stoops to pick up the broken crucifix. "That's not reassuring. Who did that?"

He looks a little hurt, his poor Christian heart wounded.

She sighs. "It fell and broke as they were setting up the mirror."

The doctor huffs a breath out. "Well, I'll be offering an extra prayer tonight. Margaret, I think you should join your friends for a drink, by the looks of you. Harriet, I'd stay off it. You don't seem to have a concussion, but until we know what exactly happened and have run all the tests, best leave off the alcohol."

"Yes, Dr. Phillips. In fact, I think I might just head up to bed." My mind feels unnaturally clear, as though it's been wiped clean, despite the evening's events. I'm shaky and a bit unsettled.

I need time to collect myself.

6

I am early to breakfast after an opaque, dreamless sleep.

As I slather butter onto my second piece of toast—for I am starving this morning—my mind tries to form itself over the contours of last night's events, but their surface is too slippery.

I know something momentous happened. Something altering. I catch glimpses of shadowy memories that don't make sense, all very black and quite noxious. I vaguely remember looking at my own reflection—that would make sense, looking in the mirror was part of the ritual we'd planned—but I feel as though I remember my head being at an impossible angle too.

False memories?

It's frustrating that despite my efforts, yesterday remains a blur. Another symptom of age? Another vanishing? It does feel as though something has shifted in me, however. A subtle change. A little cleaner, as though the inside of me has been detangled.

Or possibly, it's the lingering aftereffects of shock.

The dining room is quiet this morning. Only a couple of other residents take their breakfast at seven, apparently. Somehow, I sense the silence, hearing the vibrations of nothingness on the air, as though I'm waiting for something, though I have no idea what that might be.

I wasn't aware how early the sunlight falls into the room through the tall windows in a magnificent shaft, catching the dust motes drifting quite ethereally through the room. Usually, I have a bit of a thing about dust. I think it's the knowledge that dust is primarily made up of dead skin that bothers me the most, as though each mote were a miniature cadaver. The thought of breathing in particles from other people's bodies was always abhorrent to me—that they should inhabit my unwitting body.

But today, the dust that catches the morning light seems delighted and whimsical, as though instead of particles of my fellow elderlies it's a blizzard of minute fairies pirouetting through the elegant room. What is a gathering of fairies called, I wonder? A frolic? A glitter?

Margaret shuffles in around eight. I've stayed in the breakfast room, waiting, quite content to sit with my pot of tea and look out at the gardens that are white with thick hoarfrost, reminding me of the frosty Christmas Eve when Judith was small. I took her to see *The Nutcracker*, and she was so beguiled by its festive magic.

"Look!" I motion out towards the garden as a weary-looking Margaret takes her seat. "Christmassy!"

"Ah yes, I suppose so." Margaret seems deep in thought as she pours herself a cup of tea from the pot, glancing at my cup and seeing that it's full before resting it back down.

"You'll know this," I ask. "What's the collective plural for fairies?"

"For fairies?" She looks up sharply, confusion mangling her forehead. "I couldn't say. Why on earth do you want to know that?"

"I don't know, I was just wondering."

The room still feels quiet, although there are a reasonable number of residents breakfasting now. Their chatter is more subdued than usual. Perhaps it's the distraction of the beautiful day. Imani lights a fire in the oversized hearth. I don't know why she bothers. I'm quite warm.

"Oh, good!" Margaret says, noticing. "It's rather chilly. How are you today, Harriet?"

She peers at me with scowling concern.

"I'm perfectly well, thank you," I say, shifting uncomfortably in my seat. Does she remember something I don't? My memories are so muddled. Still, I put on a brave front, hoping to change the subject. "You, on the other hand, look like you had a bad night."

"Oh, I did. I had terrible sleep. Half worrying, half—I don't know—remembering."

"Remembering what?"

Her brow furrows. "Last night, of course. The thought of you in that awful state."

I lean forwards and place a hand on hers, soothing her tightened old knuckles, as arthritic as mine. "I'm well, Margaret. Don't worry. I had some kind of weird experience, but it has not affected me negatively."

Margaret scrutinizes my face closely, as if she doesn't believe my assurances. "You don't seem quite yourself, Harriet."

Which is odd, because I feel more like myself than I have in ages. Before I can come up with a reply, Imani strides over. "Dr. Phillips has you scheduled at the local hospital for tests this morning, Harriet," she interrupts in her over-loud barking Northern tone as she collects the teapot for refilling. She's one of the few members of staff that speaks to us as though every one of us is deaf or stupid or both. Likes to feel like she's in charge.

"Right, yes." I sit back, unsettled because I still can't remember exactly what happened to me the night before. It must have been bad, though, if it requires a visit to town. The image of my head thrown back resurfaces in my mind, and I consider that I may not be fine at all.

The tests at the hospital prove to be a tedious ordeal.

Two hours after breakfast, I'm lying still in the tube of an MRI machine, my head held in place by its padded holder, as the machine knocks and clicks and jackhammers away. I wasn't expecting so much noise. Despite my advanced years, this is my first MRI scan. I suppose I'm lucky never to have needed one before.

Poor William had several. He was the kind of man who was always in excellent health until he wasn't, and was overtaken with cancer, remission, cancer, remission, cancer. Eaten away by that horrific, vampiric disease.

Dr. Phillips and Margaret both join me for the visit. Margaret's concern remains through the morning, despite my multiple attempts to reassure her. Her face looks shadowy, and she seems contrite, which is odd. She's usually so self-assured, so certain in her actions. It occurs to me for the first time that there could be something seriously wrong with me.

Epilepsy. That's what the doctor speculates, anyway. Though why I should have had my first and only seizure during a séance I have no idea.

After the MRI and the cardiac tests, I'm told I have one more. I have no idea what an EEG is until it's explained to me. An electro-encephalogram, used to measure electrical activity in the brain. Dr. Phillips seems most interested in this test.

The technician marks my head with a soft pencil then attaches electrodes to my scalp. I'm instructed to close my eyes and relax, then open them, subtract eight from twenty-three and multiply two by eleven. Mental arithmetic was never my strong suit, and I'm relieved they chose relatively simple problems. Then I'm told to read a paragraph of something, which is challenging without my glasses, but the type is large. I wonder if the passage has any significance. It's about the anatomy of a swan. Finally, I'm instructed to look at a flashing light. I'm suddenly nervous. Could I have a tumor? Or a problem with my nervous system? What damage have I done to myself?

When the test is complete and I'm waiting with Margaret for the results, Dr. Phillips emerges and notifies me the EEG will have to be repeated.

"Really?" I'm annoyed. "Why on earth would it need to be repeated?"

"Faulty equipment, they think. They're going to use a different machine." He holds up his hands and shrugs, having the grace to be apologetic, but it doesn't suit him. It makes him look inexperienced. Still,

I comply and let the test be conducted again. I perform more simple arithmetic and read the same paragraph about swans. Why swans? It makes me think of my mother. "You have an elegant, swan-like neck, dear," was one of the kinder things she said to me.

After the second test, I'm called into another room with several senior-looking doctors clustered around a screen with Dr. Phillips. I take a seat as instructed. I assume there are more technical problems with the machines, given the confused murmurs in the room.

"Mrs. Abington," one of the specialists finally addresses me. "I'm sorry we had to repeat the tests. We assumed the equipment was faulty, but even using a different machine, the results were the same. Something highly unusual is happening in your brain, and we don't understand."

I prickle with dread. What have they found?

"It's the wave patterns." Another specialist motions to a screen filled with wavy lines. "Normal results would show a single set of waves." He points at one of the lines. "But yours—"

"Have two." Dr. Phillips peers at the screen and shakes his head slightly in apparent disbelief. "Remarkable."

"I've never seen anything like it," a third consultant admits. "We'll examine all your test results again, but at this point we can only conclude you suffer from a very rare form of epilepsy. We're going to investigate, call a few more experts. There's related research being done in America, and we want to talk to the researchers there. Then we'll get back to you."

I find his comments baffling. I wanted to be seen again, to be remarkable for something, but never like this. I could be in serious trouble. "I'm not sure what to make of this. Should I be worried? What should I do until you know for sure?"

"For now, nothing. You've only had one episode, correct?" the first consultant asks. I nod. "And you're in mid-stages of dementia."

Not a question.

This catches me off guard. How can I have mid-stage dementia? This is the first I've heard of it.

Dr. Phillips nods on my behalf as I stare blankly at the doctors. Have I been told this before?

"Once we have a firm diagnosis then you should be monitored carefully. No alcohol. No driving."

I scoff. It's been years since I've driven a car.

"We'll be in touch, Mrs. Abington," the second consultant says.

"I'm a hydra," I inform Margaret as we collect her in the waiting room to leave.

Dr. Phillips snorts. "Hardly! You don't have nine heads, just two."

"Two heads?" Margaret looks dumbfounded.

"Not two heads, two sets of brain waves," Dr. Phillips elaborates. "It's . . . *unusual.*"

"They've never seen anything like it," I tell her, pointing in the direction of the office we emerged from. "I'm a medical marshal!" *Marshal?* No. I take a moment to search for the word I want before hitting upon it. "I mean marvel." I'm joking but afraid what this new condition could mean for me. "They're having to ask the Americans for help."

"They need to consult with other experts in the field," Dr. Phillips corrects.

"They think it's a rare form of epilepsy," I explain as we make our way out of the hospital. "But they aren't sure."

"Oh, dear." Margaret, usually so verbose, simply takes my hand. Hers feels small and withered in mine.

"No need to worry, ladies," Dr. Phillips instructs. "We're getting more test results back. In the meantime, Margaret, we just need to keep an eye on Harriet." His words make me feel feeble again. Diminished.

"I won't leave her side," Margaret asserts, like I am completely incompetent.

She must have known about the dementia. Has Margaret been looking after me all this time? Looking after me and not letting on? Why wasn't I told? Or was I? I'm not sure which is worse.

In the afternoon, Margaret tries to persuade me into a game of Scrabble. I'm disinclined to lose another game, for my intellectual inferiority to be underscored yet again. Instead, driven by the anxiety of my mysterious new condition, I feel the need to move.

Margaret doesn't have the energy to join me, but fortuitously, Ralph arrives as I'm leaving, and after briefly filling him in on the séance and my status Margaret persuades him to accompany me.

"You know, you visit Margaret far more than my own daughter visits me," I tell Ralph as we navigate the gravel path, which is less slippery than the flagstones. Although it's the afternoon, the temperature has dropped further, freezing the frost in place. I meant my statement kindly, but naturally it comes out sounding like a complaint. "You're a good son."

Ralph puffs out a short laugh. "It's as much for my own good as for Mum's. As I get older, I find I need her more and more. Her advice always centers me."

Centers me. Such a young person's expression. "Your mother's a wise lady," I agree with a nod. "I'm not sure what I would do without her."

"I think she feels the same about you." Ralph's comment falls flat, probably because he has defaulted to the mechanical, generic charm he's likely relied on his whole life. The false charm that suffocates his genuine goodness. "Tell me more about this séance."

I take a breath and recount the peculiar events—or at least what I can remember. In its retelling, everything sounds completely fabricated, as though it were the plot of one of those terrible horror films and not events that really happened to me. I'm still struggling to accept the reality of my new diagnosis and don't yet know how to feel about it, or how much to fear it. What will this peculiar second set of brain waves do to me?

"So did it work?" Ralph asks after I finish the story.

"Did what work?"

"The séance? Did it make you feel rejuvenated?"

I can't tell if he's teasing me or not, but I stop walking for a moment to think.

"Well, I have no idea . . . I mean, I don't think it could possibly have done." I stare down at myself—arthritic hands, slight stoop, over-bright "mutton dressed as lamb" coat. "I mean, look at me."

"Ah, Harriet. Beautiful as ever," he compliments, but he delivers the comment without really looking at me, and it sounds hollow. To him, I could be anyone. I feel like a figure absentmindedly painted onto the scenery backdrop, an extra, not even part of the chorus.

I throw a dubious smile back in his direction, feeling clearer of mind today, despite the tests. My thoughts follow each other logically this afternoon. They line up. I should be exhausted after the morning's exertions, but I feel as though I could keep on walking for some time. Adrenaline after all the excitement. I wonder if that other set of brain waves is the dementia. I may have flipped over to the other setting—the clearer one—but could transition back at any time.

"Never get old, Ralph," I tell him.

"I'm not planning on it."

"You're lucky, being a man. Age is kinder on men," I assert, thinking of William.

"Are you joking? We lose our hair," he protests.

"True, some of you do." I think of poor Dr. Phillips, thinning already.

"Most."

"You're holding on to yours rather well." I smile at him.

"At the moment, just about. Already greying though." He hovers a hand self-consciously at his temples.

I give a dismissive wave. "Oh, no need to worry about that. It's sexy."

Sexy? I'm not sure I've ever used that word, let alone told someone they were sexy. I'm mortified for a short moment before he replies.

"Sexy, really? Well, that's reassuring, thank you." Ralph's genuinely laughing, his eyes properly lit. I've affected him. He's present, suddenly, and for that moment I'm more visible, too, connected to him, and it spurs me to continue.

"You should feel good about yourself, Ralph," I tell him. "You're a handsome man. Charming and talented."

"Oh, thank you." He looks uncharacteristically bashful now. It occurs to me that his confident veneer might be a barrier to receiving genuine praise when he's the kind of man who needs it.

"Margaret did a good job of raising you. That wife of yours better pay attention." I'm irritated with myself at sounding so barkingly, needlessly angry, and I pick up the pace.

There's a pause before he speaks again, his voice smaller. "How important do you think sex should be in a relationship?"

I'm shocked he should ask me such a thing.

"I'm sorry to ask," he continues, sensing my discomfort. "I know it's not really appropriate, but it's the thing I can't talk to Mum about."

I'm not sure I've ever been asked such a thing or had such a conversation with a person so much younger than myself. In fact, I can count the conversations I've ever had about sex on one hand. It's far from an appropriate topic for discussion between a man and a woman. And yet, this is what the young do these days. I see it all the time on the television. Constantly talking about sex. People seem to like it. Possibly, they think it makes them appear interesting. I don't want Ralph thinking of me as old-fashioned. Irrelevant. I don't want him to write me off again.

"Well, people say different things about the subject." My voice curdles in my throat. *Come on, Harriet, you can do this. Just say it.* "But I think . . . I think it's very important. Not just that you have enough of it, but that it's the right kind. You need to feel properly desired." I swallow, batting away the heat of embarrassment. This is Ralph, a very attractive man. We're talking about sex. "I think when you're married it's easy to think your spouse is only having sex with you because you're their only option." Did it feel like that, with William? I can't remember now. "If you make each other feel like they're the only person who you would ever want to be with, because they're the most desirable to you, things work out well. If you don't do that, then things can fall over, rather."

Ralph listens attentively. "That's right. That's what I think too. Rekindling. It's hard. Once the magic is gone. Once someone's looked at you after you've suggested sex, and you know they're trying to think how they can get out of it, or when they've done it with you enough times with their heart not in it . . ."

"It ruptures you," I finish. I think of Margaret's accusation that Ralph has no inner life. She's wrong. She hasn't understood him.

"Yes. You get it, Harriet. You really do."

We walk a little further. This is the most real conversation I've ever had with Ralph. He's genuine, now. I wonder how many people he lets see him like this. Vulnerable. He's let me inside himself, and by seeing him I feel seen once more. So rare. So precious.

"Take the séance, for instance," he continues. "An example of you acting, of trying something, to get what you want. How many people of your age do you think are doing the same thing?" I'm nervous, I realize—excited even—by Ralph's having understood something important about me. He's taken the time to try and see something in me. "You're vital, Harriet, dementia or no dementia."

My sharp breath catches coldly in my chest.

There it is again. Dementia. "I don't feel as though I'm ill," I tell him, sounding querulous, and I wonder again if the switch has flipped, my addled mind put away for now by the new brain waves.

"You do seem to be having a very clear day." He smiles at me as though it's a compliment. How clouded am I usually? Do I know myself at all? "We should turn back. I need to get back to Mum, and this is quite the walk." He huffs out a breath. "It's tired me out. You're fitter than you look, Harriet!"

He does look tired. Unusual for a healthy man of his age.

To be honest, I feel I could walk for longer. But then, that's how energy works, isn't it? When you have it, you think it will go on forever. Then it suddenly falls out from under you. Overexertion is unwise at my age and, as Margaret might point out, given my condition.

"Not really," I say. "I'm just having a surprisingly good day, all things considered."

Margaret harries as we reach Marryat Manor again. "Where have you been? I was getting so worried."

"You know where we were walking." I'm irritated, feeling like a child out after curfew, embarrassed by my berating mother.

"But you were gone for ages!" she complains.

"A brief stroll."

"For an hour and a half?" she exclaims.

Were we really gone that long? That *is* a long time.

"I know what you were really worried about," Ralph says, intervening. He wraps his arms around his mother. "You were worried Harriet and I would run off together."

Margaret returns the hug, wrapping her arms around his waist and smiling. "Well, no . . ."

"But you shouldn't have worried. Our elopement isn't scheduled until next Wednesday," Ralph adds.

Margaret and I both laugh, and despite my irritation, I'm more delighted with the joke than I should be, regardless of his returning veneer.

I stay up late that night, sitting alone in the living room in front of the friendly fire with a cup of ginger tea, enjoying how rested my mind feels. Perhaps tomorrow will be another confused day, and those other brain waves will barrel in, but today I've felt as I did a year or two ago. A flare of clarity. Tomorrow, I'll likely feel the effects of the long walk and the morning at the hospital. The anxiety of this new epilepsy will shoulder in again. I'll become acquainted with the horrible aspects of the condition, which will likely wreck what's left of my body while it takes control of my mind. But tonight, I'll stay up and think, while I can.

Our elopement isn't scheduled until next Wednesday.

I smile as I remember Ralph's joke. Then I remember other things he said on our walk. That I was vital. *Vital.* I think of his hand hovering self-consciously near his temple as he talked of his greying hair. If I were the wife of a man like Ralph, he'd never know self-doubt again. I'd make him feel adored every day of his life.

Did I do that for William? I don't think so, but then he wasn't the kind of man to need it. He lived practically, loving gently. He didn't need to feel adored. He just needed constancy and never fully understood that I had to have more.

Ralph, I think, would understand. We seem to share that need. Reaffirmation.

Age is so devastatingly unfair, with so many barriers to joy. It's not enough to find beauty in the things around me. Having lost my own, it's like standing outside life, looking in. As I've aged, I've become too flat, too *nothing*. In my younger days, I would look at myself in the mirror and know I was seen, that the world was mine. I knew I was prized, desired, envied. Beautiful, I was the best I could be, had a head start in everything I wanted to do. I wore my immaculacy and brilliance so well. I took the attention as my due.

But it wasn't just beauty. I had presence. Visibility. I felt as though my being there brought specialness to other people's lives, made them feel something. Desire, envy. I *stirred* people. Motivated them to be better. I charged a room. I was noticed. Important.

I do nothing to a room now. The air, disgruntled, shuffles aside to accommodate me, but I am an inconvenience. Most days, it's as though I'm already dead. An untidy cluster of dust.

What would I give to be seen again, if only for a short time? To come into being again, to have a powerful presence again. To be a bright splash of color, effervescent, alive, visible.

Everything, I think.

I'd give up everything.

7

"I have a clean bill of health," I inform Margaret after returning from Dr. Phillips's office. "Other than the epilepsy," I add, though it's a rather significant detail. "Although I've had no other symptoms."

The prospect of unknown effects has tugged at the edges of my days, niggling, probing, though remaining elusive.

"That's wonderful, dear."

"In fact, I'm feeling rather good, comparatively. Less creaky. Must be the fish oil finally kicking in."

Margaret smiles weakly. "I wish I could say the same. You know me, I don't like to complain, but I feel about a hundred years old today. This winter is getting into the bones." She looks out the window at the gardens, at the sluggish browns and barely hued greens under a graphite sky. "*There's a certain slant of light, on winter afternoons, that oppresses, like the weight of cathedral tunes.*' Emily Dickinson."

"That's quite lovely." I smile and she looks mildly surprised at my comment. I suppose I am usually more curmudgeonly when it comes to her literary references.

"You know, you do look good, Harriet. Fresher. You've taken my energy and made me older!"

I offer another grin. Usually, I would bat away these compliments as nonsense, as one of the hundred politenesses we elders exchange with each other daily, but for once I think she's right. Somehow, I do look better. A little smoother, more upright. My bright clothes lift me again rather than underscore my greyness. It's remarkable what a few days of proper sleep will do for you. The nightmares have gone too—looked after by the other part of my brain? The house no longer claims to be possessed. It feels different to be here, the creepiness evaporated. Like it's just a house again.

"Hello, Mummy."

Startled, I turn to see Judith here. "Hello, dear."

I stand to embrace her, and now it's my daughter's turn to look startled. I suppose it's uncommon for me to rise to greet her. Usually, she bends to hug her passive mother, like she does next to a seated but warmly smiling Margaret. "Lovely to see you."

"No Molly today?" Margaret asks.

"Not today, no. She . . . had an afterschool club." Judith's fingers hover at her mouth the way they always do when she's fibbing. I wonder why Molly doesn't want to join her mother. Something to do with her experience in the basement? Judith turns her attention back to me. "Mummy, you look remarkably well."

"*Remarkably?*"

"Well, yes, much more energetic than usual." She looks to Margaret for affirmation, and Margaret nods in agreement.

I'm wearing my favorite blouse. Cornflower blue. I wouldn't have thought it would complement a scarlet skirt, but somehow it works. I'm reclaiming a fragment of my former exuberance today. "I'm glad you said that, Judith, because I wanted to request for you to take me out shopping the next time you visit."

"Shopping?"

"For Christmas. I'd very much like to go into town."

"Of course, Mummy." Judith sounds hesitant. The blatancy of her reluctance to spend time with me is painful, though I pretend to ignore it. "But you always shop online now, don't you remember? The staff help you with the iPad."

"Yes, yes." I wave her comment away impatiently. "But where's the fun in that? Where's the spontaneity?"

Judith looks doubtful. An unbecoming expression on her.

"I'm not sure I want a spontaneous gift," Margaret chips in, dubiously.

"And the iPad is not very festive," I add.

"Festive?" Judith says. "You care about festive?"

"Naturally, Judith! I love Christmas!" I say, confused as to why this should be a surprise to her. "You remember when we used to go Christmas shopping, Judith? We'd stop for a mince pie and a cup of tea. There were always groups of singers—you know, for Christmas—from the local Am Dram society."

"Carol singers?" Margaret prompts, and I nod curtly. She needn't cut in every time I forget a word, though perhaps she thinks she's being helpful.

"I remember." Judith smiles uncertainly. "Just about. It was forty years ago." I look at my daughter. She has the puffiness of someone deeply tired, over-caffeinated and sugared, and deprived of nutrients.

"Are you sleeping, dear?" I ask. She takes a moment to look surprised. I'm not sure why it's such a bewildering question. It's possible I haven't paid her enough attention in recent months, given my soreness at being deposited here.

"I am . . . well, I suppose I'm not getting the best sleep. Always a lot of things going on in my head." She laughs self-consciously, and I bristle uncomfortably. Too close to an emotional discussion for us.

"You should talk to Dr. Phillips," Margaret suggests. "He gave me a tincture for sleep once. It worked quite well. I can't remember what it was. Lavender? No . . ." She remains still while she thinks. It's unlike Margaret to forget the names of things. That's usually my forte.

Melissa, whose hair is now blue, brings tea to the table, and Judith immediately reaches for one of the ginger biscuits. More sugar.

"What would you like for Christmas, dear?" I ask Judith while I pour, making a mental note not to give her the Fortnum and Mason chocolates I usually do. She chews quietly while looking expectantly at Margaret, and not receiving a reply, turns to me in surprise.

"Oh, you're talking to me?" I nod. "Oh! Well, I'm not sure, really."

"Maybe some nice clothes?" I ask, looking at her outfit—another of her Boden catalogue ensembles.

"I have plenty of clothes." She smiles.

"I'm sure, but I mean something really special."

She shrugs. Shrugs are uncharacteristic of Judith. She is usually a firmly positive person. Indifference isn't really her thing. She's polka-dot cheerful, a trait I find particularly difficult to manage. It's unusual that I should be brighter than her. I find myself wondering if, as Margaret claims about Ralph, she has a lackluster inner life. Does Margaret think this of my daughter too? Perhaps it's a generational thing.

"Are you okay?" I ask Judith. "Is everything . . . good at home?" I can't bring myself to utter her husband's name. It's an uncomfortable question. Too personal, again. I feel intrusive, unentitled to probe. I'm not sure why that is, how we got here. I never intended to be like my mother. I intended to be a gentle parent.

"It is. I'm fine. I just . . . to be honest I'm not feeling well, all of a sudden." She raises a hand to her temple. "My head is throbbing." She sips too much of her tea at once, then quickly runs her tongue over her top lip. "I think I should go home."

"But you've only just arrived," I protest, disappointed and feeling useless.

"I think maybe . . . maybe there's an allergen in here or something."

"Keep the windows open as you drive home," Margaret advises. "You look tired. The cold air will keep you awake."

Judith says perfunctory goodbyes then slips away, leaving me wilted. I wonder if something I said distressed her, and if she was feigning the headache.

"Valerian!" Margaret declares suddenly. At my confused look, she explains, "The tincture. I think I might follow Judith's lead and take a nap myself."

Margaret acts as though coming up with the name of the tincture has exhausted her. Odd. I look at my watch. Not even 2 p.m. Much earlier than her usual nap.

"What's wrong with everyone today?" I ask no one in particular, observing the nodding heads of the other residents in the room. It reminds me of the scene in *The Wizard of Oz* when Dorothy and her friends fall asleep in the poisoned poppy field. Everyone seems to be exhausted or coming down with something. At least I am spared this last indignity, after so many previous ones. It occurs to me that perhaps everyone is always like this, and it's me who feels different—more awake than usual. A pleasant side effect, maybe, of one of my new medications. Or perhaps this epilepsy renders me immune to whatever's going around.

Once Margaret disappears upstairs—taking the stairlift—I decide to head outside again, feeling restless.

"You're not going out there, Harriet," Alyson objects as she notices me slipping on my coat.

"Why not?" I ask, trying not to be irritable with her for being the object of Ralph's flirting. "It's not pouring."

"But it's a miserable day. Very damp. The kind of cold that gets into the bones." She shivers, dark circles ringing her eyes. Quite unlike her. Is she unwell too?

"It's perfectly fine. I need a good airing," I tell her, and she half-smiles.

"You do seem to have a lot of energy today," she comments, almost enviously.

"I do! I think someone is slipping something in the tea." I look at her with mock sharpness since Alyson is the one who makes it.

She laughs genuinely. "If I had something that made people feel more energetic, I'd slip it into my own tea, not just yours."

"I suppose we're easier to deal with when we're sleepy," I concede. I gesture at my burnt orange coat. "Don't worry. You'll be able to see me from the house."

"We certainly will," she agrees, still smiling. "Like a buoy on the horizon."

In general, I find England in winter quite miserable. It rarely snows, and the cold is damp and drizzly. The sodden muddy ground freezes overnight, making an ice rink of the mornings.

Usually, I feel dragged down by days like these. They creep into the sinuses, seep in through the soles of my shoes. But today, I feel a fraction brighter, as though I've managed to drag a foot from the mud, despite the fact that everyone and everything else around me seems tired. Colorless.

The seeming departure of my overwhelming decrepitude feels liberating, if only temporarily, as though the sky is suddenly cleared of the overhang of ominous grey clouds. And yet the absence is a presence in itself. A vast void to fill with my thoughts, uncontaminated with the dread of invisibility, of inevitable decline and disappearance.

Only positive thoughts, for now.

Like Christmas.

I must find something special for Margaret after everything she's done for me, and all that she puts up with. What she suffers through with me.

Dementia. *Mid-stage* dementia.

The words still make me queasy. How did I not know?

I'm not sure. The only thing I'm sure of is that since my albeit tentative diagnosis of epilepsy, I *do* feel clearer. As though my new condition has placed a firm foot on top of the dementia.

Or perhaps I'm kidding myself and, in reality, thinking myself getting better *is* a symptom of the condition.

The days have followed each other consecutively, lined up predictably like soldiers. No more absconding with the weekends. I even remembered my regular appointment with Dr. Phillips this morning for the first time in months. Attentive as usual, he'd looked at me curiously, commenting, "Your word recall is excellent today."

Even now, hours later, I'm not sure how to respond to that. It wasn't exactly a compliment. I couldn't thank him.

Should I give Dr. Phillips a Christmas present? A bottle of something. Port, maybe? Is that the done thing? I have no idea. No. Port is an old person's drink. But then he's churchy, so perhaps he doesn't drink at all. And come to think of it, I'm not sure I remember ever giving him a gift, but then I am forgetful, apparently.

How different Christmas is for Christians. All nativity and angels. Advent and Christmas Day church. Molly was an angel in the ghastly nativity play Judith hauled me along to see last year. It wasn't the best casting. She looked terrified on stage.

I wonder what life can be like for little Molly. Judith is attentive and cheerful enough, which I suppose is what you'd want from a mother, but to be that size and shape as a little girl must be difficult. Over-indulged. She does not have my genes in that area. I was always whippet-lean, all the way until menopause, when everything thickened, then sagged, then dropped, regardless of my diet, regardless of the exercise. What is poor Molly's destiny if she's already round at ten? She could be horsey. Unattractive women often are, using makeup to hide their mare-ness.

I consider whether this epilepsy is hereditary, and if I've already passed the genes down to Judith, to Molly. Dementia certainly is. I think of my mother in her final years and shudder. Beaky, poky, and nonsensical. There's some aspect of Molly that reminds me of her—that mannerism of turning her head before her eyes follow. Watchful, suspecting.

I've completed several laps of the house before it starts to rain, and I finally head back inside. I'm still restless, reluctant to sit or make idle conversation with someone who will forget me moments later. I wish I could go somewhere—anywhere—else. Instead, I wander towards the kitchen. As a rule, residents aren't allowed in there unless invited. I've never been there before.

"Hello?" I call as I walk in. A youngish man in his thirties—I recognize him as one of the men who carried the mirror into the library for the séance—raises his head from whatever he's cooking. For the umpteenth time today, I arouse surprise.

"Hello. Can I help you with something?" He stops what he's doing. "Do you need a cloth?"

"A cloth?"

"People who come into the kitchen usually need a cloth. Something's spilled . . ."

"Oh." How curious. "No, I don't need a cloth. I'm trying to make myself useful. I thought I could help with something."

Silence hangs between us. Apparently, it's quite the bizarre offer. Residents never offer to help with anything. That's why we're here, I suppose. To retire. To stop working. And I . . . well, I never help if I'm paying for something. But today I'm too antsy. I need to prove myself capable of something. It's an unfamiliar sensation. A kind of strengthening. Another unusual symptom of this epilepsy.

"Er, okay." The young man seems hesitant, suspicious even, the sepia country kitchen air hanging awkwardly between us. I suspect he's not used to interacting with residents. It's not his job. Marryat Manor is a curious place—a smattering of young people being paid to attend to the elderly. To notice us. "Thank you. You could cut slices of cake?"

"Yes! Afternoon tea is coming up, I suppose. And I can absolutely cut slices of cake."

The man unboxes a fruitcake they must have batch-cooked earlier and places it on a cutting board before handing me a cake knife.

"About twenty small slices," he instructs, eyeing the blade I'm holding, possibly worried about liability.

I set about the task, cutting slices the size I've been offered and declined hundreds of times before.

"Aren't you here to get away from all these domestic duties?" the cook asks as I work.

"Well . . ." I murmur noncommittally. I have rarely performed domestic tasks. Before now it never occurred to me that helpfulness makes one visible. Being an encumbrance, as I suppose I am these days here at the Manor, tends to dissolve one's substance. As if I don't have enough problems with that already. At Haywood Hall, we always had help. My work was running a household. Hiring staff, setting menus, paying bills, entertaining. Things I was rather good at, actually, at least until William died and the edges of my days blurred together.

"How did your séance go?" he asks.

"Oh." I'm surprised at the question. Not many people have wanted to discuss the séance. I've been given rather a wide berth by the other residents who attended, and even those who didn't. "You know, I'm not sure how it went. They say I had some sort of fit, and I've been diagnosed with a rare kind of epilepsy that emerged during the séance. But to be honest, ever since, I feel much better. I don't know for sure, but I believe it's something to do with my condition. It could be that the fit unlocked something."

The cook hums interestedly. "My mother was a medium, before she passed away," he tells me, in his thick London accent. "She was clairaudient. Which means she heard voices but didn't see anything. No visions or signs, just the voices of the dead."

An unexpectedly fascinating disclosure.

"And her doctors ruled out schizophrenia?" I ask before thinking, but he doesn't seem offended.

"No, my mother wasn't mentally ill. She really did hear messages from the dead. She helped people by passing them on." He seems un-embarrassed, matter of fact. It's interesting that this woman found a meaningful purpose in the occult. I wonder what it must be like, to genuinely feel connected to another realm.

"Were any of the messages negative?" I ask.

He's cutting lemon cake at the counter across from me. He smiles slightly. "She didn't pass any of those on."

"Have you received any messages from her? Since she died?"

"Nah. Not her style. I think she said everything she had to say in life. She died early, but lived very fully, if you know what I mean. She fit more into her sixty-three years than most people would in eighty."

A full life. Can I say I have lived a full life? Not full enough. I yearn for more, yet I'm spending my days playing board games, taking the same walk day after day, and now, cutting cake in the kitchen of the retirement home I'm paying to be at. My spirits flag slightly again.

"I wish I'd lived more," I surprise myself by admitting to him. "Before being stuck here, doing very little, feeling confused, and losing track of days. I feel as though I'm stuck in one of those horrible dreams where you're screaming for help at the top of your lungs, but no one can hear you. I'm so very tired of being invisible. I've been moved to the end of the sentence although I'm still somewhere in the middle." My cheeks heat at my vehemence, my over-exposure. I'm never this open, particularly with the help.

He seems unfazed. The young are more used to such conversations. "I see you."

"Thank you," I say, though I doubt he really means it. He doesn't even know my name.

"I'm Angel, by the way." Angel. Quite charming. Very different, for a man. I suppose it's a nickname and wonder if his real name is Gabriel.

"Harriet."

"Yeah, I know who you are."

This unsettles me. How does he know who I am? Am I complained about in the kitchen? I hadn't thought I was particularly difficult, but then it seems there is a lot about myself I don't know. Another side effect of the dementia. Pathetic, really.

Changing the subject, I say, "You make awfully good food."

"Cheers, that's nice to hear. I don't make everything as I'd eat it at home."

I nod. "I suppose you're making things easier on the digestion?"

"Yep. And the teeth. And people of your generation like the food they're used to rather than anything more modern."

"It must be rather boring for you," I comment, depressed by his observation. We sound awfully dull. Perhaps this is why we older folk are so ignored.

"Not boring, exactly, no. It's nice making food people enjoy, regardless of what it is."

I think about that for a moment and wonder about my former staff. Did they take pleasure in my satisfaction? I had high standards. I shouldn't have thought they did. I suppose my entertaining gave other people pleasure—people like me.

"A very giving job," I say quietly, then gesture towards the platter of cake. "I think I'm finished."

Margaret emerges from her room in time for afternoon tea. Her skin looks translucent, tinged with the same purple as the frozen afternoon sky. I watch her as she bites into her fruitcake.

"You know, I cut that slice today." She looks at me quizzically, and I shrug. "I was a little restless, so I helped Angel in the kitchen."

Margaret finishes chewing before she speaks. "What have you done with my friend Harriet?"

My laugh is at odds with the continuing drizzle tapping on the window. "I need to get out."

"Didn't you take a walk already today?"

"I did, but I'm still restless."

"Your arthritis isn't bothering you?" she asks.

I look down at my hands and move my fingers, surprised not to feel the usual pain in my joints. I waggle them in front of my face so Margaret can see too. "Remarkable, given this weather."

"I wish I could say the same for my hip." Margaret groans.

"The jippy hippy?"

"Indeed. Every time I wake up lately it feels stiffer. Like someone comes in while I sleep and tightens its screw. Forget the stairs, I'm using the stairlift from now on."

"Oh, you poor thing," I sympathize, realizing how easy I've found the stairs the past few days.

"You seem much more . . ." Margaret frowns, as if searching for the right word. "Unfuddled."

Unfuddled. An apt description.

"I know it's odd, but I do feel much clearer. Less clouded. I think maybe that fit I had reset things a little. Did you know I have dementia, Margaret?"

She looks at me thoughtfully, considers her response before speaking. "We all know, Harriet. And you've been told multiple times."

"But I forgot every time?"

"Yes." She looks at me meaningfully, though not unsympathetically.

"Has it been difficult . . . dealing with me?" I sound so needy, so vulnerable, but I must know.

"No, my dear, not difficult. You're always Harriet, whether you're back to front or inside out." A funny description. "I just feel for you. You've been so confused, so aimless recently. It's why—the séance—I thought having a purpose would help you. Something to do. An activity."

It's distressing hearing her talk about how she's thought of me, of her approaches to handling me, like someone who tells you later how they looked after you during a drunken evening. I imagine Margaret conspiring with Dr. Phillips, discussing their strategies to "manage poor Harriet" and bristle. "An activity?" I snap, irritated. "I am not a child. I do not need to be managed."

Instead of addressing my comment, Margaret rubs her arms and shivers. "It's so dark in here. So cold. When are they going to light the fire?" She looks around the room for one of the staff. "Winter never used to bother me, but this season the cold seems to go straight through me. The house feels different suddenly, with this turn in the weather." She meets my eyes again. "But truth be told, although you really do seem a lot brighter, a lot more energetic since, I feel as though something's shifted in the house, like everything's tilted at an angle, a little darker. It's a coincidence of timing. The change in seasons."

"Poetic," I comment. "But no, I don't think I've noticed the sudden change in season." Too distracted, I suppose. Epilepsy. Dementia. Darker? I feel the opposite. Everything seems brighter, more real than it did before. No more nightmares! I suppose I'm less scared of the house now. I see its colors, and not just its shadows. "The weather *is* frightful today though. And this old house does nothing to keep out the chill and damp," I add, even though I am not cold. "William and I went on holiday once to a little cabin by a lake. Really not my sort of thing, but he had it stuck in his mind he wanted to go fishing. He thought roughing it in a cabin would be fun, but I felt dreadful the entire time. I'm sure it was the mildew. You could smell it."

"Mold," Margaret corrects.

"Possibly."

Strange how these old memories are still so vivid, so real, I can remember them with such clarity while I can't think of the correct word I want to say. But then, I've heard that's another thing with dementia—the short-term memory goes first. Or is that Alzheimer's? Now I'm getting my illnesses mixed up too.

"But they keep Marryat Manor well maintained," Margaret says, picking up the thread of our conversation. It takes me a moment to realize where we left off. "It's what we pay for."

I look around the oak-paneled room, its floors plush with expensive rugs, its large windows framed with heavy brocade curtains with an intricate design woven in purples and golds. Gilt-framed oil paintings. Antique brass table lamps. Nothing out of place. She's right. We pay too much to be here for the house to slip into disrepair. "I suppose you're right."

"Maybe I'm coming down with something," Margaret says, shivering again. "Perhaps they brought up a virus along with the mirror from the basement. It was rather dank down there."

"Perhaps," I say, shuddering inside as I remember that huge mirror, its foreboding dark surface, like infinite nothing. I glance at my friend, frowning. There are new shadows on her face, a slight wobble of grip, and I wonder if she really is unwell.

I catch the eye of one of the staff and point to the fireplace for them to light it, then say to Margaret, the clarity of my voice contrasting with the rasp of hers, "We'll get a nice bright day soon. It will get unseasonably warm and completely un-Christmassy, and you'll feel a lot better. A good meal, that's what you need. Something with iron in it." But I'm worried. This is so unlike Margaret, this drop in energy, this lack of literary quotations or quips, this new frailty, and I'm suddenly afraid she'll leave me too.

8

It can't be just the morning light that's smoothed my skin, nor just a good night's sleep that's erased the dark circles beneath my eyes. And there's no accounting for the quite sudden reduction of stains on my teeth. Unless something about my new condition causes hallucination, I think I look at least fifteen years younger, around sixty-five perhaps—just in the two weeks since the séance. Not just my face, either, but also my hair, which feels softer and thicker, and my body, which is straighter, more upright and limber. It's remarkable. Were it not for the comments from others on my appearance, I would think it were a figment of my imagination, a result of my dementia. The other set of brain waves taken over.

Today, I'm wearing the matching earrings to my sapphire pendant and a purple knitted dress with a low neckline that before made me look like a scraggly piece of gristly chicken. It's been years since I've worn it and I have no idea why I've kept it, but I'm glad I did. I even slide my feet into a pair of elegant designer velvet shoes that have a small heel. A heel! Evening shoes really, but I can't resist them. It's such a difference from my everyday look, as though I'm dressed up for an event. A luncheon, a fundraiser, full of accomplished women to see and be seen by. Vain of me, I know, but it's remarkable, this difference. I don't quite trust it, this rapid improvement.

I briefly wonder if I've traveled in time, before realizing that if I had, I wouldn't be here. I'd be back at Haywood Hall with William. "If anyone could will away age and decrepitude, it's my Harriet," he would say. He valued my gumption. I was the social mastermind behind his business, enabling new acquisitions, strategic appointments, and the sealing of contracts, all through putting the right people in the right room at the perfect time. If it weren't for me, the business would have been a tenth of the size. William would have loved to see that Harriet back—the one that made us a formidable team.

Then I consider that if this isn't real and if the dementia and epilepsy *has* rattled my brain into a new delusional state, then to everyone else I must seem ridiculous.

A pitiful emperor in her new clothes.

If they see me at all.

After spending close to half an hour examining my reflection, I make my way downstairs to breakfast.

"Good lord!" Margaret exclaims when she sees me. "Look at you. You look like a glamor model. What on earth?"

I shrug to cover my shiver of pleasure. While Margaret's hyperbole is charming, it's clear she can see my improvement. I haven't hallucinated the changes to my appearance. "I can't explain it, but I'm going to enjoy it while it lasts."

"I mean . . ." Margaret's face is frozen in genuine shock. She's not just being kind.

"We'll see if everyone else around here has the same reaction as you," I joke. "Honestly, it's been so long since I've had this much energy, I'd forgotten how it feels."

"I know what you mean." Margaret nods towards me, taking in my newly upright posture. "Even when I was younger, I was nothing much to look at. I've always had a bit of a pointy chin. And I'm oddly shaped. Not that I minded. There are advantages to not being beautiful." There are? "I was always secure in the knowledge that my husband married me for my brain. Always seen, always heard. I let the content of my character say everything there was to say about me. Seen for my brain." She chuckles. "But I could use a little of your energy."

I knew other women who were exchanged, but never feared it from William. Yes, he liked the way I looked, but it was my spirit he loved. The presence I brought to a room. My steel. My strategic mind and relentless determination.

"Perhaps it's the epilepsy," I offer. "Changing my brain chemistry, forcing an unexpected resurgence of collagen." I speak with mock medical seriousness.

"Of course! A sound observation. What does Dr. Phillips think?"

"I'm not sure he knows. He cancelled my appointment today. Too many sick residents needing his attention." We both glance around the room at the empty seats. Elderlies taken to their beds. "I thought perhaps it was a virus, but Alyson tells me it's all sorts of different ailments affecting people. Or the winter. It hits the elderly harder. Or diet? Has the menu changed lately? Less iron?"

"I don't think I've noticed any difference." Margaret shrugs, lowering her eyes to her breakfast.

We're quiet for a while, eating our toast and eggs and drinking tea, and watching as one by one, the few fellow residents in the dining room shuffle out. June looks particularly gaunt as she stumbles from her chair. No power walking today, it would seem. I'd always thought of her as my junior but right now she looks positively elderly. Illness can do that, I suppose, eating away at the body, erasing any hint of color. She should be in bed.

Thinking about it, very few residents have ventured out for walks over the past week or so, and I've noticed fewer playing board games or visiting the library too. They've mostly been in their rooms or by the fire or television. Passive activities.

I resolve to enjoy my improved health while I have it. Even if sitting here amongst the severely fatigued and sick seems brazenly indecent.

"I'm going into town today," I announce to Margaret. "Getting a taxi. Do you want to join me? Spot of shopping, a bit of lunch?" I can't wait for Judith to take me. It's apparent I'm nowhere near the top of her list of priorities.

"Oh, no. Thank you, but I'm going to curl up with this." Margaret motions to the book on the table in front of her. I read the title. *The Hidden Histories of Manors in the South of England.*

"More history?" I thought since my nightmares had ceased, she had stopped looking into the Manor's past.

"There is so much I don't know about the story of this place. I feel like I'm missing something. These diaries of the original Mistress Marryat—they stop very suddenly. I think it's curious."

"Good lord, do you think there was a murder?" I ask, appalled. Perhaps that's where my nightmares came from—somehow, I'd picked up on the haunting, charred blackness of what happened here.

"I have no idea," Margaret continues, tapping the book. "But these Victorians were very secretive, you know. I'm going to see if there's anything in here that might give me a clue."

Farnham is dressed for Christmas, adorned with tasteful evergreen, red-ribboned wreaths and strings of lights draping between the Georgian buildings of the narrow streets. It's a quietly expensive market town with just enough boutiques to counter the ghastly chains that appear in every town center: WH Smiths, Boots, HSBC, NatWest, blah blah blah. Their corporate flatness has always seemed out of place with the cobbled courtyards, old churches, and castle. Still, I am fond of the place. It is designed for the comfort and leisure of the middle and upper classes, made for people like me. Expensive shopping, plus what seems like hundreds of coffee shops, restaurants, and wine bars.

William and I spent a lot of time here after he retired. Sharing the broadsheets over tea, occupying ourselves with small tasks—buying gifts for friends, browsing the bookshop's new titles, replacing watch batteries. A happy, gentle time of assured love and comfort. Before his cancer took hold.

I enjoy the puffs of condensation my breath makes into the morning's frigid air as I make my way from boutique to boutique. It's been a long time since I've not minded this kind of cold, since it's felt invigorating rather than draining.

Despite the air still deeply encased in its frost, a brilliant blue butterfly sails in front of me, dancing on the breeze as though it's still September. Another sign of William, I think, enchanted. Is this an acknowledgement of our time spent here together? The butterfly disappears in front of the department store, and it's as though William is dropping me off there while taking himself elsewhere, to buy a newspaper, or a bottle of wine.

Although I'm here to shop for Christmas gifts, I find myself browsing the department store for makeup and jewelry for myself. It feels as though William endorsed this indulgence, supportive of my newfound energy, keen to help me find color again after so many years of fading into a distorted graphite sketch of a person. It's a familiar sensation, that delight of buying something you know becomes you. Something improving.

Over the last twenty years, I've spent a small fortune on creams and serums that promised smoothing and lifting—to redeem, to rescue—that invariably failed. Today, I avoid anything "anti-aging" and buy makeup in brighter hues. Under the advice of a sales assistant, I purchase a metallic eyeshadow that will make my eyes "pop"—a ghastly American expression the younger Brits seem to insist on. I buy a scarlet cashmere beret, which makes me feel like Marilyn Monroe, and which William would have called "very fetching."

I'll probably wake up in a few days, recovered from my odd, brief stint of health, and wonder what I was thinking, buying these items. Not for a lady pushed into her eighties. But regardless, I'll be noticed. Not dead yet, flittering girlishly up and away from my tomb.

The pavement is narrow, and a man emerges from a shop in front of me and apologizes. As he moves aside, I catch sight of the butterfly again. I'm awed by the magic of it, that symbol of summer, the same blue as the ocean.

This time it doesn't disappear but hovers a little way in front of me. As I move towards it, it flutters further away. I follow, feeling like Alice chasing the White Rabbit. Absurd. Whimsical. But my focus hooks on what is beyond it. A man. Old, though not elderly. Striding around the corner onto Downing Street.

It can't be William. I watched him die. And yet . . .

I follow his grey hair and navy overcoat—the same cashmere overcoat I'd bought for William the Christmas he retired—down the narrow street, quickening my pace to catch up. My heart is racing, uncomprehending. My nerve endings fizz with adrenaline as my face heats with the realization of this insanity. It's possible the dementia has not left me after all. My heel catches between the cobblestones of the stunted private street leading to Spire Church. A place of happy memories—of carol services with friends, of Judith's performances with the Farnham Youth Choir.

Is he leading me there? This William? *My* William? This . . . ghost? The figure disappears inside the old church ahead of me.

Adrenaline gnaws deeper into my body as I cross the entryway into the churchyard. A peculiar wavering pulses through me, as though I'm filled with an entire ocean, tumultuous and turbulent. The gentle harmony of the hymn practice emerging from the church sounds discordant, threatening.

William. I must find him.

I stumble deeper into the churchyard towards the benches, while the wavering increases, as though there's a storm inside me. Black shapes fizz and pop in front of my eyes. *I'm having another fit!* I drop onto a bench, thinking a little rest will set me right, but the wavering and wobbling continue, so different from my fit during the séance. My alarm quickly changes to panic. *What's happening to me?* I should seek help. William will help me. If he knew I had this condition, he would find a way to help me.

I stumble to my feet and gather up the bags, taking a few steps towards the church—if I can't find William, the vicar must be there—but it feels as though someone, or something, is screaming directly into my ears. I back away from the building and the screaming dissipates. I take a few more steps in the other direction and the wavering eases a fraction. I'm being pulled away from the church, but I must get in! William will know what to do. He'll help me. An inner voice that sounds like Margaret reminds me again that I watched my husband die, that it can't be him. But I saw him. I know it was my William.

I push forwards, and finally I'm inside the church. My ears ring as though a thousand voices are screaming directly into them. I'm being crushed from the inside, my dementia and my epilepsy warring against each other, using my body as a brutal battleground. I fall to the ground, and something clatters down beside me. The light is fading. Blackening. Blackening.

I'm on my back, pinned down by pain. A shape emerges from the blackness. A silhouette. A figure. William. I recognize the shape of his head, the upturned collar. He's come to help me! His features emerge. But no, this can't be right. It's William, but he's different. God no! His cheeks are dropping down towards me. Not just sagging but falling—falling in crusty, bloodied chunks, landing on me like dust.

I add my own scream to the cacophony as my eyes squeeze themselves shut. My head has splintered. This is what death feels like. I open my eyes again, sure I was mistaken, that he's not decomposing. But a skull in the shape of William's head stares back at me, descending towards me.

"*Sum quod eris*," it snarls.

And the blackness consumes me.

***

"Tell me what happened, Harriet." Dr. Phillips has already checked my blood pressure and listened to my heart and my lungs, and now his expression is one of curiosity and concern. He saw me immediately upon my return to the Manor, after an ambulance arrived at Spire Church and I was revived with fresh air and a little medical attention.

"Oh, it was nothing," I dismiss, and then I relay to him the physical aspects of what I experienced at the churchyard but leave out my hallucination. The screaming black horror. How it felt like an assault, how I still feel severely bruised, how I'm not entirely convinced it wasn't real. While he needs to know how my condition is developing, I can't risk him thinking I've fully lost my marbles. That I'm too feeble, too dementia-ridden. Who can tell what the medical professionals would decide to do with me then? Leave me to rot or ditch me in a ghastly institution, perhaps.

"I'll report the episode to Dr. Fry and the other specialists. But these things are going to happen, Harriet. And when you least expect them. My best explanation is that it's part of the epilepsy, I'm afraid. You're not taking any medication I'm not giving you?"

"Nothing. In fact, my arthritis seems to have improved greatly these days. Look." I bend the fingers of each hand backwards in turn then stand and bend over to touch my toes. "See?"

"This new condition does seem to have a remarkable effect on your mobility," he admits. "And your energy."

"Yes," I say flatly. The morning's disturbance has stamped out my jubilance for the day. "What's happening to me, Dr. Phillips?"

He watches me closely for a few seconds. "I don't know, Harriet. Honestly. But where there are positive side effects, enjoy them if you can. Do you know how many people here are sick, struggling with what would be an ordinary virus in another person?" He looks wearier today, older by a good couple of years than he did just last week. Must be the strain of this new illness going around. He deserves a vacation once all this is over. "Thank God you're feeling good."

At the mention of God, I automatically glance at the crucifix on the wall behind him and feel slightly queasy. A lingering negative association with the church, given this morning. I look away again quickly.

"Take care of yourself," Dr. Phillips says. "Try not to spend too much time alone in case you have another fit."

Another day passes and I'm craving the outdoors again, to fill my lungs with delicious cold air. The picture of yesterday's decaying William has continued to rattle around my head. I dreamt darkly, though I can't remember the substance. The Manor is stuffy and overheated, and naturally I'm eager to avoid its many viruses.

I head through the hallway and slip on my coat when I happen upon Ralph. I smile, ready to greet him, but hesitate for a moment as a wave of confusion passes over his features before he recognizes me.

"Harriet?" His neat eyebrows raise in perfect shock.

"Yes. How are you, dear?" I smile encouragingly at him.

"But you seem . . . I mean, you were looking lovely last time I saw you, you always look lovely, but today you seem . . . well, so much more energetic, younger even." His cheeks color slightly, uncharacteristic for Ralph. The antithesis of William's melting skull. I shake away the thought, unwilling to let that trauma interfere with my joy. I realize this is the first time Ralph's seen me since our last walk, the day after the séance, and his reaction is a good one. His compliment was delivered authentically again, his slathered-on charm removed. If only others could see the genuine warmth underneath his veneer.

I beam back at him in pleasure. Oh, to be seen again. Really seen. Not as a woman in her eighties, but as a vibrant, vital human being. Interesting. Incandescent. My word, how I've fantasized about this moment, of being truly *seen* by Ralph. But I can't let myself get carried away, knowing all too well how fleeting it might be. "Dr. Phillips thinks it might be a rather nice side effect of my new epilepsy, though I have no idea why it would do things like this. It must be hormonal."

"You should offer yourself up for experiments. If they could bottle whatever you've got, people would pay thousands for it."

Thousands for epilepsy? I tinkle a laugh, pushing thoughts of William to the back of my mind. "I expect you're right."

He's quiet for a moment, watching me, so I study him in return. He's wearing a disappointingly shabby jumper, yellowish grey and pilled, the color unflattering to his complexion. The kind of garment I usually despise, but in this moment, it's somehow touching. It makes him seem fallible, less shiny. And that fallibility only adds to his sincerity. It's been a long time since I've held a man's attention like this.

His gaze eventually slides away. "I wish you'd give some of this elixir to Mum. She's slowed down so much in the last two weeks. She doesn't seem ill, just . . . not quite herself. A little . . . I don't know the word . . ."

"Shadowed?" Ever since the séance. Perhaps due to her concern for me.

"Yes. Shadowed. I think that's it." Ralph nods with a pained twist of the mouth, then finally seems to notice I'm wearing a coat. "Are you going out?"

"I am." I want to stay with him, to absorb more of his attention, but not obviously so. It's unbecoming for a lady to be seen seeking attention. I smile as I pass him. "I'll see you soon, Ralph."

"Oof!" I hear from behind me and turn to see he has knocked into the oversized Christmas tree centered in the hall and is trying unsuccessfully to steady the disruption. As he does so, I wonder if his carelessness was a result of being distracted by me. *Lovely indeed.*

I burst through the heavy door to the outside and realize the heat I'm experiencing internally is desire. Not the half-remembered kind I'm used to these days, weak like the elderlies' tea, but powerfully waving, literally weakening my knees and dampening my underwear. A sensation I haven't experienced for well over a decade. It's quite overwhelming, this sensation, like the moment you realize you've started menstruating for the first time. That you are whole. A woman.

I hold onto the wall to steady myself, and as I lean there, Angel's voice slices the cold air.

"Are you okay, Harriet?" the cook asks, on his way inside for his next shift.

"Quite well, thank you." I flash him a quick smile of polite reassurance as I right myself and unhand the wall. "I just . . . I'm fine."

"I hope you don't mind me saying this, but you're looking really good today." He's taking in my face, my newly upright posture. "I mean, you don't look like you're one of the residents, but more like you're one of the visitors."

Like a visitor! I'm delighted.

"Thank you, Angel." Although I don't know him well, I find his attention intoxicating and turn away from his gaze before I become drunk on it. "Off for a walk. See you soon!"

Although not conscious of my decision, I head towards the maze at a pace, almost running. From the house I must look quite deranged. But behind the cover of the hedge, I lift the skirt of my dress. My legs are cold, and my upper thighs emerging from my stockings are freezing, but I can't help myself. Desperately, I slip my hand into my underwear. The sensation of feeling myself, so immensely wet, as I haven't been for so long, with my cold fingers, brings me to orgasm in moments. So soon I had barely the chance to picture Ralph or Angel. I'm so unsteady on my feet with the power of this nearly forgotten sensation I find myself almost tipping into the tall hedge walls. I want to keep going, but the absurdity of the situation—hiding in a maze and masturbating like a lusty teen—dawns on me, and I correct myself, wiping my glistening fingers on the leaves, scratching my hand.

Absurdly, a blue butterfly lands there and I freeze. William again? No. I will not have another hallucination. I shan't give into it. This is *mine*, this feeling, this awakening. It's private, even from William. I shake the butterfly off my hand, and it disappears into nothingness. Yesterday's residue, nothing more.

Once reassembled, I emerge from the maze. Had anyone seen me from the house and wondered what I was doing there? They would have thought I needed to urinate, I tell myself. But as I continue to walk, the tremors of orgasm still giving me the occasional tug, I think about how wonderful it would be to have sex again. A man inside me. Young and hard and needing all this wetness. Someone who wants to peel my clothes away from my body and look at it because it's beautiful.

I pass the remainder of the afternoon in my room in front of the mirror, quite frankly turned on by my own reflection, exploring my lifted curves, the suppleness of my skin. I imagine Ralph's gaze, his touch, and I pleasure myself over and over until I'm aching and drained. Despite this, I'm unsatisfied. I need flesh against mine, inside me. I feel hollow, unfilled, disappointed. Like an empty stocking on Christmas morning.

"You look pleased with yourself," Margaret comments over dinner.

I feel the corners of my mouth tucking upwards in a secret smile, and I color with embarrassment. I need to be more careful. Less transparent. I lie, "Oh, I am. I've nearly finished my Christmas shopping already."

"Well done, you," she congratulates genuinely. "I'm about a third of the way through. I thought it got easier, this kind of thing, when you're retired. But I don't feel as though I know what's available these days. I haven't seen Lisa in months. What do I buy for her?"

At the mention of Ralph's wife, I picture him choosing a gift for her, peering into glass cases in one of Farnham's premier jewelers, and my stomach drops a little. I put my forkful of chicken pie down. What would he buy her? Jewelry, or possibly lingerie. Something romantic to rekindle the romance between them. I suppress the fluttering that comes with the memory of Ralph's attention, how it brought me into being again.

"What are you giving Ralph?" I ask Margaret, imagining something expensive in leather, an item of designer clothing, or a first edition of a meaningful book.

"Electric toothbrush," she says instead. "You know me, I like to give useful presents."

"Ah, yes," I agree, shaking off the probing amorousness in the background of my thoughts.

"What have you bought for Judith?"

"Diamond earrings," I tell her, thinking of the expensive gift I know my daughter will be shocked by.

"Gosh!" Margaret is shocked too.

"Well . . . it's been years since I bought her anything special." I don't add that I bought myself an identical pair, that when imagining them on her, I'd held them up to my own ears and liked the way they looked. I couldn't not buy them for Judith when buying them for myself.

"And Molly?"

"A few of those awful things she likes. What are they called? Shopins? Or Shopkins, even?" I try to recall, remembering all that horrible American brightly colored plastic. "And a silver locket."

"Oh, how lovely." Margaret looks touched on Molly's behalf. "A wonderful gift from a grandmother."

"It's silly. Something Judith said a couple of years ago. Just offhand, I don't think she meant anything offensive. But when helping me pack away my jewelry when moving here, she found one of my old lockets and told me how much she'd always wanted one as a little girl. But I never gave her one."

"There are always things we want as children that we're never given." Margaret smiles warmly at me. My own mother never thought to ask me what I wanted either. A failing of our bloodline, countered by the side effects of my condition.

"Naturally. But I remember being annoyed with myself that I hadn't thought of it. It's the kind of thing she would have loved. She so loved magic and secrets."

"So did Ralph, actually," Margeret comments, which surprises me. He doesn't seem the imaginative type. "Don't we all love magic and secrets?"

9

Mirror, mirror, on the wall, who is the fairest of them all?
Like all little girls, when I was young, I was enchanted by
fairy tales and magic. Hair so long it would span the height
of a tower. Sleeping for a hundred years. Your mirror telling you that
you were the fairest in all the land. Oh, how I fantasized about having
a magic mirror! Physical beauty was prized above all other attributes in
my house, and I grew up thinking nothing could be greater than being
recognized as the most beautiful.

Now, I consider my mirror may well be telling me this, given the
astonishing reflection shimmering back at me, the invisible made visible. I am reminded of the summer I slipped from girlishness into wom-
anhood. Disconcerting, at thirteen, transitioned overnight and looking
at least sixteen, suddenly the source of hungry stares from fully grown
men. I soon learned how to fend off the handsier ones—those without
self-control, who stroked, and groped, and tried to kiss me. "Be flattered," my mother told me. Thankfully, I avoided rape.

But it wasn't only men who noticed me. Women, too, spoke to me
as one of them. I wasn't talked down to as I had been before. It wasn't
just about being pretty. It was about coming into being. Changing
from being one who sees and admires, to one who *is* seen and admired.
Shortly afterward, I took over from my mother in visibility, in importance, and predictably, she shook our household with anger at the

injustice. I'd not been sympathetic. Only victorious. My world, my turn. I regret that now, given what I've learned as I age.

Wearing this new glamor as my fellow residents decline around me feels incongruous. I hear their coughs echo down the corridors as I indulge in my new sexual urges. I feel as I did as a teen staying at my grandparents' house during the summer when I discovered my body. Indecent, though guiltily thrilling, I give into it, reasoning I'm not harming anyone, and any of the others would also indulge these desires if they experienced them again.

I shop for lingerie online. I'd rather someone else see me in it, but I'll enjoy my own reflection. It's something I used to do as a young married woman when William was away. Dress myself up in my most becoming French lace and pleasure myself for hours in front of the mirror. For a while, when I was younger, I thought no experience with a man would be as satisfying as time alone with my reflection. That changed when people stopped looking, and when my reflection revealed the absence of what had been.

It's snowing. We don't usually get snow in the south of England before Christmas, and it's not even December yet. Much too early for snow. Not just a light dusting, either, but thick, blizzarding conditions. At least four or five inches accumulated so far.

I feel trapped in the Manor, as though in a snow globe, unable to move away from all this illness, from this landslide of decaying people tumbling down, down, as I am lifted by unknown forces.

From the dining room window, the grounds are quite wondrous, so breathtakingly white, hushing the disgruntled browns and muddied greens beneath. It's the kind of heavy, wet snow that sticks to the tree trunks as well as resting atop branches, weighing down the hedgerows and suffocating the shrubberies, making hulking monsters of those overgrown topiaries. A barging, barreling snow, quite unlike the apologetic, meagre flakes that occasionally make a tentative appearance at some inconvenient time in January.

It's quite distracting. So much so that everyone's attention seems more focused on the weather than the striking changes occurring with me. I suppose it's warranted, given the illnesses still running rampant within the Manor and the drop in temperature that this house's old heating and mile-long fireplaces can't keep up with.

The live-in staff are run off their feet, and the road conditions are too hazardous for the rest of the staff to travel in to relieve them.

"Maybe I should go and help in the kitchen," I ponder aloud. Being the most able-bodied of the residents surely gives me the responsibility of at least offering. Margaret is at first startled by my suggestion but then measures her reaction. She is getting used to my unpredictability.

"That would be kind, dear, but I should have thought they'll be just fine. Help can often be a hindrance, you know. The chef will just make something more simple than usual. And we'll just have to wait longer for our tea." She looks around. Still no sign of Alyson with our teapot.

I suppose I have been quite unlike myself recently. Or rather, unlike myself at eighty-two.

I feel like I did in my mid-fifties, which I think is only a little younger than I look now. At sixty, my calendar was still quite full. Social and charity events—both attending and planning them—and taking vacations, making sure the staff kept up with the house, then fitness classes and endless hair and beauty appointments.

My walks about the Manor grounds, online ordering, and bouts of self-pleasuring aren't enough anymore. I yearn to get out in the world, to *live* and be seen by non-elderlies.

"Look what I found." Margaret signals to the book on the table in front of her. "*The Blood of the Vampire* by Florence Marryat herself."

"Dear lord, she wrote a book?"

"Quite a famous book. I'm rather annoyed with myself that I didn't remember it. When I moved here, I thought I recognized the name Marryat, but I didn't link it to the novel. Of course, the Victorian gothic was not my specialism." Margaret looks more deeply hollowed than usual, as though something is devouring her from the inside. With the bright white of the window behind her, I can see the outline of her skull. Her hair has thinned so much, the short, fine curls give the impression of a halo.

"What's it about?" I ask.

"Funnily enough, the protagonist is a woman named Harriet."

"Oh, gosh! Well, a lovely name."

"Agreed! She's some sort of psychic vampire who goes around killing people unintentionally." She grins weakly at me as if it's a joke.

I think of my two sets of brain waves—dementia Harriet, and epileptic Harriet—of the uncanny feeling of there being two of me, twin selves inside one unpredictable shell. I can understand the compulsion to want to explain away medical incongruities with theories of the supernatural. It's peculiar, feeling dominated by dueling conditions, having no control over either. Were it not for the fact that I have daily evidence that the epileptic side is winning, and with positive effect, I'd be more alarmed.

"She wrote it around the time of *Dracula*, I believe," Margaret continues. "Far less known than Bram Stoker, but I've read that what's particularly interesting is the way Marryat portrays vampires—she has a medical rather than supernatural take on them."

"In what way?"

"Not sure. I need to read it, then I'll let you know. You can have it once I'm finished." Margaret knows I'm not a great reader. I don't have the attention span. Nothing to do with a lack of inner life. "I happened upon this book mentioned in one of the diaries I found. I thought I'd see if I could find it."

"And this is the same woman who wrote about the séance?" I ask.

"The very same." Margaret coughs a little, unearthing a deep rattle in her chest.

"Who had an apparent intense interest in the supernatural."

"The supernatural, collided with the natural, it seems." Margaret flips through the book. "She was interested, as many were at the time, in the medicinal aspects of the occult."

"Like the séance making her feel revitalized and younger?" I offer.

She gives me a careful glance, swallowing audibly and looking awfully pale. "I wonder when they're going to be able to bring us that tea. I'm feeling a little unwell."

"May I have a carrot?" I ask.

"A carrot?" Angel looks up from the kitchen counter.

"Oh, you're here! I thought it was only live-in staff today." I'm pleased to see him.

"I borrowed a jeep from a friend in town." He smiles. "We can't have the old folk going hungry, can we?" I snort. He gives me a full-body appraisal before settling back on my face. "Not that you're all old, of course."

"Of course." I twinkle back at him, glad he sees me differently. Not old. Younger. Vital. Does he wonder if I'm sexually active now? Does he know I pleasure myself? Does he imagine me doing it? The thought is delicious and makes me shiver a little.

My lack of attraction to Angel is mainly because of his height. I'm moderately tall myself so am naturally drawn to tall men. I once declined the offer of marriage from a viscount because he was only five foot and eight inches, even though the size of his manor was considerable—practically a palace. But regardless of height, Angel is a well-proportioned and neatly contained man. His forearms are a little too thick—he probably has farmers in his gene pool—but he has an appealing mouth, despite being a little weak in the chin.

"I mean, you're looking well, Harriet," he says. "Considering how sick everyone else here seems to be."

"Yes, it's terrible. Margaret and I were speculating there's some kind of virus here making everyone unwell." Maybe the virus has positive side effects for me. Perhaps my epilepsy or dementia warp my body's responses.

"Could be. This time of year is always virus season." Angel looks thoughtful. "Poor Alyson is run off her feet at the moment, now that Melissa has gone." I didn't know she left. "She's not looking her usual self. I've been feeling pretty run down too."

I notice his hairline seems to have receded over the past couple of weeks. I suppose viruses can have all kinds of effects on the body.

"Sorry to hear that," I offer weakly.

He waves a hand to bat it away. "But you're okay, Harriet?"

"Apparently impervious!"

He nods. "Right. What is this about a carrot?"

By mid-afternoon, the snow has eased to a gentler fall. As I work in the garden, I think of Christmases past, of the partridge and pheasant dinners at Haywood Hall, the always spectacular tree decorated with baubles from Liberty in London, the pristinely wrapped gifts, the doll's house for Judith. The Boxing Day shoots, the cold meat lunches, the open fires. None of it feels blurry anymore. I remember it all clearly as though I could reach in and retrieve it easily from somewhere it's been resting at the back of a drawer. All that joy.

Dr. Phillips emerges from his office during one of his too few breaks to admire my frozen-fingered work. I wonder if he's seeking distraction.

"I didn't have you down for a snowman kind of a lady, Harriet," he comments, sounding delighted as he approaches. I fix Angel's carrot to the front of its face. The snowman reminds me of a colonel I once knew. He was quite taken with me but with a nose that large, I couldn't take a courtship seriously. William's nose was sized more sensibly.

I've built the snowman far bigger than I'd intended, somehow getting carried away. It stands tall at six feet and is eye level with Dr. Phillips. "I'm not really. We're not getting on. In fact, he's been giving me the cold shoulder."

The doctor indulges me with a laugh louder than the joke warrants, attempting one in return. "Bit of a chilly disposition. What's his name? Parson Brown?"

I find the *Winter Wonderland* reference charming and try to picture Dr. Phillips as a young child enchanted by Christmas, learning the songs. But I find I can barely imagine him wearing anything other than his doctor's coat. It's disconcerting that he's wearing a winter coat over the top of it now.

"Doesn't that mean you and I are about to get married in the town?" I ask.

This time his laugh sounds forced, and I notice him watching me carefully, giving me what the young people call "the side eye."

"You know, I'm not sure I've ever built a snowman before," I admit.

"Even with your daughter?" Dr. Phillips looks surprised.

I know the comment wasn't meant as a criticism, but still my heart drops. Little Judith would have loved to build a snowman with me on the odd occasion when we were lucky enough to get enough snow, or on one of our ski breaks to St. Moritz. I have to stop myself from becoming defensive. "That was William—my husband's—domain. He took care of most of the more physical, fun activities. Swimming, skiing, sailing."

I was always too afraid of making a fool of myself, of falling, losing my dignity, looking less beautiful, less together. I become quiet for a moment, thinking about William, him matching our Great Danes in reliable energy.

"How did your husband die?" Dr. Phillips asks with a respectful tone.

"Prostate cancer. Nasty disease."

"Indeed." He nods gravely, professionally.

What it must be to care for the elderly, to see patient after patient decline and die. He's a courageous man. I think of Margaret, and her rapidly increasing frailty, remembering William's decline, his hollowing.

"Dr. Phillips, I'm a little worried about Margaret."

He nods.

We both keep our eyes fixed to the snowman, deep in thought. Losing her—the closest person in the world to me—is too much to bear. Margaret's usually so vital, if not in body, then in spirit, in mind.

"It's the way with some people. A sudden, rapid decline. They can resurface just as quickly though," Dr. Phillips says. "I mean, look at you, Harriet. You had mid-stage dementia and epilepsy, then—"

"I know. It makes Margaret's decline seem worse, somehow, given how much better I feel. And, quite frankly, not just her. Everyone is getting ill, seeming older."

Even Dr. Phillips, I realize as I say it. There are new lines around his eyes, a slight sagging at the neck. He looks almost gaunt. Like a man pushed well into his forties. Then again, he's been working hard, staying at the Manor in case of emergencies at night, his own quality of sleep forgotten.

"A very nasty virus season. Even with geriatrics, it's . . . unusual."

I rarely hear the term "geriatrics" anymore. It could be that it's only used in reference to the elderly, not directed towards them. Does this mean Dr. Phillips no longer thinks of me as old?

We're quiet for another moment, and I wonder if, like me, he's thinking about the likely impending deaths. Elizabeth passed away earlier this week, and ambulances have arrived on four separate occasions, taking the most unstable residents to intensive care units at the local hospital. I wonder if they'll return. It's an odd sensation, feeling so alive and well while others fall around you. It's as though I'm a bird taking flight as the earthquake hits.

"I'll tell you who I'm most worried about." His tone is serious.

"Who?" I'm alarmed. It's Margaret. It must be. My dear friend. My ally.

"This fellow." He gestures to the snowman, and my tension deflates. "He's looking very, very pale."

"Yes," I agree, smiling.

"Immobility, discoloration of the nose, a stony look in the eyes." I'd used small stones in replacement of the traditional coal. "And quite frankly, he has no limbs."

"Limbs!" I exclaim. "I need some sticks for the arms."

Dr. Phillips helps me find some from the sweep of perennial branches at the corner of the house, and we push them into the body of the snowman.

"Still a bit stiff," Dr. Phillips mutters.

"Arthritis," I point out, knowingly. "He needs some piroxicam. You should prescribe some."

Dr. Phillips holds up his hands. "He's not my patient. I have none of his medical records. I'm afraid that's impossible."

"I have some I'm not using any more. I'll slip him some." I grin, and Dr. Phillips gives me a genuinely warm smile.

"I'm glad you're feeling so much better, Harriet." His smile changes to concern as he returns to doctor mode. "But please be vigilant. We know so little about this illness."

He walks away, and I am left alone again in the garden.

"Knowing very little" is an exaggeration. They know nothing at all about my epilepsy. Dr. Phillips is required to give detailed reports about my symptoms back to the specialists at the hospital. Not that he has the time.

And my dementia . . . I wonder if that's why he came out here—to assess me in a different environment.

I catch sight of the snowman's orange nose in the periphery of my vision, but its head morphs, quite suddenly, into something else. A face. My breath stops. Not just a face, but a man. A hostile presence. Very slowly I turn, knowing deep inside what I'll see. The same horrific visage I saw in the church. A contorted gargoyle of William, now resting on a mound of snow. He's watching me, a statue, as frozen as the landscape. His grotesque expression seems like a punishment for something. A penance for my wellness amongst all this illness.

I close my eyes to steady my breath and lessen my dizziness, reminding myself this is just another hallucination. A part of my condition, my dementia, seeing things that aren't there.

When I open my eyes again, the snowman is back, but the carrot has fallen to the ground.

I pick it up and shove it into the globe of snow, back into the center of the snowman's face, then leave before it can decide to change again.

"Oh, hello," Tom greets me in the hallway. I don't think I've run into him since the séance. He stands slowly and gingerly, transporting his weight from the stairlift chair onto a cane I've not seen before. He looks sunken, his skin more liver-spotted than I remember, his head topped with merely a suggestion of hair. A wisp, like the finest spun sugar.

"Hello, Tom."

"Are you here to see someone?" he asks me.

"You mean Margaret?" I ask, confused.

"You're visiting Margaret? What, are you her niece?"

Niece? He doesn't know who I am? "It's me, Tom. Harriet."

He peers at me closely, then shakes his head. "No, you can't possibly be Harriet. She's over eighty. You, my dear, have some years before contending with seventy."

Tom laughs a little as if he made a joke, but I'm unsettled. It hasn't occurred to me I would stop being recognized by my fellow residents. But then I suppose the combination of my drastically altered appearance and the rapid onset of illness in many of the residents could create confusion.

"Oh!" A thought occurs to him. "You mean you're a visitor, and your name is also Harriet? Fair enough, yes. Common enough name."

I bristle. "Common" is not a term I welcome being associated with in any way, and I have met very few Harriets.

"Don't worry, dear. It's a good thing you're not the other Harriet." I take a breath in, aghast, but Tom doesn't seem to notice. Instead, he leans in conspiratorially to whisper, "She's a bit of a snob. Very snooty."

A snob? Snooty? I have no words.

"Have a lovely visit. Be careful with Margaret, she's very frail," he says before hobbling away towards the living room.

I am stunned, unsure what to make of the interaction, of his unsolicited criticism. I should be offended. But instead, I find myself laughing. A deep, full-body kind of chortle that would have been painful or even dangerous a few weeks ago, given my health issues. But I'm not offended, I realize, because I don't feel like that Harriet anymore. It's as if I have emerged from her hard shell, her cocoon, now bright and dazzling.

What should I do with this new surge of energy and youth? I'm practically bursting with frustrated buoyancy. Being here, around all these old, decrepit people, these motionless sunken rocks, seems so wrong. I am not a Tom. Nor am I a Margaret.

I've become, what, spritely? No, that's only ever used to describe old people who move with unexpected vigor. I'm more than that.

I think back to Angel asking me what kind of adventure I want to have. An affair. A grand affair. It's what I ache for. Not only to satisfy my lust but also my desperate need for attention. To adore and be adored. To not only feel alive but that I'm living, that I'm seen and loved for who I am now, and not who I once was.

But how? How can I have the adventure I crave stuck in a place such as this?

10

"Dear God!" Margaret startles, staring out at the snowman through the dining room window, a shaky hand to her chest, her face white as a ghost.

For a moment I panic, thinking she sees William as I did—that my hallucination was an actual flight of the supernatural. I'm choked as I follow her eyeline, but no, it's just the snowman.

I'd built it directly in front of the window where we sit for afternoon tea, looking in. At the time, I'd thought it would amuse her. But in the dwindling afternoon light, I suppose it does look a little more threatening than a couple of hours ago, even without a trace of gargoyle William.

After taking a moment to recover, Margaret smiles slightly, an uneasy concession to the humor of the situation.

"Don't you like him? I spent all afternoon making that. While you were napping away, I erected old Chilly Fingers!" I laugh and Margaret joins in, though hers seems hollow, half-hearted.

"Well, I . . . he's unexpected!" she attempts to chirp brightly. "How on earth did you have the energy to assemble him?"

I'm about to tell her my energy feels boundless these days, but it seems indelicate, given her obvious exhaustion. The circles under her eyes are so dark they could be bruises.

"I thought we could use a new Scrabble partner," I say instead.

"Well, there's not a snowball's chance in hell I could beat him." Her quip seems disembodied from the rest of her, as though she's been emptied of her natural humor.

After placing a small pile of leather-bound books on the table, Margaret sits—or rather collapses—into her chair, and I pour her tea.

"He has quite the intense stare." Sitting opposite me, she glances out the window again. "Quite disconcerting, how he's looking right at me."

I giggle uncertainly. Does she see something of my earlier instilled horrors? Are she and I so close she senses it in me?

"I made another discovery," she tells me finally, and I wonder if I'm mistaken. Perhaps her discomfort has nothing to do with the snowman, but what she's read instead. "While you were dallying around making him." She nods towards the window without looking out. "The diary—not of Florence, but of her husband."

"Her husband?"

"Yes. Well, more of a journal than a diary."

"These Victorians had a lot of time on their hands, it seems," I say. "Sitting around all day writing to nobody at all."

"True. But it's quite . . . disturbing. Listen to this." Margaret takes a sip of tea before finding her place in a slim green leather-bound book and beginning to read.

"'*I can barely comprehend the events of the last few months. Indeed, I have not been able to eat, let alone write! I thought—and I can barely believe I'm writing this—that by now I would be resting in my coffin. The cause being my darling Florence, my darling, beautiful wife. Oh! What a monstrous series of occurrences. All because she was predisposed to believe in the supernatural, beguiled by its secrets and promises. It turns out that such a belief is a fate worse than death of a different kind.*'"

Margaret looks up to check I'm paying attention.

"Go on," I urge.

"'*Unwound after finding herself victim to the petty tortures of her advancing years, Florence tried a variety of firstly traditional methods of feeling rejuvenated. She visited spas, spent a good deal of time at the ocean in summer, tried salts and tinctures, and even dabbled in the Eastern art of meditation, but nothing garnered her the effects she yearned for. In truth, I suspect she missed the comments of others, the regard of people and their attentions, more than anything else. Growing up such a beauty, the center of it all, how would it have been possible not to? To me, her explanation was more delicate. She said she wanted to feel more alive, younger, that she felt invisible despite my continuing and constant regard, but I do suspect what she found, or didn't find, in the mirror was her real motivation. A need to be a lady of consequence. I've never been enough. I know that now. She needs to be admired. Visible, yes—she claims her age has made others dismiss her too readily—but admired.'"*

Margaret pauses again and looks up at me over the top of her glasses.

My chest feels as though it caves in on itself. He could be writing about me, not Florence Marryat.

Margaret continues to read. *"'When Florence started to appear more youthful, with the energy and vigor of a young puppy, I was delighted, regardless of the cause. She came to me again, happy, joyful even, as she had been when we were first married. I was satisfied with just that—with her feeling better, more rejuvenated—but her appearance continued to alter quite dramatically.'"*

I begin to wonder if this *is* Florence Marryat's husband's journal or if Margaret has made it up as some elaborate practical joke. It's too real. Too on the nose to my situation. I lean forwards to catch a glimpse of the pages and do not see Margaret's handwriting, but rather a quite unfamiliar and elaborate penmanship scrawled over time-aged, yellowed pages.

Genuine, then, it seems.

"'She became younger, truly younger. A once-faded thing restored to new. Over the course of just a few weeks, her skin tightened, her figure slimmed and straightened, her breasts became small, high, and round as they were before she birthed our children. Her hair lost its steely threads and blackened to ebony once more, thick and shining like polished wood.

She became the woman I first loved. No, even more than the woman I first loved because on rediscovering her youth and vitality, she prized it so much more. She shone so much more brightly.'"

My face grew uncomfortably hot with shame. Can Margaret see this woman in me? The similarities are striking. I'm shining. My attractiveness is increasing. I'm getting younger, as she had. I'm more vital. People are noticing me again. But how? Why?

Did Florence Marryat suffer from the same rare type of epilepsy as I do?

"'At the time, I did not know the source of her change. That came later, and not from her own lips but from those of her friends who'd attended the séance. She knew I did not approve of the occult, that I scoffed at its baseless claims. And at first, none of us saw the effect her improved youthfulness was having on the rest of us, including me. But we aged, oh how we aged. As quickly as she became younger, we became so much older. I, myself, aged years in only a few days. I lost my hair, my cheeks hollowed and the skin at my jaw sagged. My joints ached, and my natural fitness evaporated overnight.

"'And it wasn't just me. The biggest changes occurred in our staff. Our young chamber maid advanced into middle age in weeks. A scullery maid lost her baby though she was quite advanced in her pregnancy, emerging from her miscarriage older by a good twenty years. Our dear housekeeper, Mrs. Baker, became ill quite rapidly and her disease progressed faster than it could be diagnosed. She died. Old Mr. Hartley could pass away any day now.'"

I tense. What is Margaret saying? That I'm causing all this illness around me? That not only am I not suffering the same as everyone else, but that I'm the direct cause?

Hot and wobbly, I swipe a hand over my forehead to steady my reaction, to allow time for my brain to catch up with my horror, but she presses onward.

"'Florence is a good woman, concerned for those around her and their sudden decline, but she was also distracted by her sudden good health,

enjoying her youth, reveling in her beauty and the reactions of those around her, savoring being a notable person again.

"*'The rest of us became quite desperate with the situation—losing people so quickly, and all with different ailments. There was no pandemic. Our dear friend Mrs. Mason finally told me about the séance Florence had invited her to here at the Manor and that she saw something taking over Florence's body in the course of the event. The Shadow, she called it. She told me she believed that dear Florence's body had been possessed by a daemon.'*"

I scoff, outraged. That couldn't possibly be true.

Margaret looks up. "You don't believe it?"

"Do you?" I ask, incredulous. How could logical Margaret even entertain such an idea? The fact that she's considering the possibility means either she's mentally as well as physically unwell, or . . .

Well, I don't want to consider the other option. It's too absurd.

Instead of answering, she returns to the journal. "*'I have never thought myself to be the kind of man to seek an exorcism. If I were told I would do such a thing even a few months ago, I would have called them a liar. And yet here I found myself desperately seeking the services of the church. And after the blasted thing was done, Florence—my darling Florence—aged so rapidly again that she dissolved to nothing but bones in my very hands within seconds.*

"*'Nothing is left of her now but the book she wrote a few years before all of this took place.* The Blood of the Vampire *is its title.'*"

"Dear lord." I grip the arms of the chair so tightly that I must force myself to release my fingers before they break. Part of me is admittedly terrified, and yet another part thinks—knows—it's all complete nonsense. Daemons and exorcisms and the occult. How could any of it be real?

My level-headed friend would never believe such an outlandish claim. Surely, this new delusion of Margaret's is a symptom of whatever illness has taken hold of her. "You can't possibly think that's true. That she was possessed?"

Margaret coughs severely into her elbow, winces, and takes another sip of her now cold tea.

"I believe there's something very unusual going on here, Harriet." She gestures around the room at the other residents, sorrow further clouding her expression. "And look at you. You look twenty years younger than you did last week. You're making snowmen, for God's sake!" She tips her head towards the window.

"A snow*man*, singular," I correct, childishly.

She ignores me. "We're all suddenly older, Harriet. Sick. Dying."

"And you're blaming that on me?"

"I'm not blaming—"

My terror is manifesting as anger, bubbling up my throat.

"Yes, you are, you're saying all this is my fault. I have epilepsy, Margaret. I was diagnosed." Outrage pushes me to my feet.

"You were hardly—"

"I have a rare condition that nobody understands. The only comforting side effect is my increase in energy and vitality. It must be hormonal. Dr. Phillips has already warned me to enjoy it while it lasts because he doesn't believe it will." I realize I'm telling myself as much as Margaret. "Dear lord, Margaret, you're claiming I'm possessed!"

"I know it's upsetting—" she starts, but I interrupt.

"Upsetting? It's not upsetting, it's ludicrous. You're . . ." My voice has risen, drawing the attention of those around us, but for once I don't want it. I remind myself that Margaret is ill, and that these claims are likely a product of that. I take a deep breath and lower my voice, resuming my seat again. "I think you're unwell, Margaret. I think you have some kind of rapidly advancing illness, and it's affecting your reasoning."

My friend looks down at her hands, folded in her lap.

"I wish you'd consider what I'm saying, Harriet," she tells me finally, and when she looks up, I see her eyes fill with tears. I've never seen Margaret cry, and it frightens me. For a fraction of a moment, I let myself imagine it's true, that Florence Marryat was and now I have been possessed by a daemon that makes us younger, the price being we steal youth from those around us. It's grotesque, too awful to contemplate. Absurdity bursts my imagining. Science is struggling to explain what's happening to me and to my fellow residents, so Margaret has sought an explanation in the supernatural. A tale as old as time.

As I get up from the table, I catch sight of the snowman leering at me as I leave the dining room. I need time alone to think.

Though spacious, my room is crammed with furniture and not designed for pacing. I suppose the elderly seldom pace. How could Margaret think I'm possessed by a bloody daemon? She's not even religious, not that I remember anyway. She can't believe this nonsense. If she did, why would she have sat there, day after day, having tea, playing Scrabble and Monopoly, dining with a daemon, for God's sake? *Oh, here, daemon, I'd like to buy Trafalgar Square. Excuse me, daemon, you've just landed on my station.*

Then again, she sat there day after day, knowing about my dementia without telling me . . .

I snatch up an empty makeup box from my dressing table and throw it against the wall, attempting to sate my angry frustration. But it's so small and light it wanders through the air quite pathetically, and its collision with the wall is barely audible.

Suddenly I hate this room, with its cream and peach sweet pea wallpaper, and even my own teak furniture I brought with me from Haywood Hall. I despise the self-important paintings by artists who were once popular but are now generally forgotten. The silly porcelain boxes and trinkets gifted by friends, most of whom have passed away. It all seems so meaningless. So *old*. A meagre collection of *things* to make an elderly lady feel at home, to be bundled up and cleared out on the same day as her death. It's insulting that this is what I'm left with, these reminders that I haven't been in control of my own life in recent years.

I sit down heavily on the bed and look into my long mirror. Despite my clouded expression, I think I look even more youthful than I did this morning, my skin smoother and complexion brightened in anger, my hair a little fuller. My appearance feels emblematic of my emerging agency, the regaining of my faculties, my ordered thinking, as if the dementia has been shaken away.

Though while I remain here at Marryat Manor, categorized as elderly, my freedoms are still compromised. I'm still caged. Still pinned to that butterfly board.

I had my third and final affair at the age of fifty-five. Not an affair, more of a brief dalliance, entirely born from a need for validation. I chose a mediocre actor, whose face was more appealing, it turned out, than his body. It was actually his voice that drew me in, but he was not inclined to talk in bed, so any attraction I felt for him diffused during the act itself. He was a particularly expressionless lover. My betrayal of my husband wasn't worth it. It never was.

Perhaps that's why I see William now. Is guilt the culprit?

What was it Florence Marryat's husband had said? That he knew she wanted to be admired and craved the attention. Did William know that of me? Was I like Florence Marryat?

I see my uncertainty reflected in the mirror, uncomfortable with the wisdom of age.

All people have different gifts—intelligence, wit, guile, compassion. They all need validation, to be proven intelligent, to be found funny, etcetera. Why should it change just because of advancing years? In my younger days, I'd shoved the knowledge of my inevitable decline aside to worry about later and forgot to reconsider what could continue to make me seen and respected by others until it was too late.

Now, by some absurd medical coincidence, some catch of the light in nature's mechanics, a second chance has been given to me, and I'm not going to take it for granted as I once did, not because of the increased energy and beauty, but for what it might buy me.

Freedom, control of my own life, love even.

Regardless of Margaret's bizarre suggestions.

***

I don't want to see my friend again today, but I'm hungry and need to go down to dinner.

Unashamed, I descend the inadvisably badly lit stairs—a product of the lack of staff and lack of time to change a blown bulb, no doubt—nimbly passing a fellow resident using the stairlift.

As I do so, I notice in detail—maybe for the first time—the portraits lining the oak-paneled stairway. Very large gilt-framed paintings, fitting in so well with their surroundings that they're instantly forgettable. Florence Marryat as a young woman, and Lord Marryat, slightly older. In both portraits, their skin glows creamy and luminous from darker backgrounds and clothing. Florence is very beautiful, delicate beneath her thick dark hair. Lord Marryat looks noble, elegant even, if not conventionally handsome. Neither are smiling but instead look thoughtful, as if Florence was caught musing and her husband was engaging in conversation with the viewer. But like most Victorian paintings, both are so unnaturally posed they are not truly intimate. They look as people would if their portraits were being painted, angling themselves becomingly, keeping truth at a distance.

Idly, I remember that the photos of me that William loved best had been my least favorite—those taken off guard, my expressions clownishly dramatic. I had favored the still, considered pictures in which I looked composed and where the light flattered me.

My own version of unnaturally posed, I suppose.

As I peer at the paintings, I realize how closely I'm peering at them. Could my eyesight be declining? Is my prescription off? I remove my glasses, and suddenly the world is a great deal clearer. How has it taken this long to realize I don't need such a strong prescription anymore?

Entering the dining room, I find Margaret is not there, and I'm both relieved and concerned.

"She's quite unwell," Alyson tells me as she fills my water glass, helping with the dinner service given the lack of staff. Her brow furrows as she mentions Margaret, as if reading my thoughts.

"With what?" I'm alarmed, remembering Margaret's exhausted appearance earlier, the cough.

"Chest infection." Alyson places an empathizing hand on my arm before attending to the elderlies at the next table. She really does care about the residents, I realize. She's actually very concerned. I underestimated Alyson.

I sit on my own in the half-empty dining room, feeling more out of place than ever, as if I'm a visitor stranded here in the snow who must be accommodated reluctantly.

Every other resident appears older, ailing.

Under questioning gazes, Margaret's accusation replays in my head. *There is something very unusual going on here.* What did they name the thing that was claimed to have taken over Florence Marryat? The Shadow.

I shiver, trying to grasp at a half memory. A shadow. Am I remembering a shadow?

From the window of the dining room, I notice the flashing lights of an ambulance making painfully slow progress up the snowy drive towards the Manor. No sirens. Alyson notices the lights, too, as she serves me my rather unrefined dinner of sausages and mashed potato. She slumps a little.

"What? It's not Margaret, is it?" I ask, fear constricting my throat.

"No. Tom," she says softly. "He passed away early this evening."

Time seems to grind to a halt around me. This evening? But I saw Tom only this afternoon. He didn't recognize me. He told me Harriet was a snob. How was it possible he could have slipped away so suddenly? I say as much to Alyson.

"I know." She sighs. "A very rapid decline. He came down for tea and instantly took ill."

Alyson herself looks unwell, the bags under her eyes exaggerated, her steps heavier, almost dragging. A consequence, I suppose, of the Manor being so understaffed lately. Too few helpers, too many ailing residents. Her hair is scraped back into a ponytail as though to hide the wiry white hairs sprung at her roots. But the style only makes the slight drooping of flesh at her jawbone more visible. Maybe she's not registered that yet. Maybe it doesn't matter.

I should have offered to help today after all.

What did I do instead? Made a snowman intended to amuse my friend, but it only made her uneasy. Heard Margaret's reading from that awful journal—the story of that supposed possession and terrible exorcism. Why would he believe such awful things about his wife? He must have been trying to control her, felt her slipping away from him as he aged. His jealousy made him blame her wanting attention. He wanted it all for himself.

Is that what Margaret's doing to me now? Is she jealous of the attention I've received since my fit at the séance? No. In truth, that doesn't sound like Margaret. More likely, she's genuinely trying to find an answer to what's happening at the Manor, and an explanation for my drastic—for it is truly remarkable—transformation. In appearance and in mind.

My clarity, quickness, and order.

I've finished dinner without registering that I've eaten. Alyson doesn't offer me pudding, as I always decline, but today, for once, I ask for it. My recently reduced waistline can endure the butterscotch tart. And in truth, I want to put off my return to my room, where I feel contained in a box within a box.

This place, this entire Manor—decaying, festering, forlorn, with its histories of resentments, disgruntlements, and mental illnesses—feels like a grave. Trying to hold me under when I want to live. I want to float above, stay buoyant against this current dragging the rest of the people here down, down, down.

But I can't leave Margaret, my friend, my soul's champion.

If only I could find a different way forwards, a new way to be happy as the fresher me, illnesses or no, whilst staying with her.

I could help her, I'm sure. Listened to, seen, as I am now, I could find a way.

11

In my late forties there was a brief rekindling of my sexual relationship with William. Our skiing holiday was overtaken by storms, and he had neglected to bring his usual reading material. The endless blank whiteness outside and the warmer, creamier firelight within our suite stirred our old and almost forgotten chemistry into something spectacular, possibly inspired by the energy of the storm. I felt adored and treasured in a way that had been absent for a while. Having sex in front of windows, knowing the conditions meant nobody looked in from outside, lit us.

The magic evaporated too quickly, however, when other, more important things rushed to the forefront of William's focus again—work and appointments and associates, at a time when it was less important that I entertain his clients—leaving me feeling useless and abandoned. Yearning to be the center of someone's attention again, when feeling particularly ignored I accepted the advances of the first man who proffered a brief dalliance. Boringly, he was the business partner of our accountant, someone I'd actually managed to get work for a couple of times through a contact of William's, and to thank me, he invited me to lunch.

At first it had seemed exciting, as he calmly suggested sex in the same tone as he suggested we order a second cup of coffee, and I thought him smooth, suave even, rather than soulless. But his expression during the act was identical to his expression doing anything else I'd witnessed. Reading papers, pouring tea, ordering lunch, climaxing—all the same. Being with him left me dissatisfied and questioning who on earth I thought I was and what I was doing on that dirty grey spring afternoon that spat inconvenient rain. We'd had a few minutes of quietly mechanical sex in his too-dark, brownly decorated townhouse bedroom in—not on—a cold, hard bed. I was administered to as he might have administered to a toaster or an electric kettle.

That day clarified for me the difference between beauty and visibility. I was beautiful, everyone said so, therefore I should have been seen and had purpose. But that accountant's almost pathological dispassion made me feel like I was nothing. Less than nothing.

After that day, I rarely confused the two again.

I should have been content with William's busy complacency.

I think of this as I wait for Ralph, who is visiting his mother in her room. How different might my marriage have been if I'd been with a man like Ralph instead of William? Would we have avoided those dwindling, mediocre days of marriage? Would someone like Ralph have been worth leaving William for? The prospect of losing Haywood Hall in a divorce would have been unimaginable but survivable, for love. For feeling seen and cherished.

Undivided attention trumps gentle respect.

The focus in my marriage changed over time, as is normal. From passion and sex at the beginning, life gradually became about companionship, growing the business together, and supporting each other through the trials of everyday life. I was glad I'd stayed with William and that my brief affairs hadn't scuttled things between us.

By the time I was forced to leave Haywood Hall, I was merely a prop for its majesty. Irrelevant, like a coat stand. If I'd had more of a voice, a perspective, Margaret's intellect, I might have been able to stay relevant, visible. To the younger world, there is little difference between an old woman in a bright Jaeger dress and one in a tweed suit, but an established scholar is more respected than a former socialite.

The world will still read Margaret's books once she's gone.

My entrails will be sold for a few pounds in a charity shop.

"Harriet?" Ralph's expression is timid as he approaches me.

He looks worn down, tired, upset, unshaven. His hair is more unruly than usual, and his usually smart clothes are crumpled. Somehow, this makes the blue of his eyes bluer, like two gems emerging from a pile of coal.

"Ralph!" I try to look like I haven't been waiting for him in the hall by taking a sudden interest in reading a plaque about the house's history bolted to the wall of the entranceway.

In truth, I took in none of it. An undignified performance.

He steps forwards and hugs me for a fraction too long, his tension releasing an inch. His body is warmer than I imagined. Firmer, too, beneath the rumpled shirt. Must be down to all that time he spends in the gym.

"I haven't seen your mother today, how is she?" I ask.

"Not well. Dr. Phillips is with her now. She has a fever. He's given her something to reduce it. Also—" Ralph's concerned expression deepens. "He asked her if her illness would keep her from her sexual exploits?"

I remember how much their banter used to annoy me, because I wasn't part of it.

How transparent, that self-centeredness. How unbecoming.

"Don't worry, it's a running joke between them."

Ralph seems relieved at my reassurance. "Then he asked if she wanted him to read to her from the Bible?"

"That's also normal for Dr. Phillips. Most of the residents like it. What did Margaret say?"

He grins. "She'd rather hear some Robert Frost."

I laugh, because that's exactly what my friend would say. "And did he?"

"He did!" Ralph laughs too. "I think he was taken a little off guard. I left them to it."

But as the extent of his mother's illness occurs to him afresh, the merriment drops from his eyes. The seriousness of the situation hits me too. Margaret's accusation that I might be the cause hovers, unwanted, in the periphery of my speculations, so I refocus on Ralph.

"Your mother's in good hands." I place a reassuring hand on his arm. "She couldn't get any better care than she's getting here."

Ralph releases a breath. "I know. I . . . would you walk with me, Harriet? I need to clear my head before driving home."

"Absolutely," I reply, glad he's suggested it, since I was too nervous. "I'll get my coat."

I opted for my thinner, more fitted red wool coat that gives me an almost Kate Middleton shape, but I'm cold.

It's another flat, grey day, the snow now disappeared, revealing dull, dead earth—the winters in England are awfully dreary—and I stand out against the gloom. A sprig of holly in the mist. Walks feel different now than they did before, as though I'm breaking free from my shackles rather than merely wandering the perimeter on a leash. Ralph offers me his arm as a gentleman might, not because I need it but because he's noble, as William might have done years ago.

"You've quite changed, Harriet," he tells me, his tone more considered now than a few weeks prior. He's not trotting out inauthentic compliments.

I tingle. "Changed how?"

"You're so energetic, so much younger seeming. I didn't know such a change was possible. How do you look so young at your age? Did you get secret surgery at some point?"

"Lord, no!" I scoff. Surgery is distasteful. It has the appearance of desperation. "I'm just, I mean, I believe it's a side effect of this epilepsy.

Albeit a mysterious one. My eyesight has improved too. I must need an altered prescription."

"A medical marvel!" Ralph smiles warmly at me, and I ache with the gentle authenticity of his words.

"I don't believe I've ever been called a marvel before."

His grin widens even more, before his brow shifts into a squint. "Funny you mention glasses though. I just got reading glasses, I couldn't see my computer screen clearly anymore. It came out of nowhere. Bizarre."

Bizarre indeed. Though I suppose late forties is about the time I first needed reading glasses too. I decide to shift the subject away from issues of aging. "How are things at home with the run up to Christmas?"

"Not great. I thought it would be an opportunity to reconnect. You know, buying Lisa something, letting her know I still care?" I nod. "But she found my gift for her."

The dejection in the poor man's voice breaks my heart. "I'm sorry. What was it?"

"A necklace. A sapphire solitaire pendant, surrounded by diamonds, on a gold chain." He stops and smiles at me uncertainly, self-consciously. "I was . . . inspired by the one you wear. It always looks so nice on you."

His statement surprises me. I'd always secretly hoped someone would notice, but . . . I realize he's waiting for a response and say, "It sounds lovely."

Ralph frowns at the snow-smattered gravel beneath our feet. "Lisa said it was too expensive and old-fashioned. That I didn't know her at all if that was what I thought she'd like. That it was thoughtless, given the problems we're having." He sounds dejected rather than resentful. I imagine him visiting a jeweler, selecting the necklace with great care, making the decision to spend the money on something special for his wife. I feel bad on his behalf.

"That's awful. Did she at least appreciate the effort?"

He shakes his head and shrugs. "So I returned it, like she told me to. And I haven't given it a lot of thought since. I've been distracting myself with work. It's been busier than usual. Clients want holiday landing pages associated with promotions."

"Well, she should appreciate the fact you wanted to do something nice for her." I try to show I understand him. "My husband always gave me such thoughtful gifts. And even when he got it wrong on occasion, I appreciated the thought. He once gave me a blue enamel butterfly brooch. It was worth nothing but beautiful, and so thoughtful. I think I loved it even more than the expensive pieces."

"Because you're a lady." He emphasizes the final word. "You put value in the right places. You have class, and dignity, and strength, and warmth."

"Oh, gosh!" I laugh off the compliments as three spiky crows land on the path ahead of us, inky black against the frost. They rattle out reprimanding caws, twitch with judgement, pick at the gravel for a moment, then—disgusted—fly off.

Ralph changes the subject as we keep walking. "Tell me about William." I'm surprised he remembered his name. "Did you have a happy marriage?"

I pause. The horrifying hallucinations have unmoored me slightly from missing William. Zombie. Gargoyle. Snow monster. Thinking about him now brings fear along with comfort.

Noticing my hesitation, Ralph adds, "Of course, if that's too personal a question, ignore me."

He has such excellent manners.

"No, no, it's fine." I don't tell him about my recent visions, about my dread. "We had a happy marriage of sorts. A . . . *kind* marriage. The passion wore off, and the complacency became too great. I always wanted more attention than he had the time to give. Of course, he valued how I ran the house and finessed his clients, but the business took up so much of his attention. There was always kindness, though, always understanding. William was . . . impossible to leave."

"Kindness sustains." Ralph understands.

"Yes, it does. But the lack of passion, whether physical or mental, can wear you down eventually. As we've spoken before, it eats away at your self-worth, frustrates the soul."

I wonder if William hears me somehow, if his uncharacteristically disgruntled spirit is taking notes, preparing itself for another appearance.

Ralph murmurs in agreement, and it occurs to me he has that same level of kindness and conviviality as William, but unlike my late husband, he also values passion as much as me.

"Can you see yourself having a relationship again?" he asks. "Given the side effects of the epilepsy?"

I fizz inside. "You're the first person to ask me that. Yes, I can imagine it. If it's with the right man, the right situation. But I need spark. I'm not after simple companionship. I want real passion again."

Probably too honest, but I need more than hollow adoration. I need real, lasting regard and respect.

"That's . . . refreshing to hear."

Refreshing? Something about Ralph's raw vulnerability in that moment—his need to love and be loved, to feel a genuine connection with his partner—makes me feel as though I'm seeing my soul's twin. I'm stunned and a bit shaken.

We've completed a loop of the garden nearest the house.

"Look!" Ralph points at something behind me. I turn to find the snowman, all snow thankfully, with no trace of William. "Someone built him. Isn't that funny?"

"That was me, I'm afraid." I feel self-conscious and slightly queasy at the memory of yesterday's hallucination.

"What?" Ralph laughs—deep, sustained, joyous, not at all mocking—throwing his head back to give way to it, until he finally pauses. "*You* did that?"

"And why not?" I ask with mock-indignance. "I think he's rather jolly!"

"He is! I just could never have imagined it. I love your sense of fun, Harriet."

I laugh, too, and when we stop, Ralph is studying me, as though seeing me for the first time, trying to make sense of me. His eyes take in each of my features before finally settling on my mouth. Instinctively, I lick my lips.

"You're very beautiful, Harriet," he says, his eyes returning to mine. I see the truth of his words in his oceanic blue gaze. I feel them in every part of me. It's not a line. He's not trying to be charming. He seems as surprised by his confession as I am.

"That's—" I start.

"Don't say kind," he cuts in. "It's true. There's magic in you, Harriet. And not just because of your altered appearance. There's magic in your spirit too. I'm very drawn to you."

I swallow down my nervous joy, feeling like I'm eighteen again, being told I'm beautiful for the first time, being truly seen for the first time. I have no idea how to respond or what this means, but I feel the same way about him.

"You don't have to reply," Ralph tells me, smiling, saving me, as we turn and walk back towards the house. "Do you ever get bored with this place?" He looks up at the grand façade of the Manor, flatly brown against the snow.

"God, yes!" I answer with feeling, relieved he's diverted the subject away from my awkwardness. "I would do anything to get out of here."

My cage. My prison.

"Well, would you like to go out to dinner with me, Harriet? Tonight?"

A date! A proper date, not a walk, a date. "I would absolutely love that, Ralph, thank you."

He turns to me, his face lit, his smile warm. Given his earlier distress at his marital situation, being the reason for this new ebullience spins my innards skywards. "Excellent. Where would you like to go?"

"Anywhere. Your choice," I tell him and then regret it, wondering if he'll take me to one of those awful "hipster" restaurants with terribly

loud music and odd things on the menu, but I don't say anything.
We're at the front of the house now.

"Then I'll pick you up at seven, okay?"

"Perfect!" I beam.

As soon as Ralph leaves, I'm back inside my room, facing the mirror
with my hand up my skirt, letting his name fall from my lips over and
over. As I touch myself, I hear a moan of pain from the room next door,
the sound cracked and agonized. Awful wracking guilt joins my illicit
pleasure as my orgasm shatters through me, practically taunting my
neighbor: *I'm alive, you're not.* As though my sexual energy has feasted
on the nearest available life source. Vampiric.

I shake these thoughts away and switch on the radio to Classic FM
as I collect myself. But the groans of the ill compete with the music,
and I hear the scuffled footsteps of a staff member entering their room.
Vivaldi's *Four Seasons.* Muffled conversation. The cries convert into a
wail, shaking, harrowing, the sound of death's prelude.

Age is so cruel. That could have been me, weeks ago.

I focus on Vivaldi's *Autumn,* as I visit my dresser and consider the
contents of the top drawer—my lingerie. Plum lace, or coffee-colored
French silk? I want to wear it to dinner, to know it's there, an alluring
secret inside my dress, next to my skin. A reminder I came earlier in
the day while others my age succumbed to their viruses, infections, and
diseases.

A reminder I am vital.

As I wait in the lobby for Ralph to pick me up, I wonder what it's like
to be him. At his computer all day, vapidly tinkering with websites,
hosting inauthentically upbeat meetings with clients, going to the gym
and working tired muscles, and occasionally crossing paths with a busy
and indifferent wife.

How can he feel important in that life? Is he taken seriously? Is his tenderness valued? He has too much soul for that desert-dry existence. Is he suffocated by its monotony, its somber dullness? Does he still have sex with his wife, or only his hand? I imagine him pleasuring himself. Perhaps he thinks of me when he does it, as I did of him earlier.

Even though I still look older than him by some years, his attraction was obvious earlier today. Only lustful eyes linger on lips in that way.

The hall is too brightly lit in the evenings, the glare of the bulbs in the chandelier not particularly flattering. Standing by the door, I walk through it as soon as it starts to open, partly to avoid the lighting effect and partly because I don't want anyone noticing I'm leaving for the evening with Ralph. Whilst it might not be unusual for residents to leave the Manor with visitors, me leaving with Margaret's son is. *Margaret's son!* But my concerns evaporate as I catch sight of him in his black wool overcoat, open to reveal a shirt and tie beneath. This isn't a charitable affair, taking his mother's friend out to alleviate her boredom—he's dressed for a date.

"You're ready." He seems mildly surprised that I'm hurrying us out.

"I am. Ready to get out of here." I flash him a smile as I lead us away from the Manor and towards the parked cars on the far left of the driveway.

"Are you okay with those shoes on this gravel?" he asks. He's noticed the new Prada high heels I'd ordered online a few weeks ago. At the time, I thought I'd just keep them in the closet, admire them when the mood struck me. But now having a chance to wear them out is rather thrilling.

"I'll have to be." I shrug good-naturedly. I don't care about my shoes, designer or not, only about how I appear to Ralph in this moment. I want him to be impressed, but also to see beyond the exterior.

"No, no, wait here. I'll bring the car around," he insists and leaves me on the front steps while he jogs over to his car, then pulls up shortly after in the black BMW, hopping out to open my door for me as William had for the nearly five decades of our marriage.

We don't speak at first in the car. I'm enjoying its interior darkness, the only light the red glow of the dashboard and headlights on the drive. It's been a long time since I've gone out at night, and I love the coldness, the ink-dipped depth, the sense of adventure and possibility. I'm aware of Ralph's physical presence, the movements of his arms as he drives, his hands on the steering wheel then closer to mine as he changes gear.

"You look lovely tonight, by the way," he says finally, though his eyes are on the road, not on me. I detect the slightest quaver in his voice. He's nervous. I'm delighted. I'm wearing my most form-fitting navy dress, which flares out to just above the knee—a shorter skirt than he's seen me in before, my calves lean and flattered by the new shoes I had to practice walking in. I chose the outfit partly to complement my figure and partly to complement the sapphire pendant he mentioned admiring earlier. My neck is now leaner, so the pendant rests lower down on my smoother chest rather than dangling at my once-ugly clavicle.

"Thank you. As do you." I return the compliment with the slightest tinkle of a laugh, a bit nervous myself.

"I'm so glad for this evening." He takes my hand, which was resting on my knee. "So glad for you, Magic Harriet."

"Magic Harriet," I murmur back at him, enjoying the warmth of his hand, the softness of his fingers, the newly familiar tug of lust between my thighs.

"Nothing has felt this right for a long time." His voice is soft. Being enclosed in this space with him feels intimate in a way I don't think being in a car with anyone else ever has. "That we should be out tonight together," Ralph continues, "feels . . . I don't know, oddly inevitable."

Inevitable sounds promising. His gentle sincerity makes me feel even more special, as though I've been singled out as the recipient of his most genuine of attentions. He chose me, because of this inevitability. "I know what you mean."

We haven't even arrived at the restaurant yet, but the evening has a weight to it, a heady promise. He *sees* me, this beautiful, sensitive man.

The illuminated snow-covered buildings and Christmas lights of the town ahead spins even more enchantment into the evening's fiber. It feels as though I'm caught in a dream, long and vivid. A hallucination of the best kind. The séance, this recovered energy, wellness, a return of my energy and beauty. My sexual reawakening. The reemergence of myself, like a butterfly from a chrysalis. All of it has brought me closer to this man, opened Ralph's eyes to not only my external appearance, but my true self—the best version of me.

If there weren't a medical explanation, I'd think it was magic too.

12

Ralph has chosen an old inn, close to Guildford, lit with hurricane lamps and decorated with twinkly fairy lights and swags of real greenery. It wears its romance as if it is central to its core character, not cheaply manufactured or fabricated by some awful "brand specialist." It's the kind of authentic place people go to fall in love or to propose. Both old and new me love it. I feel joyful to be somewhere that doesn't smell of illness and death. Diners here have their own teeth. They are not worn down, crumbling away. This is a place that holds itself upright and exults in being the special part of somebody's week.

"The food here is great," Ralph tells me as we're seated at a window without a view but that reflects the room's hundreds of lights. "A superb classic menu."

Classic sounds wonderful. I wonder if he selected it on purpose, suspecting my tastes might be similar to his mother's. *Don't think of Margaret.* Thoughts of her, of the possible reality of the situation, will make things awkward. I'm pretty sure Ralph feels the same because he doesn't mention her either.

"Shall we order some wine?" He's smiling with a new kind of charm, unlike the type I've seen him use on Alyson and occasionally Imani. A special kind reserved for me, revealed only to *me.*

"Definitely." I beam back. It's been a long time since I've been on anything resembling a date, and I'm not sure how to act. I've been accused of being a flirt in recent years, but that kind of flirtation was different. There was a freedom in it because it was so utterly futile. I could afford to act scandalously. But my new vitality and more youthful appearance has come along and sat squarely on top of that kind of behavior. Possibility changes everything.

"Red or white?" Ralph glances at the menu. "Oh, I suppose it depends on dinner."

"I'm rather fond of duck," I tell him after perusing the choices. "I haven't had it in years. Too rich for most Marryat residents."

"Then you should get the duck. The ragu?" He points to it on the menu, and I nod. "Do you think it comes with quackers?" he quips, and I laugh, delighted at his spirit if not the joke. "I think I might be a typical man, I'm afraid, and go for steak."

"You have a young person's digestive system to handle it," I say and immediately wish I hadn't, having simultaneously drawn attention to my own age and digestive ailments. Luckily, he doesn't seem to notice.

"At the moment. But I'm closing in on fifty now. I'm just waiting for something to drop off."

"You've got some time before that happens. Things must droop and waggle about first."

"Waggle about?" He laughs. "I hadn't heard about this. Exactly what is it that waggles?"

I giggle. I'm not a giggling sort but given the nerves, I can't help it. "Anything you can imagine will probably end up waggling."

"Unless I convince you to share some of your elixir of youth." He means it as a compliment, but his comment makes me uneasy, as though he suspects me of keeping some strange secret. Magic Harriet. Double-brain-wave Harriet. Dementia Harriet.

We place our order, Ralph selecting an appropriate bottle of wine to pair with both duck and steak. I wonder, fleetingly, how wealthy Ralph is. He's a web designer, his wife a lawyer, so they must be fairly well-off, yes? I wonder if he's told me before, but I don't remember. I can't remember the last time I checked on my own finances. Other than paying the bills, money was never my concern. That was William's domain. Still, I believe at the last check a few years ago there were many millions resting in my accounts and investments. Judith has been handling all of that. Everything of mine is *managed* by somebody else. Maybe it's time I learned to take over.

I realize I've lost track of my thoughts again and glance over to find Ralph fiddling with his fancy watch. I'm glad he's distracted, giving me time to consider if I should pay for dinner or if he'd find it offensive.

I have no idea what the modern etiquette is for such things, and I despise not knowing.

"What's it like being a stepfather?" I ask while we wait for our first courses. I'm enjoying the banter but am also keen to deepen our connection and know I need to ask more personal questions. Ralph's face drops a fraction, and he looks down at his glass of wine, turning the stem on the tablecloth until it has completed a circle.

"I mean, it could be worse. But it's strange. I am not Justin's dad. His actual dad, he idolizes. Me? He tolerates. He's indifferent, really." I stay quiet, so he'll tell me more. "To be honest, I think he's a bit confused about why his mother left his father, and why she chose me to replace him. It's obvious he regards me as a lesser man."

"That sounds difficult." I reach out across the table and place a hand on his. "And unfair. You're such a *kind* man, Ralph. I bet you're a wonderful stepfather."

He smiles sadly. "Yes, well . . . Justin's dad is . . . a big man. A man's man, you know? All muscles on top of muscles, beer, footie. Less intellectual." Interesting, I hadn't thought of Ralph as intellectual. Margaret certainly doesn't. "With my parents, it would have been weird for me not to be at least somewhat intelligent, curious." I nod. "But obviously, I'm less interesting to a teen boy. We were closer when he was little."

"Isn't that the case with all children though?" I think of Judith. "They drift away as teens."

"Justin's still close to Lisa." Ralph sips his wine. "But to be honest, and this is brutal, I don't really mind all that much. I mean, I love the boy, I guess, but I don't enjoy his company. If he's not invested in me, well, I can spend my time developing relationships that matter." Ralph meets my eye and then looks away, a little embarrassed at his brazenness. He diverts the attention to me. "And you have a daughter?"

"Judith, yes." I don't mention Molly. No sense highlighting my being a grandmother.

"Are you close?"

"Not especially." I smile gently, covering the sadness. "She married a difficult man. She's always been . . . cheerful," I concede, "but a little meek. Quite unlike me." I brighten.

Ralph laughs. "You are definitely not meek."

"And her husband is quite dominant. Abrasive. He and I do not see eye to eye. And I can't stand it when she goes along with everything he thinks and says as if she doesn't have a mind of her own. She has a perfectly good brain, but you wouldn't know it to talk to her. Honestly, if you met her, you'd think she was vapid. That's how she comes across."

A little unfair, maybe, and I worry I've been too harsh, too honest, that Ralph thinks less of me for my opinion of my daughter. Guilt bites at me. I do love Judith, regardless of her messing.

"It's painful when people aren't who you expect them to be," he says.

"It's disappointing," I agree. "But it's not okay to be disappointed by people these days. When I was a girl, I was constantly being told I was a disappointment. Now it's not on, of course." Ralph nods. "Not that I'd tell Judith that. I am more sensitive to others' feelings than my mother was."

Or am I?

"Mother-daughter relationships can be difficult, I hear. Mother-son relationships are simpler, I think." He doesn't directly mention Margaret and looks relieved as the waitress arrives with our salads.

* * *

"If you could go anywhere in the world, where would you go?" Ralph asks me later in the evening.

"That's a good question." I smile. "I'm fortunate. I traveled a lot with William. I've been to many places. The Americas, naturally. Most countries in Europe, save a few of the odd ones. Bali, India, Thailand, China, Japan . . . Morocco, oh, and Australia and New Zealand."

"Which was your favorite?" he asks encouragingly, his eyes lit with interest. Although I treasure the memories of traveling with my husband, they also account for the severity of my claustrophobia in recent years.

Widowhood, age, and compromised mobility ripped away my liberty.

"I couldn't say, they're all so different. I loved Norway, for reasons I can't articulate accurately. The fjords are my favorite kind of vista. Majestic. Surprisingly colorful. And I love a mountain you don't have to climb to enjoy," I add. "What was it Shelley said? 'A dizzy ravine'?"

He shakes his head. He's not his mother's son in the literature department.

"I think that was Mont Blanc." I wave it away. "Nothing to do with fjords. I'm always mixing my quotes up."

"Mum is a flawless reciter of quotes," he says finally, giving in to the inevitability of Margaret coming up in conversation.

"Oh, yes!" I roll my eyes comically, taking care to keep the tone of the conversation light. "Flawless. I feel like an absolute dunce around her. Like I'm a little girl and she's my teacher." My words sound a touch too desperate, as if I'm trying too hard to fabricate a distance between Margaret and I to show we're now at different points in our lives and have different stations. And it's true. I wonder if, given Margaret's absurd claims about my possession, the dementia I've seemingly lost has found its way into her. Ralph smiles politely but he's staring at his wineglass again, and he pushes his dinner plate a little further away from him.

"So, what about you?" I ask, distracting him from thoughts of Margaret.

"I'm sorry?"

"Where would you travel, of all the places in the world?"

Ralph clears his throat. "I've come to realize I don't mind too much where I go. It matters more who I'm with." His words come with a weight and a meaningful lingering gaze. There's longing lodged in there somewhere too. A man full of want, full of unfulfilled need.

His brazen words fill me with a fizz of nerves, but I keep my eyes locked onto his. I'm suddenly confused about what we're doing here. "Ralph—"

"Harriet."

"What's happening here, exactly? I mean, this evening is wonderful, but is this a *real* date?" I hold my breath, unsure of how he'll answer.

"I . . . honestly have no idea. But I feel like I can be myself around you, Harriet. It's been a long time since I felt listened to, taken seriously."

I deflate a fraction, then worry it shows on my face. Is that what I am to him? A listening ear? A fill-in for his ailing mother?

"Ah, well, I'm glad I can be of some help," I say brightly, sounding a little too much like Judith. Too polka-dot. Too normal.

"But there's more." He takes my hand atop the table, and my psyche soars once more. "I just love your company. You're interesting, and thoughtful, and quite honestly, very beautiful."

Ralph's realness with me is what I'm drawn to, as though I'm seeing a special side of him. A deeper, more meaningful center he's choosing to share with only me. Because . . . why? Inevitability?

"That's a lovely thing to say," I offer. His words are delicious, but I'm still nervous. "I . . ." Should I return the compliment? If he has no plans on this being anything other than a pleasant meal out with one of his mother's friends, I don't want to embarrass myself. "I'm delighted to be taken out by such a charming, handsome man." I smile. A safe comment?

"There are no other men chasing you, then?" Ralph's grin is cheeky, but he waits for me to respond. Does that mean *he's* chasing me?

"Not that I'm aware of, but you have to watch the octogenarians," I say mock-conspiratorially, as though I'm not one of them. "They're a surprisingly randy bunch." He laughs. I take a deep sip of my wine, readying myself before continuing a bit more boldly, "Don't worry, if anyone's getting into my knickers, you've got first refusal."

Ralph stops laughing, his face coloring.

"I'm making you blush," I tease, leaning forwards.

"No," he protests, glancing around us. "But Harriet, this is a nice establishment." He teases back in a way that, confusingly, reminds me of Margaret. "You're not supposed to invite people into your knickers here."

"Well, I wasn't expecting we'd do it *here*," I counter. "I didn't know you were that kind of man."

"*What* kind of man?" His blue eyes are dancing now, merry, relaxing into the flirt.

"A naughty one. An *in public* kind of man," I say in a stage whisper.

"I'm not, I'm not!" Ralph holds up his hands in mock protest. "At least not in public in a restaurant."

"Unhygienic?" I ask.

He nods. "That, and too many poky implements." He picks up a fork to demonstrate. "I'm not adverse to trying something up my bum, but a fork is too . . ."

"Prong-y?"

"That's it."

"Well, I'm a fan of being pronged. I rather like to be the prong-ee." I giggle.

"That's interesting. I'm quite the opposite! A pronger."

I feel warm—full of wine and deliciously admired—by the time we leave the restaurant and make our way to the car. I realize, shockingly, we've been here over three hours. It felt like barely a quarter of that time. Outside, our laughter has a different timbre, echoing out into the frigid air so it sounds more like we're barking. Or howling. Animal, regardless. Euphoric laughter outside the lines of the Manor's polite and gentle titters.

"Stars," Ralph says, and I look up to see a whole glorious rash of them. It's so rare that I'm outside at night. I forgot what it was like to see the galaxy winking its "I see you."

"And moon," I add, which is full tonight, captured in a filigreed cage of tree branches.

"A magical night with Magic Harriet." Ralph opens the car door for me.

I bat away my memories of the séance, of the husband's horrible journal, of Margaret's implication of there being a supernatural cause to what's happening to me.

"Thank you." I flash a smile, pretending not to notice him inhaling me as I slip into the car.

During brief pauses on the drive home, I find myself wondering if Ralph will kiss me when he drops me off. It must be too much to hope for. I didn't think I'd ever be kissed again, let alone by *this* man. This beautiful, warm-hearted, tender man full of need. If only I'd met him thirty years ago, instead of the grey accountants and whippet-y-impatient sports men I was subjected to.

Still, what was it he asked? *There are no other men chasing you, then?* "Other," as in, he was one. Is Ralph chasing me? All that flirting about having sex in the restaurant, being pronged and pronging . . . Did that mean there's something here? Although, he's an unashamed flirt. *It takes one to know one,* Margaret would say. Briefly, I think of my best friend again, ill in bed, declining rapidly. If she saw how well we got on and how good we felt in other's company, she'd have to be pleased, wouldn't she?

***

"Harriet?" Ralph murmurs gently as he opens the car door for me, parked a short distance from the front of Marryat Manor.

"Yes?" I emerge from the car. The light from the full moon is quite bright now, resting atop his cheekbones and along his jaw. Those blue eyes of his shimmer like exotic gems in the gloom, flecked with the tiniest suggestion of moonglow.

Ralph takes a deep breath. "I think I might be about to kiss you. Is that okay?"

I'm not sure how to respond adequately, so I just nod.

Tenderly, he wraps his arms around my waist and draws me in, so our bodies are fully against each other. Our coats are open, and I feel every ridge and hard plane of his body pressing into my soft curves. His hand moves up into my hair, cradling my neck as his thumb strokes my jaw. He studies my lips a moment before kissing me. Gently at first, then more passionate, his tongue sliding along mine, his groan filling my mouth as he clasps me closer.

It's spectacular, and ridiculous, this perfect kiss in floods of moonlight, our bodies warming each other in the cold. Quite Mills and Boon. Picture-perfect. And completely addictive.

"Thank you, Magic Harriet," he whispers after pulling back. I can feel his erection pressing into my lower abdomen and consider reaching down to stroke it, but he steps away. Too much for a first date.

"Thank you, Ralph. Raucous Ralph."

"Raucous?" He laughs.

"Ridiculous? Rampant?" I raise an eyebrow, and he chuckles again. "I'll see you very soon."

I turn, regrettably, towards the looming old prison, flashing him a last smile before saying, "Thank you for a wonderful evening."

I walk past the drawing room on the lower floor on my way to the entrance. As I pass the black window, I see a face, skeletally gaunt. I waver unsteadily on my feet, the gravel beneath my stilettos suddenly an impossible surface to walk on. Why would anybody be standing at the window in the dark?

But it's not the face of a resident. My guilt has fabricated William's ghost again. Dead, shrunken, his face twisted into a seething, furious expression he would never have chosen. He'd not be angry with me for looking for love after he died.

It's not William, I reassure myself. It's not real. Just another hallucination. A projection. Dementia rearing its ugly self again, perhaps not fully gone after all. Guilt, it seems, is the cost of youth. Adrenaline surges through me, boiling me despite the cold air, making short work of my nerves. I shake my head, attempt to blink him away.

Suddenly, the thin line of his mouth is no longer a line but a gaping hole, an unnaturally huge scream. William's head is flung back, but his eyes still taser to mine. An unholy wail, not of pain but of ungodly, daemonic malice. Unnatural. Molten. Too real to be an apparition. Too dimensional. Meagre flesh and bone.

It's an elderly. An elderly who looks like William and who's in pain.

I hobble my way across the gravel, feeling more like the other Harriet now, the old one I'm smothering.

Inside, I dare to glance into the drawing room, to see if the person there needs help. But the room is empty, the air undisturbed, all residents having tucked themselves away hours before.

It's the fault of my new condition. Must be. This second set of brain waves shuns dementia at certain times, then allows these ghastly hallucinations at others. This new version of my soul picks up my fear and guilt and manifests them into morbid, horrifying shapes of my beloved. But despite Margaret's beliefs about the supernatural, I do not feel—I am *not*—daemonic.

Still, these projections, these visions . . . terrify me.

13

I'm aching to open a window. The air in Margaret's room is stuffy, acrid with breathed-out phlegm. The curtains are drawn, and it's too dark and cavernous here. Brown and mauve with a sticky yellow blob of light suggested by a lamp in the corner. I'd forgotten her room was so much smaller than mine. I want to be here for her, but I don't want to physically *be* here, in this room that smells of near-death, of decrepitude, of nothing that up until now I associated with my lively, sharp-witted friend.

Margaret is awake, though barely. I'm unused to seeing her without glasses, and her face practically disappears without them. The rattle of her chest has dissipated somewhat, but she looks so small, so withered. Almost a skeleton, I think, before I remember last night's hallucination and shake the thought away.

It's quiet in the room. Too still. I sit beside Margaret's bed, waiting for her to summon the energy to talk. After a while she coughs suddenly, releasing more putrid air into the room. She tries to cover her mouth as her body is overtaken, succumbing to the severity of the fit. I help her sit up slightly, propping her against the pillows, but she waves me away, holding up a finger, indicating I should wait. She has something to say to me.

"You have some nerve," she finally splutters. "Being here."

"I-I'm sorry?" I ask tentatively, giving a short, uncertain laugh. She must be joking with me, as she often does. Or is this related to her theory that I'm somehow responsible for all this illness? Or a comment about my not visiting her enough?

"I saw you last night. I was returning from the bathroom—yes, I'm just about managing to go to the bathroom myself—and glanced out of the window at the full moon and I saw you there. With Ralph. Kissing!" She hisses the final word, like a curse.

I take a sharp breath, guilt smothering indignation and prickling my skin. Was it her eyes I felt on me last night instead of that hideous skeletal monstrosity masquerading as my William?

"Down there, in front of the building." Speaking is a struggle, as though it hurts her to talk. I'm silent, my excitement from last night buried under a deep shame. I hadn't meant to hurt anyone. I'd just wanted to have fun, be seen again.

"What do you think you were doing? He's my son!" Margaret scrapes out her admonishment.

"I . . . we didn't plan it. He was very kind in taking me out to din-ner. I was getting stir-crazy. And the kiss just happened. Ralph is a very wonderful man."

"He's forty-eight!" Margaret barks again, her eyes widening in anger and deepening into their almost-black-ringed sockets. "And married. And *my* son! It's disgusting. I'm ashamed of you! Of you both!"

I'm taken aback by her vehemence and rage. I wouldn't have imag-ined Margaret would be so angry. Shocked? Yes. Displeased? Certainly. But disgusted?

Still, I try to explain myself. "I know it must seem strange, given the age gap, but we're actually quite similar people and—"

"Yes! You are similar. Both selfish. Selfish, vain people. What about his wife, Harriet? His son?"

"They have an unhappy marriage—" I manage feebly before she cuts me off again.

"Don't even start with that. He and Lisa are going through a rough patch, and you're taking advantage. I thought you were my friend but turns out you're a sex-crazed slut! A whore!" I never imagined Margaret would be capable of speaking to me with such venom and hatred in her voice. That she would see me as nothing but cheap trash.

"I can't bear to look at you. Get out of my sight!" she bellows with a sickening rattle before collapsing into yet another coughing fit, one hand on her chest and another on her head, obviously in pain.

"Let me get the doctor," I say, hating the timidity in my voice.

I walk to the door, shaken, and Margaret calls after me, "And stay away from my son!"

I almost collide with Dr. Phillips on the way out of the room and have no idea how long he's been there or what he's overheard. His expression, though, grey and questioning, makes me suspect he heard it all.

I am unused to arguments with loved ones. Yes, I can be tetchy and frequently disagree with others, but rarely does it result in a row. I can count on one hand the number of times I've been told off in my life. I'm usually the one doing the berating.

A sex-crazed slut? A whore?

I know Margaret was furious, even confused, but that insult is beneath us both. It makes me wonder if her gentle teasing over the years came from a real place of scorn and disapproval. Something in me wobbles, like turbulence. An anchor pulled, leaving me unmoored.

Who am I, without my friend? Without Margaret's love and respect, am I real?

I feel like a paper boat on a pond, buffeted this way and that by life's blowing gusts. Bile, along with this morning's coffee, burns my throat. I'm not sure how I will bear feeling so isolated.

But then I remember my connection with Ralph. I see depth in him where others see only charm. He sees the real me—sensitive, inquisitive, thoughtful—where others see only brusqueness, snobbishness even.

Margaret used to see the real me too. Or at least I thought she did. Now, she only sees me as a harlot, a home-wrecker. Is it the immorality she objects to in my being with Ralph or does she truly not think me worthy of him? What was it H.G. Wells said? *Moral indignation is jealousy with a halo?* Perhaps my friend's outrage is really masking jealousy of my good health when she is so frail and unwell. Perhaps she is envious that I've taken several steps back towards youthfulness, whilst she's plummeting headlong towards the grave. That by kissing Ralph, I have now placed myself in another generation, in a longer-living, socially superior place away from her.

Or—I hardly want to consider it—is it because she truly believes me daemonic? That her son is subject to my inner evil.

My skin feels too tight and itches terribly, as though covered with mites or something equally dreadful. I rub at it, trying not to scratch. It must be due to stress. My friend's upset and my own.

I glance at the clock in the hall and see it's 11 a.m. Too late for tea, too early for lunch, caught in refreshment purgatory. Through the living room windows I see clouds have marched in overnight and released a billion arrows of untidy raindrops, washing away the lingering remnants of snow and with it my excitement for Christmas, now only a couple of weeks away. The landscape has lost its festiveness, sludging its browns together, the ground slick with mud. A dirge of a day. Last night's brilliance has been trampled on by today's disgruntlement.

And yet I stare outside, craving any sort of light, a glimpse of Ralph's car, unwilling to engage in activities that remind me of passing time with Margaret. Is that all lost now? Will she forgive me once recovered? Already I miss our board games and gentle conversation, the comfort of our friendship, even as my renewed energy grows more restless by the second.

I feel desolate. Quite alone.

***

"Mummy?"

I turn to see Alyson showing Judith into the living room. My daughter wears the same look of incredulity at my improved appearance that I've seen on the faces of the staff and residents over the past few weeks.

"Is that you?" Judith asks, her eyebrows knit together. "Dr. Phillips said you were improved, but this is astonishing."

Despite the upset of the morning—and the fact Judith is again here to speak to Dr. Phillips behind my back—I stand straighter, taller.

"Hello, dear!" I greet, genuinely delighted to see her, particularly given my loss of Margaret's companionship, and as we hug, it feels different than other careful embraces we've had in the last few years. Our bodies are similarly upright, similarly supple. In fact, I am far leaner than her. Though Judith looks younger than me still, it feels like a hug between equals rather than a mother and daughter. Her puffiness has increased since I last saw her, something she's inherited from William. And she did always have a penchant for custard creams. "I'm so glad to see you, Judith. Have you come to take me out?"

"Take you out?" Judith looks confused and shakes her head slightly. "No, I . . . Dr. Phillips called. But Mum . . ." She inspects my face more closely, her scowl deepening in concentration. "How do you look like this? It's like you've reversed your age by twenty years. It's quite miraculous. Quite scary, even."

She seems legitimately frightened.

"Scary? What, no, not scary. I have epilepsy, Judith. Didn't Dr. Phillips tell you?" What on earth had they been talking about, if not that? "A very rare form of it, apparently. The specialists in town are monitoring me, but so far, apart from a couple of weird episodes, the side effects have been only positive. I think it's hormonal too. I have all this energy now and my arthritis is gone. Plus, the illness seems to have done wonderful things for my skin and hair." I realize I've been eager to share all this with someone in as buoyant a way as I truly feel. I won't share the horrific visions of her father though. I'm still trying to understand those myself. If they're just figments of my overactive imagination or . . .

"He mentioned the epilepsy, but I thought it was just another sign of decline, I didn't realize you would look so . . . And I . . . it's remarkable. We could be sisters." Judith offers this with a small smile, though she still seems uncomfortable with the shift. At least she's not talking down to me any longer, as if I'm a child or a doting old woman. "I hope I inherit this condition."

"Well, yes, although I'm not sure it's hereditary. My mother certainly did not become younger-looking in old age. And where's Molly today?" I ask, realizing this is the second time Judith's visited without my granddaughter.

"School." Her expression becomes clouded. "She's been a little . . . different since coming here. The episode with the mirror in the basement quite terrified her, I'm afraid. She's refusing to return to the Manor, at least for now."

"Oh, dear." I'm genuinely dismayed. "Poor thing. What a shame she's taken her little fright so seriously."

"It was more than a 'little fright,' Mummy. I'm worried about her, honestly. She's been drawing such strange things. I might need to take her to a child psychologist."

"Oh, nonsense," I declare, thinking about everything I've experienced in the last few weeks. Seeking any sort of therapy has not once crossed my mind. "What that girl needs is a bit of exercise."

"Mummy!" Judith exclaims.

"Not a comment on her weight, dear, just that exercise invigorates. It brightens the mind. Children need more fresh air than they get these days." I don't mean to sound quite so opinionated or assertive. And I don't mean to belittle Molly's feelings either. But it's a bad habit of my generation, irritability with the emotional care of children. A result of how we ourselves were treated.

"You're not very tactful, Mummy," Judith grumbles. A fair point.

"I'm sorry." The apology sounds unusual in my mouth. Judith looks up sharply again, assessing, noticing that this is uncharacteristic for me. I am not an apologetic sort of person. "Whatever you think best, dear. You're a good mother."

"Thank you," she accepts, sounding uncertain again.

The compliment is real. It's a shame Judith only has the one child. Her abundant warmth is made for mothering. But she had difficulties in conceiving. So many rounds of IVF, poor thing. I thought William and I had Judith late, but she was well into her forties before finally conceiving little Molly.

"Changing the subject, Judith, I really would like it if we could go out one of these days. I feel trapped here. I can get a taxi into town on my own, but they're so unreliable, and I would love to go further afield! London, maybe? A day shopping in London? Or on a mild day Brighton might be rather fun. Lunch out, a walk along the pier? Shopping in the Lanes?"

But as I suggest this, I'm picturing the day with Ralph, not with my daughter. I wish I hadn't brought it up.

"Perhaps," Judith says warily. "It's a rather busy time of year." She has ample time to arrange my affairs, to discuss me with the staff, but not to actually spend with me. I wonder if this could change, now that I am so improved.

"Well, whenever you're free then, let me know. It would be awfully nice to have a girl's day out like we used to."

She looks at me suspiciously. I don't blame her. We've rarely gone out together, just the two of us, since she left home at eighteen. Apparently, I thought I had better things to do. It's then I realize the mistakes I've made due to my own self-importance. My snobbishness, and lack of willingness to participate in children's activities. I never played with Judith. Old Tom may have seen the truth of it. I may have been wrong to be so incredulous over his comment.

"Sorry, Mummy. I-I'm just a little overwhelmed with all of this." Judith motions to my face. "And I feel quite drained all the sudden."

She does look pale. "This is the second time visiting me when you've felt unwell, dear."

"Maybe there *is* a virus here after all." She idly glances around the room, then asks, "Where's Margaret?"

My heart drops. I swallow hard past the constriction in my throat. "In her room. She's rather poorly."

"Oh, dear!" Judith's concern increases. "What's wrong with her?"

"Mainly a chest infection, but she's generally very weak. Awfully frail."

Judith reaches over and takes my hand. "Have you been keeping her company up there?"

"I've visited, yes. But we had a bit of an argument. She doesn't want to see me for now." The words are crushing to say, painful in my mouth and catching in my throat, and my daughter must pick up on it because she squeezes my hand.

"Oh, Mummy!" Judith sighs. "What did you say?"

Funny how she just assumes it's my fault. It is, of course, but the truth still hurts. "I'd rather not discuss it now, if you don't mind."

I know I'm being evasive, but it's too complicated, too raw. And I don't enjoy being reprimanded by my own daughter. Especially when she understands nothing of my current situation—of this beautiful but bruising other me, emerging magnificently, catastrophically, uncontrollably.

"Well, I'm sure you two will make up eventually."

I hope she's right. That things aren't irretrievably broken between us as I fear they are.

"She has Ralph, who visits her regularly," I tell her. My comment feels so small in front of this emotional backdrop. The injustice of being misunderstood by those closest to me feels doubly isolating.

"Tea, Harriet? Judith?" offers a harangued-looking Alyson as she clears cups away from a nearby coffee table. It's customary for tea to be offered when visitors arrive, but I know it's not convenient for her. It must be nearing lunch now.

"No, thank you," I tell her.

The poor girl needs a break from this place. I say girl, but her hair is so much duller than before, and the puffy patches at the corners of her mouth make her appear quite a bit older than usual. Or she's been comfort eating and not hydrating enough. The Christmas season really does take it out of people. And then there's the illness at the Manor . . .

"Are you okay, Alyson?" I ask. "You're looking a little wan."

"Wan?" She puffs out an exasperated sigh. "Not sure I needed to hear *that*, Harriet. But yes, I'm fine, thank you."

She whisks away then, and I turn my attention back to my daughter.

"I'm worried about you," Judith says once Alyson is out of earshot. "This is all so different."

"I am perfectly fine. Better than I've been in decades. There is absolutely no need to worry about me. The only thing I need is to get out of this place. I'm being driven slowly mad. And you needn't discuss me with Dr. Phillips quite so often. As you can see, I am perfectly capable now of overseeing my own medical needs."

"I saw that your daughter visited you this morning, after she and I met," Dr. Phillips comments as he passes me in the hall after lunch.

"She did," I confirm. "She seemed surprised at my condition. I assumed you were keeping her apprised of the situation."

"I did explain, but I don't think she fully understood. I'm glad she saw you for herself. And it's nice for you to see family. Margaret's son visits her very frequently too," he adds unsubtly.

"Yes, he's so attentive."

"Indeed. Indeed." The doctor looks down thoughtfully. "You know, it's very important for Margaret not to get upset, Harriet. For her health. Her current condition is unstable."

"I'm not planning on upsetting her further," I agree, disgruntled. It's not his place to get involved with personal business, and he's doing so under the guise of his interest in Margaret's health. I'm also feeling

something else. Some strange cocktail of guilt, fear, and shame bubbling up inside of me again, fizzing uncomfortably.

"Good, good." Dr. Phillips nods. "I realize being here must be
quite frustrating for you at the moment." I'm quiet, waiting for him
to continue. He's right, and I'm curious what he's going to suggest.
"But please be careful with yourself, Harriet. We don't know the real
nature of your condition. This . . . new energy . . . could be temporary.
Epilepsy isn't a joke. If you exert yourself too much, you may have another episode, and end up in a dangerous situation."

"Then what do you suggest, doctor? Can one die of boredom?"

"It's unproven." He smiles then suggests, "How about a visit to the
library? When I'm a little underwhelmed with my circumstances, I
find escaping into the pages of a good book does me a world of good."

"Thirty cubits by twenty cubits," I pretend to recite the most achingly dull part of, I think, Leviticus. "You're right, the good book is
riveting."

I'm being cheeky, intending to tease him, but I must get it wrong
because he looks offended.

"Whatever kind of book you enjoy," he says simply and heads towards his office.

Today is apparently a day when I can do nothing but offend. I
slump away, feeling like a child whose offer of play is rejected by every friend.

Ralph isn't due back at the Manor until tomorrow.

This is perhaps the one and only time when I wish I had a mobile
phone to contact him, tell him his mother knows about our kiss, tell
him to beware. Her admonishment still upsets me, *scorches* me, and I'm
not sure how I'll manage if she continues to shun me.

Still, I can't bring myself to regret the kiss. How could I? It was
too right, too—to use Ralph's word—inevitable. The longed-for

connection elevating the moment, drawing us together, magnet-close. Furthermore, I can't—*won't*—stop it continuing. It is too delicious. And I'm alive and still able to taste.

Now that Ralph and I have found each other, stopping whatever's between us from unfurling is absurd. More absurd than the séance, than this strange epilepsy and its dramatic youthfulness, than these sightings of William, than this . . . twin self, twin brain waves, whatever they are. My connection with Ralph feels like the truest thing I have known for a long time. I hope he feels the same. He can't turn away from what we have, despite his lackluster marriage. He is a good man, and I do so wish he does not have an attack of conscience.

I spend the evening at the mirror, newly enraptured with my appearance, the lifting and blooming of middle-age. The whites of my eyes have become even whiter, my lips plumper, although maybe that's my imagination. Perhaps they're just reawakened after having been kissed. My inner energy finally matches my outward appearance, much as my former lack of energy showed on my withered frame.

In the dim light of the bedroom, I shimmer, sparkling and glamorous.

I want Ralph to see me, to want me. Be fascinated by me.

14

I hardly notice as a hundred tiny twigs tangle themselves into my hair as Ralph presses me back against the maze wall, his mouth insistent, his tongue dueling with mine, his hands grasping my waist. I needn't have worried that his lust for me would cool in the day we've been apart. To the contrary, it has elevated, become its own animal.

"Harriet. Oh, Harriet." He groans, pulling away slightly before his mouth reconnects with mine. I'm not sure I remember the last time I was kissed with such lust. "Are we bad? Is this bad?"

That spiky, dangerous conscience.

"No, Ralph," I pant back to him as he grazes his lips down my neck, nudging my coat open with his nose. "This is very right. Can you imagine how wrong it would be to deny this?"

His hands move to my breasts, outlining their shape with his fingertips before gently cupping each in his palms. "You're right, it would be very, very wrong." I relax a fraction before he adds, "But Harriet, our ages. No matter how youthful you look we are so far apart in years. You were born in the forties. The forties! I'm a child of the seventies. That's—"

"Shhh." I cover his mouth with mine once more, moving my hand down to his groin. His breath catches as I stroke his erection with a finger, enjoying this sexual power that's been vacant for so long.

"And besides," I continue. "I don't look much older than you now. And as you said, we're the same, you and I . . . the same in spirit."

Ralph takes my face between his hands. His gaze locks with mine as if desperately seeking an answer. Then he breaks away, turns in the other direction before turning back. "And Mum definitely saw us kissing?"

"She definitely did."

"And she hates it?"

"She hates it. Loathes me."

"I'm sorry, Harriet. So very sorry."

I reach for his hand. "No, *I'm* sorry. But you see, the damage is already done. Why not continue? We can't do more harm."

That's an obvious lie. We could easily do more harm, but I need to convince him not to abandon us. Despite having damaged my friendship with Margaret so irrevocably, being with Ralph feels right, inevitable, too tantalizing. Intimacy with Ralph feels, in a horrible way, owed to me.

My fingers rest at his temple for a moment before stroking the new crop of grey hairs that have sprung forth from his hairline, virtually overnight. An attack of my conscience overtakes me then, not for Margaret but for Ralph. "I know you'd be giving up a lot to be with me. You have a wife, a stepson . . . and this is all so sudden." Margaret's words echo through me. "It's true I look younger than my years, but I am as old as I am. I can't imagine this new disease will have me live longer. Ralph, I've not known anything like this before. This thing between us . . . it feels so deep, so *true*."

"I know. I know. That's what I think too. It's there, isn't it? It's not an everyday kind of attraction?"

"No," I agree. "It's a big, inconvenient but inevitable connection."

"Two star-crossed lovers?" he suggests, and I smile sadly. "Okay. I'm going now, but I'll be back tomorrow. Let me leave the maze before you. I won't visit Mum today. Allow her another day or two to collect herself." He looks guiltily towards the exit of the maze.

"Sure," I say, an odd mix of apprehension and anticipation welling inside me. "It's quite usual for visitors to explore the maze by themselves in the middle of winter."

He barks out a short laugh. "They'll think I was caught short."

Were we further in our relationship, I'd tell him about my own version of being caught short in this maze, but it feels too soon. We haven't even shared a bed together.

"Harriet, I want to be with you, spend the night in your arms," he says earnestly, as though reading my thoughts.

My chest constricts. "I want that too."

"Then let's make it happen." He grins and kisses me again before leaving.

I wait for a while after he's left to exit the maze and head towards the house, my boots sinking into the mulchy ground. Despite our mutual attraction and connection, Ralph is right to have doubts in this unusual situation. I have doubts too. But my yearning for him—physically, emotionally, and mentally—supersedes everything else. He has become my oxygen, my beacon of hope in the darkness of the Manor.

I spot a figure heading up the path towards the house. Tom, I think, and catch myself. *Tom is dead.* I look again. Someone who looks like Tom, a brother, come to visit the property, or a relative planning his funeral.

Then the man turns suddenly and looks at me. I'm suspended in what I can only describe as a death stare. *Tom's* death stare. He's glaring at me as though I've stolen his life. As though my indecency in the maze is the most contemptuous act in the face of so much fatality.

Another hallucination. That's all this is. Not William this time. Tom. But still just an illusion. My old dementia, my new Harriet brain, sliding off reality again, slipping off the living realm. He's not there, I remind myself. I close my eyes and shake my head, expecting him to remain as William had in the window two nights ago.

But this time Tom has disappeared, his contempt communicated, my guilt re-manifested.

As I near the house, and my boots find the solidity of gravel, I hear voices, a man and woman, young voices—or at least not old. Shaken by my recent vision, I'm momentarily relieved to be around people again, until I register the tone of their conversation, discordant and sharp. Cautiously, I walk toward the sound, following the path around the left side of the Manor, until I see them. Angel and Alyson.

I don't think I've ever seen any kind of altercation between staff at Marryat Manor. They're so careful to remain professional in front of the residents.

"I said no," Alyson says.

"Where's the spontaneity?" Angel appeals to her charmingly, but his arms block her in, resting on either side of her as she leans against the wall, a dominant position. They're roughly the same height, but Angel is so much stronger than her. I've seen that look in a man before—the knowledge that he can take whatever he wants. I remember the way Angel looked at me in the kitchen—brazenly taking in my body. At the time, I was flattered. It didn't occur to me to think him predatory.

"Spontaneity?" Alyson tries to move past him, to no avail. "Let me go, please. I don't even want to date you, let alone get up to anything *at work*."

"Have you seen yourself lately?" Angel asks, his tone aggressively derogatory now. A verbal sneer. Is he drunk? This man doesn't resemble the kind person I've encountered several times now. "The light in you has gone, Alyson. You got *old*. You should be grateful anyone is paying you any attention at all."

I suck in a breath on Alyson's behalf. I hadn't thought Angel could be so cruel.

Angel? Daemon, more like.

"Fuck you!" The words don't sound right on Alyson, too flabby and weak. She tries to move away from him again, attempting to duck under one of his arms, but he shoves her against the wall, the painful thud of her body against three-hundred-year-old bricks, pinning her there.

Alyson continues to struggle against him. "Have you seen yourself? You've practically lost all your hair. Is that why you're doing this? Because you're feeling less than a man?" Angel shakes her now with concussion-inducing force, but somehow, Alyson manages to continue fighting. "Trying to prove you've still got it?"

"Hey!" I yell then, striding towards them, unable to stand by and watch anymore. "Let her go!"

Angel looks over at me while maintaining his position, still trapping Alyson.

"This is a private conversation," he snarls, nostrils flaring, his normal visage replaced by an ugly little goblin face.

"Not anymore, it's not. Off her. Now!"

It feels as though the particles in the air are spacing out, making it difficult to wade through them from one moment to the next. My temples pulse hard, my eyelids throb, and a strange current of energy surges through the circuits of my body, lightning fast.

Perhaps this is another fit, though it feels different than the others. As though one part of me, angry and molten, carbon-black, is holding the other, more-known part of me inside myself. I feel like I'm watching from outside myself as I bellow at Angel in an ungodly, unearthly roar, "Off her!"

Angel's arms drop to his sides, the look in his eyes going from feral to unexpected terror in a flash. I see his fear, yes, but also something else—a blackness, an absence, nothing but negative space—reflected in his eyes.

Alyson uses the distraction to tear away from Angel and dart towards me, pulling at my elbow.

"Come on, Harriet!" She sounds desperate.

But it's some moments before I'm able to leave, before this unknown side allows my departure. I think of the second set of brain waves again and wonder for the first time if perhaps there is truly another being inside me. This is quickly swept aside, though, as the triumph of my effective intervention fills me with the power of authority. Heard. Seen. Affecting.

"Are you okay?" I ask Alyson once we get back inside the house.

"Yes." She rubs her arms, which I suspect are bruised from Angel's rough handling.

"I hope you're going to report him," I say in a brusque tone. She's just been through an ordeal.

"I—no, it's complicated." She touches her red cheek, and I wonder if the brute hit her too.

"Complicated how?" I ask incredulously.

"Angel comes from difficult circumstances. He has bad days, but he's trying. It's difficult for him to find work."

"I can see why!"

"Harriet, please let me handle it." Alyson gives me a beseeching look, and I wonder why on earth she's protecting him. Does she love him? Women do tend to love abusive men. Or if not love, then excuse them, as though we're just stepping stones in their journey and we need to let them evolve and find themselves.

"Well, if you need a witness, let me know. And get yourself a stiff whisky, dear!" I tell her, then leave to head back to my room.

Perhaps I should get a drink myself. I'm shaken too. Angel. A wolf in sheep's clothing. Thankfully, Ralph is a gentleman. A sensitive soul. A man made for loving, not dominance.

Not an everyday kind of attraction.

I feel vertiginous, thrown from Ralph's touch to hallucination to horrifying intervention. Each time I close my eyes I picture those dueling sets of brain waves—roving around like maddened snakes in my head. Flailing. Reacting.

And although I've felt so much more in control since the dementia-ridden Harriet has been muted, today I don't feel in control at all. Not as though I've lost it, but that I'm being controlled by something I can't see or know.

Dr. Phillips finds me in my room before lunch. He looks drained.

"Harriet? Would you mind coming with me, please?" he asks, and I wonder if I'm going to get a ticking off about Ralph. Maybe Dr. Phillips saw us, somehow, in the maze. Will I be sent to the headmaster's office?

"Am I being punished for something?" I ask, mildly affronted.

"What?" His expression is weary, worn, concerned. His joyful lightness is gone, as though his faith has dropped out of him. "No, of course not. I just want to talk to you in the library."

"The library?" That's a new one.

"I want to show you some books."

I remember that recently he suggested I visit the library to distract myself from restlessness. Perhaps this is related. He's found something he thinks will entertain me. I'm surprised he has the time or energy to bother, given his current patient load.

I feel thrown about today, from one emotion to another, one scene to the next, person to person, with soap-opera alacrity. The feeling continues once we reach the library and he hands me a familiar-looking leather-bound book.

"Here."

The light in the room is brighter at midday, though it deepens the many shadows. The wrong time of day for a room like this. More a bilious, outdoor hour, not a fusty oak-paneled one. The Manor's dwindled choir is practicing their carols in the next room. *Once in Royal David's City.* Every so often a cough or sneeze emerges from the singing.

I stare down at the book, hating the damned thing, but noting how easily I can read the title without my glasses. It's green leather reminding me of the skin of a snake. "I've seen this before. It's Lord Marryat's diary. Or journal."

"Quite." Dr. Phillips nods. "What do you think about what it contains?"

I remember my conversation with Margaret. It seems so long ago now, though it was less than a couple of weeks. Her reading from it, our argument, my confusion, my indignance, my stifled horror. I'm startled he should ask me about it now. "What do I think of it? It's nonsense."

"Nonsense?"

"Yes!" I'm baffled. "That a woman here was possessed by a dae-mon, and it made her grow younger and everyone else so much older? How can you, a medical professional, even ask me that question?" I harrumph audibly, incredulous. I would never have dreamt that Dr. Phillips would entertain such a ludicrous idea.

"*Mary was the mother mild*—" the choir sings. Lackluster, fatigued, slightly off-key in places.

I'm getting a headache, between the carol and Dr. Phillips wres-tling for my brain's attention. This religion, this magic, this nonsense, angers me.

"I've been reading other books too," he says.

"I'm surprised you have the time."

He ignores my sarcasm. "Books on mysticism, the occult. And yes, I agree with you, Harriet. On paper, as it were, the idea of daemonic possession is absurd. And if the idea of it were limited only to these old books, the diaries and the novel, I would dismiss it as nonsense too."

"As you should."

Dr. Phillips studies me carefully before perching on the arm of one of the heavy leather armchairs. "Please, sit down."

I'm hovering, keen to leave, but I comply, and sit towards the edge of the armchair opposite him.

"Harriet, I want you to consider, really consider, your condition."

"My epilepsy?"

"We don't know definitively that it's epilepsy," he says, holding up a hand. "That's just the working medical hypothesis."

"*He came down to earth from heaven*—" The choir is short on baritones, the sound tinny, jangling at my nerves.

"Your side effects are unparalleled, Harriet. Getting younger. So much younger. I've checked in all the medical sources I could find. Every corner of PubMed. The specialists have consulted every other specialist in the country. Unparalleled."

I've knowingly ignored its novelty, not wanting to hear that it's temporary, that I will hurtle back towards decrepitude soon.

"Were it not for how many sick patients I currently have," Dr. Phillips continued, "I'd work with other doctors, getting you more specialized testing."

My respect for the man shrivels and evaporates before my eyes, like ash. I don't tell him about the increasing hallucinations—William, Tom. I know they're not real. I keep my voice calm as I say, "I'm perfectly well."

Dr. Phillips pauses, regarding me. "But that's the point, Harriet. *You're* perfectly well."

His gaze bores into mine, pleading with me to understand.

"And?" I ask, being deliberately obtuse. *Don't convince me of this. I can't survive it.*

"While everyone else, *everyone* around you becomes older, Harriet. Every single person. And the timing with the start of your epilepsy? That séance? It was exact."

"Don't be ridiculous." I stand, hot and juddering.

"Please, you have to consider—"

"I must consider nothing at all. You've been listening to Margaret, haven't you? The musings of a daft, sick old woman. She was a professor of literature, Dr. Phillips, not medicine, not the occult."

"Margaret's concerned, as I am, that you're harming people. They're dying, Harriet."

Harming them?

I pace towards him and jab a finger against his chest. We're both surprised by my vehemence, but I continue anyway. "I'm not harming anyone! In fact, I've been trying to help people. You should be struck off, Dr. Phillips. You have no business being a doctor if this—whatever this is, thinking I've been overtaken by a daemon—is your hypothesis."

He gently presses down on my pointed finger until I move my hand back to my side. "I know how it sounds, Harriet. I denied it myself for a long time. And if it affected just the elderly residents in this place, I would put the deaths down to a bad virus season. But it's everyone, Harriet. The younger staff as well. We've all aged rather dramatically in only a few weeks. I've also checked other facilities in the area, and this issue isn't happening anywhere else. This isn't widespread. No reports of rapid deaths outside this facility. Nowhere, except for where you are, Harriet."

I'm shaking now, unnerved, discombobulated. "Have you considered it's not me? That it might be this ghastly building?" That's still the most reasonable explanation. "Some virus trapped in these ancient walls that my new illness has made me impervious to?"

"Yes," Dr. Phillips answers, surprising me. "That was the first thing I considered, actually. And why I had the place tested from top to bottom."

"You did?" This catches me off guard. "I didn't see anyone."

"I made sure they were discreet. Didn't want to startle the residents. And there was nothing, Harriet."

No virus? Perhaps it's something non-testable, unusual. "They could have missed it."

Dr. Phillips sighs. "Possibly, but—"

"No buts. No. I'm done here, thank you very much!" I barrel my way out of the traitorous library with its billion dust motes, shadows, and conspiracies.

Inside me there's a flicker, a dart, that green snake maneuvering, ready to act.

The choir fades as I stride away, the final line of the carol echoing through the hall, my ears: "*Jesus Christ, her little child.*"

***

I want to pace the grounds, work this all through in my mind, but it's lunchtime, and I'm ravenous.

In the dining room, I find Alyson and Imani rushing around, filling water glasses, Imani trying to order elderlies around as usual. No food sits in front of the admittedly fewer seated residents, even though I'm late.

"What's wrong?" I ask Alyson as she passes.

She looks at me with dark-ringed racoon eyes. "We can't find Angel."

"Can't find him?"

"He's disappeared since earlier. The chef is cooking alone with no-one to help him." She motions between herself and Imani. "We've done our best, but we're not cooks. Lunch will be late for everyone, I'm afraid."

I sink into a chair, Dr. Phillips's words rattling around uncomfortably in my head. Is he right? Is my being here negatively affecting the others? Is there something, a daemon, inside of me, sucking life from them?

It sounds absurd, utterly absurd.

And yet two of the people I trust most are convinced of it.

I'm hurt and aching, realizing how little you really know people. How keen they are to believe fantastical explanations despite their education, their common sense.

My insides are tense, coiled, waiting for the next ball to drop.

The next hallucination, the next accusation.

Abandoning lunch, I return to my room where I tear into one of the boxes of expensive chocolates I bought from the chocolatiers in Farnham as Christmas gifts for staff, eating greedily, ignoring that I'm making myself sick.

It's been years since I've let myself indulge like this. The candy is more delicious than I remember, and I congratulate myself for my former self-control before my mind wanders back to my altercation—*another* altercation; I'm becoming quite contrary, apparently—with Dr. Phillips.

Coffee cream. How dare he claim I'm possessed by a bloody daemon? Caramel. That I'm killing people? Me? Violet cream. How can a medical man be convinced by the idle musings of a bitter, ill old woman? Fudge. And find the occult more convincing than science? Orange cream. He's a Christian, that's why! Predisposed to imagine miracles are more believable than hard facts. He really should be struck off. Who should I report him to? I'm eating more chocolate than I have since I was a bored teen.

Shocking, how the religious can so easily blend their beliefs with those of the supernatural. Isn't God meant to be real? Jesus, fully man?

I am not a believer. William would have scoffed at all of this. And yet, I agreed to the séance. It was my dementia, I tell myself. I didn't really believe the boasts of rejuvenation from the diary Margaret found. And yet, that's exactly what's happened. Youth. Vigor. Clarity of the mind. Haven't I become visible again? Respected even? Wasn't this what I longed for?

I'm distracted by my reflection and the feeling of looseness at my waist. The lines at my forehead and corners of my eyes have smoothed, and I'm leaner still. Such sudden weight loss. Isn't that a sign of cancer? I whip my clothes off to inspect my body. My breasts are higher, skin smoother. My buttocks have tightened. I've moved beyond acceptable naked to beautiful. I haven't looked like this since my forties. Enviable. Desirable.

Not bothering to dress, I return to the chocolates and finish the entire box. All two layers.

There's something deliciously illicit about eating chocolate naked, and my thoughts return to Ralph, to how he agreed to making spending the night together happen. I run my hands over my own body, imagining they're his.

There's a knock at the door. Instinctively, I cover myself with the blanket on the bed, although the door is locked.

"Harriet?" It's Alyson. I wonder if Margaret's okay. I haven't checked on her.

"Yes?"

"Ralph's downstairs to see you."

"Send him up, please," I call back as I start to dress.

Ralph waits, looking nervous, as he sits on the bed while I pack a bag.

I wish I hadn't eaten so many chocolates. I feel quite nauseous now, partly due to my overindulgence, but also due to the excitement of leaving this place, even if only overnight, and the prospect of being with Ralph.

"What did you tell your wife?" I ask, then wish I hadn't.

"You don't need to worry about that. We've decided to separate." He smiles a little sadly. "Mum doesn't know. And this isn't about Lisa, or our sham of a marriage, anyway. It's about you and me and what we've found together."

I stand next to where he's seated and slip my arms around his shoulders. He buries his face in my torso, just below my breasts, and I feel an automatic jolt of excitement between my legs. I kiss his head, and inexplicably, can't help but imagine it's Dr. Phillips there instead of Ralph. That I'm comforting him after a deep trauma. I can't explain it and move away. This is about Ralph and me.

"Thank you," I tell him as I pack the last few items into my overnight bag.

The murmur of voices echoes outside on the landing. Staff assisting residents.

"I'll tell them you're giving me a lift to Judith's," I say. "And that I'm not sure when I'll be back."

15

My explanation goes mostly unnoticed, as it happens, given the circumstances.

As Ralph and I prepare to leave, we're met with flashing blue lights in front of the building and several police officers in the hall, amidst a clamor of confusion and upset. I am used to the emergency services making appearances to take residents to hospital, but I don't think the police have ever visited.

"What's happening?" I ask Imani. Her brow is contorted, and she's holding both hands tucked into her chest defensively, obviously upset, not quite in control of herself. Unusual, for Imani.

"Angel," she replies low, under her breath. "He was found dead on the Manor grounds this afternoon."

"Angel? Dead?" But he isn't even one of the elderlies! And I just saw him alive this morning.

I try to recall our encounter, only I can't seem to land on any specifics. My memory has been crystal clear lately, but this one experience is blurring over. Was I the other Harriet—dementia Harriet—during the exchange? Is that why I don't remember? I think we had words. Something about Alyson. I try to spot her. She's towards the front of the hall, at the entrance, talking with two police officers. Dr. Phillips is consoling her, an arm placed firmly around her shoulders. But, I notice, his eyes are fixed directly on me.

"Oh, wow. Poor guy." Ralph's is the reaction of any stranger to the news of any untimely death.

"What happened?" I ask Imani.

"Suspected overdose." Talking quietly, for once, she shrugs, pointing left. "He was found by the side of the building."

I think that's where I last saw him, but I can't be sure. That foggy memory.

"They found drugs on him, syringes and things?"

"Not that we saw."

"*You* saw? You found him?"

Imani lowers her gaze and nods. "Yes, it was horrible, Harriet. His face—his eyes were open, and he looked . . . well, he looked petrified. Literally frozen in fear." She shakes her head. "I've never seen anything like it."

It's unusual for a staff member to be so open, indiscrete, and particularly Imani, who loves to give the impression of being in charge, although technically she's Alyson's subordinate. She seems vulnerable, like a child. How we change in the face of tragedy. For a moment, I'm shamefully pleased to be confided in, thought of differently than the other residents. I'm not a sympathetic person, but I manage to put an arm around her shoulders.

"That must have been horrible for you."

"Yes," she agrees with a whimper.

"How awful." Did he look afraid when I saw him? Was he using drugs at the time? Could he have been high? I don't think I remember. But I *was* there with him earlier. I remember that much.

And why would Dr. Phillips imagine I'm responsible? Surely, he doesn't think me capable of murder? Since his earlier speculation about the authenticity of those damned journal claims, I no longer trust the man's judgement.

Frozen in fear. Imani's words rattle their way through my skull, dizzying.

Something tells me I need to avoid police questioning, to get out of here and away with Ralph. I'm not guilty of murder. It's not possible. But I have the impression of having some fractional culpability, although I can't remember it. The same feeling I get when I enter a room immediately after an event and sense a disturbance in the air. I sense a disturbance in *me.* Something to do with Angel.

"Gosh," I continue after a short time. "Well, I think we might slip out the back. Ralph is giving me a lift to Judith's. A family birthday." Imani nods. I fizz with the lie, and with everything it implies. "I won't be here for dinner. Or breakfast."

Between Angel and my impending night with Ralph, I feel as though I'm erring. Getting into trouble. Like the time I let myself be fingered by the son of a family friend while at a wake. Undignified. Disrespectful.

"Probably good," Imani murmurs vaguely. "We're down a cook now and short-staffed anyway. Chef's considering ordering delivery. I'll sign you out." She nods to me, and with a parting sympathetic smile, Ralph and I slip out the back exit.

"An inauspicious start," I declare once we're safely in the car and headed down the long and winding drive away from Marryat Manor.

"Yes, poor chap," Ralph says again. "An addict. I'm surprised he wasn't screened for drugs when he hired in."

"Well, he must have been. Perhaps there were problems in his past."

I remember an earlier conversation with Angel about his mother, how she spoke to the dead and carried their messages to the living. I wonder if he's found her. I'm not a believer, but Angel was. He believed in some kind of "other." He may not have been wrong, but I don't want to think about him, his death feeling disturbingly personal.

"Let's not have it spoil things," Ralph says in a brighter tone, shifting the mood, Angel's fate apparently forgotten for now. "This is *our* start, Harriet. I've been aching for you. Literally aching."

Aching. For me.

His comment is thrilling, and incongruent given the backdrop of death. Probing fingers at a funeral.

"And I for you." I mentally trample Angel. It becomes easier the more distance Ralph puts between us and the Manor. I'm increasingly nervous now, excited, filled with a hundred helium balloons, trying to keep myself from bursting or floating away I'm so light.

I place my hand over his on the gear stick, feeling his muscles work as he changes gear. "Where are we going?"

"I've found us an inn, a perfect distance away, tucked in near Blackheath village."

"Lovely." Not too different, not too scary. It's been so long since I've been away, particularly when unimpeded by physical ailments, that painful arthritis, that ghastly dementia. Recovered from the unrecoverable. Is the dementia merely dormant? The epilepsy holding it down? Will one of these fits release it again, along with that other Harriet—hunched, shrunken, invisible? I twist the past away and focus on the present—my night with Ralph.

"I got us a suite. It should be comfortable. And should you wish to stay for more than one night, it's available."

Should *I* wish to stay for more than one night? Does he mean for me to stay there alone after tonight? Or does he assume he'll want to stay for longer too? That *we'll* want to stay for longer?

"Very thoughtful."

"Are we doing the right thing?" he asks after a while, and his hand slackens slightly.

"It's not right *not* to do this, with a connection like ours," I reassure. "Like denying life."

How different it is, his need for reassurance. None of the other men I've been in relationships with have sought it. I wonder if it's more reflective of the younger generation or the kind of man I used to find attractive.

I remember my first night with William. We weren't yet married but were engaged. It had been unplanned. We were overtaken by our youthful lust. Outside, at night. A field near the church. I recall the feeling of giving in to something, of letting myself be engulfed by emotion, and sensing a similar feeling in William. Afterwards, we were giddy with what we'd done, holding the delicious secret between us— *look what we discovered*—finding more opportunities to meet to do the same.

Will sex now have the same effect for me? Ralph hasn't had the long hiatus I have, but maybe our deep connection will make it similarly new for him? I think of the intensity of our time in the maze, but that also brings memories of my horrifying encounter with Tom's ghost.

I refocus on the present.

The inn is the picture of discretion—a jewel of an old farmhouse, overgrown with extensions, tucked away from the road amongst tall firs still dusted with snow. The windows, lit with soft amber light, are inviting in the glowering, wheezy dusk.

Ralph takes the bags as we make our way up the path and into the building. I'm not expecting a rush of nerves when we enter, but they come like stinging nettles brushed against my skin. I stand back and let him check us in with the woman waiting for us at the front desk. The foyer is decorated with white lights strung from its beams and a Christmas tree nestled comfortably in the corner. As though it was made for us. Suitably different from Marryat Manor, from Hayward Hall.

"Mr. and Mrs. Haverhill," I hear Ralph say. I try not to feel cheap, as if I'm merely Lisa's understudy, her fill-in. Has he taken her here before, I wonder? Or another lover, perhaps?

"Up the stairs." The woman points behind her at a staircase as she hands Ralph a key with a smile. "It's the only room on that floor. We have no in-house restaurant for dinner, but we do work with the local restaurants that deliver, and you can order from us as you would any other room service. Menus are in the suite."

Ralph thanks the woman and turns to me to indicate we should go to our room.

I follow him. The staircase is narrow and dimly lit, and I wonder if the room will be similarly cramped but find the suite to be so large it's practically the size of an apartment, with an ensuite bathroom next to the bedroom and a separate sitting area sectioned by a wall. The windows are vast, looking out over dense woodland.

It's decorated quite unlike anything I've seen before, probably because I'm used to rooms designed for my generation—traditional, old-fashioned. This room is modern, but not austere. A black four-poster bed with contrasting creamy linens, a sheepskin rug, and tan leather furniture in a Swedish design. The paintings lining the available walls are muted and abstract, textured and expressive, and the lamps are interestingly structural, all smoked glass and modernly faceted edges. Several lit hurricane lamps dot the space, flickering romantically.

A room designed for contemplation. A comfortable and comforting space, shielding one from the intensity of the woodland. All that green, now darkly viridian, soon black, as the night draws in.

"Do you like the room, Harriet?" Ralph asks, surprising me out of my wonder.

"I do, yes. It's quite lovely." His kind of room? A perfect place for a younger person. Though I am younger now, too, of course. I must adapt my tastes to be more appropriate for a woman of my appearance.

"Would you like me to leave you to get situated?" he asks. I see a nervousness in him. Over-considerateness. An inability to decide what to do with his hands. "To settle in? I can nip out to find us some wine or champagne?"

How thoughtful. He wants this as much as I do. He needs to feel seen too—wanted, alive.

"I think champagne might be quite festive," I agree, glad for the opportunity to prepare myself for him, to freshen up and slip into lingerie under my clothes.

I choose the coffee silk camisole and French knickers under my dress, which has a deep neckline to display the sapphire pendant beautifully. The necklace doesn't only belong to my marriage anymore, it has become significant in my relationship with Ralph too. A long oval mirror hangs on the sectioning wall facing the bed, and I see my full reflection as I perch there. I'm surprised by my appearance. I look Ralph's age, and beautiful, my cheekbones high, my lips now full.

But I also look sultry. Sultry without trying. Something to do with the light, creating sweeping cats eye shapes at my eye sockets and catching on my exposed skin, so it looks almost polished, making the contours of my body even more alluring.

This situation is impossible. How can I look over thirty years younger than I did a month ago? How can I be here in an inn, preparing to have sex for the first time in over fifteen years, with a handsome man three decades my junior?

I consider again the possibility that I'm living in an extended dream, a long hallucination brought on by my dementia. Or perhaps the incident at the séance caused some head injury, leaving me in a coma? Have I been dreaming this warped, vertiginous life since? Are sexual awakenings common during comas?

All at once I'm terrified it's true and my realization will cause me to wake in Harriet's old broken body, in her disease-ridden mind.

Ralph arrives back with a bottle of champagne in one hand and glasses in the other.

"Success!" he declares, setting the glasses down on the bedside table so he can set about opening the bottle while kicking off his shoes.

"I'm glad that champagne is still in vogue," I say, shaking off my disturbing thoughts as he hands me a glass. I force a grin. "It was always the most romantic of beverages."

"I'm happy you think so. I love it. What else was romantic, back . . ." I think he's about to say "in your day" but he diverts to "when you were first dating?"

"Oh, gosh, I don't know. The same as now, I should have thought."

"Yes, I can't remember what Mum and Dad did . . ." Ralph trails off, opening an awkward silence between us. It's difficult to avoid the topic of age. After a few moments I catch his mortified eyes, my tight smile loosening a bit, and we giggle.

"I'm not looking for you to woo me, Ralph. You've already done that. I don't need anything to feel romantic. I have you." I was never one for romantic expression, and I'm embarrassed as I speak. I take a sip of champagne, feeling absurdly girlish.

"You are quite something, Harriet." He sits on the bed next to me, then, still awkward, leans back against the pillows. "Tell me, are you quite certain you want this?"

"More than anything. You?"

"Desperately." His smile shimmers back at me, reigniting my desire. I'm disappointed as he withdraws his cell phone—the young have the dreadful habit of constantly looking at the blasted things—but relax after he fiddles with it for only a moment and then music starts playing, some woman singing melancholy and soulful, a relatively timeless choice.

Ralph carefully takes the glass of champagne from me and sets his and mine next to each other on the table beside him. I hold my breath—it's happening, really happening—as he leans closer. He strokes the side of my face, telling me gently, "You really are the most beautiful woman."

I think he's going to put his mouth on mine, and my lips tingle, but he lowers his face to my chest instead, kissing the exposed skin there, pulling a little at the neckline of my camisole to reveal more of my skin. I'm warm and aching deliciously, desperate for him to take his sweater off, his trousers. I want him naked. I need his skin. That young, taut skin.

I'm concerned for a moment he's going to be too gentle with me, that despite my physicality he's hung up on my age, but Ralph surprises me again when his fingers suddenly slip up the leg of my French knickers and then inside me. I gasp. His hand stops moving.

"Am I hurting you?" he asks.

"No! God! Keep going!" I plead, and he complies, hesitant at first until I insist "More. More!" and he drives his fingers deeper, harder. I can't help but think again of being touched like this at that wake when I was sixteen. This feels as illicit. Unimaginable just a few weeks ago. Absurd I should find myself in this kind of time slip.

I need more. More of him. I move away to slide my own hand up inside his thin blue cashmere jumper, finding his skin warmer than my fingers. He pushes himself up and removes his sweater, revealing a lean, lightly muscled torso with the smallest amount of hair in its middle. The kind of body made to appeal to a woman. Instead of lowering himself back over me, he pulls my knickers down. I lift my legs so he can remove them completely. My nerves mount, some parts of me tingling, some parts aching, as he gently pushes my thighs apart to see the space his fingers had just probed.

"Ah, Harriet," he groans. It's the most erotic moment of my life. His eyes are glued to me as he unbuttons and removes his own trousers and underwear, but I don't have the opportunity to see him as he sinks to his forearms between my legs, licking and tasting hungrily. Too soon, my orgasm comes, powerful, dominating. My cries are too loud, but I don't care. It's been so long since I've climaxed with a man. I'm practically a virgin again, I've been so untouched. Like that first time with William in that field all those years ago. Stunned it's happening.

He penetrates me as my body is still pulsing with pleasure, his beautiful face over mine, his eyes locked to my own, contoured with need. It's too slow. I want more, harder and faster. I move under him, spurring Ralph to drive into me more forcefully, until he gives way to it.

"Yes!" I pant again, hungry for proof of his adoration, his need for me. His eyes fix on mine. Butterfly blue. Intense.

"Ah, Harriet," he whimpers then stands at the edge of the bed, pulling me to him, spreading my legs and pushing into me again. If I turn my head I can see us in the mirror—this naked, younger man with his taut muscles and full head of hair, fucking me, truly fucking me, exactly as I've dreamed. I arch back on the bed, openly enjoying the ravishing, his worship of my body, both of us vital and alive. My second orgasm rises as I meet my own expression of intense desire and deep happiness.

Ralph groans, desperate and almost wild. Quite unlike the man whose charm is so well-contained and controlled. This is him at his core. His raw self. His whole body tensing as he gives in to the ecstasy.

"Magic Harriet," he murmurs as he collapses, gazing into my eyes.

I try to remember if sex ever felt like this before. I'm not sure it did. It felt good with William, certainly, but I was never truly swept away, melded to a person.

"I'll order us some food." Ralph kisses my forehead before he gets up from the bed and pulls on his underwear.

I watch, enjoying the sight of him. Naked, he seems both stronger and more vulnerable. You can never tell how a body will look beneath the clothes—if their naked, inner personality matches their clothed self. A perfectly decent-looking man can conceal some weird lump of fat somewhere or be excessively hairy. I suppose the same goes for women. I hate to think how I looked just a few weeks ago.

Now, naked, my outsides match my insides. Strong, upright, in control.

"What do you fancy?" Ralph leafs through the fan of menus left for us on top of the small writing desk positioned in front of the window. "Thai? Sushi?"

"Oh, gosh," I say before I stop myself. I don't think I've ever had either. I imagine they contain all kinds of mystery ingredients Ralph, and his generation, are more used to. Isn't sushi raw fish? I'm keen not to appear elderly in my tastes and am about to suggest Indian before I remember it's likely not the sexiest of foods, being so heavy and with its lingering smells.

"How about something a little plainer? With all this excitement, I'm feeling a little jittery."

Ralph raises his eyebrows as if surprised.

"No, not jittery exactly," I find myself explaining. "I just ate a whole box of chocolates earlier and . . ."

He laughs. "You don't seem a whole box of chocolates kind of person."

"Usually, no," I admit.

"Italian?" he suggests. "Spaghetti carbonara?"

"Perfect." I smile, hoping the restaurant isn't heavy on the garlic.

Ralph phones down to the front desk then dresses. It's a little cold, so I do the same.

"What's that?" Ralph asks, frowning.

"A slip?" I laugh.

"What's it for?"

"Stopping my dress from sticking to my legs."

"Dresses stick to legs?"

"Yes, from static." It's a peculiar thing to have to explain.

"Huh. I've never seen one before," he says.

Never? Are the young going around without wearing petticoats these days? How do they manage? Their skirts must constantly get caught between their legs. I'm about to ask him if he hasn't noticed Margaret using one, but I stop myself. Partly because I don't want to draw attention to the fact that in years, if not in looks, I'm about the same age as his mother, and partly because Margaret always wears trousers. A Daphne du Maurier type. Femininity has never been important to her. Still, I'm self-conscious doing something other women who look my age don't.

Ralph pours us both another glass of champagne. I almost wish he wouldn't. I'm not sure how much I can drink before feeling woozy, and I don't want to start slurring.

"What are your favorite drinks?" he asks, then clarifies, "Alcoholic."

"Brandy. Vodka soda." I answer before I realize my choices might betray my age. He smiles. "You?"

"White wine—Muscadet, Chablis. Good bourbon. Whisky cocktails, Manhattans, a good old-fashioned. I also like a gimlet and an India pale ale." I nod, interested. After years of entertaining, I'm familiar with all these drinks, apart from the "India pale ale," but I didn't know they were trendy again. Maybe brandy and vodka soda are still in vogue too.

"You always look nice, Ralph. Where do you buy your clothes?" I ask.

He looks down at his shirt. "Ted Baker, Reiss, Pink."

I've heard of none of these places. Christmas is only next week, and I haven't bought anything for him. Are we that kind of "together"? A gift-giving couple? Exchanging shirts, watches, and perfume? It seems too soon, too predictable, for us.

"You always look beautiful, Harriet. You have great taste in clothes." I think he's being kind, taking care not to draw attention to my age by asking me the same question, looking down as he adds, "No hoodies and sweatpants for you."

Is he comparing me to his wife? It's a rather strange comment. "I don't go to the gym."

He laughs as if I've said something funny. I'm not sure I understand but smile as if I do.

16

"**I** love this place," I say dreamily, and it's true.

I love that the rooms are so dark, thanks to the density of the woodland filling the window. We need to light all the amber lamps, even in the middle of the day. I love the depth of the mattress, the airy linen sheets and thick wool blankets. The almost Celtic aesthetic. I adore the whirlpool bath and powerful shower with exceptional water pressure, both of which are roomy enough for two. A place built for comfort and intimacy.

Time passes in a blur of sex, food, champagne, and conversation. Ralph barely touches his phone. He doesn't seem to be communicating with Lisa. I call the Manor to tell them I will be away longer than expected and am mildly annoyed that they seem relieved. We realize that neither of us packed enough basic undergarments. My initial titillation at the idea of our being forced to go without is replaced by surprise when Ralph simply orders some using his phone, and they're delivered to our room a few hours later.

My energy is mounting, as Ralph's seems to deplete slightly, my sex drive matching, then surpassing, his. I'm not sure I've ever felt like this—incandescent, insatiable, irresistible. The times we're not having sex I'm thinking about it, about all the things I've wanted to do but that never felt right with William or other lovers. As though our bodies were meant for each other, as though sex was always planned for us.

I want to be restrained, then to dominate. I want to have sex in front of the mirror. On my request, Ralph gently wraps a handful of hair around his fist and takes me from behind. He introduces pornography. I had no idea there was so much of it available online or that it came in such variety. Although we don't need anything to spice up the lovemaking, given how much heat it has already, watching others ignites us further all the same—I'm so hot I feel as though I'm on fire—and the videos inspire new positions. Bending this way would have been inconceivable a couple of months ago. I learn from what arouses Ralph, and he gets excited by learning what arouses me. I've never known this intensity of sexual solidarity before.

We relax, laugh, express our desire openly, giving over to it. He tells me I'm beautiful, he loves my skin, my eyes, tells me how good it feels to be inside me. He loves talking to me afterward, too, sharing secrets, confidences, hopes and dreams. Oddly, given that people of my generation are not prone to sharing intimacies, I'm most comfortable with the more personal questions—those about my marriage, my affairs, my relationship with Judith and little Molly. I can be open, candid, and Ralph likes my answers, seems keen to accept all of me, and seems comforted, I think, when I confess mistakes and betrayals. He is equally open.

I am less comfortable with chitchat that reveals my age or his youthful ignorance, like the time Ralph characterized the sixties as "all flower power and short skirts" or I referred to rap music as "the music where they talk instead of singing." I worry he'll slip away from me, the more we draw attention to our differences.

In some conversations, Ralph has the upper hand. He knows more about the way the world is now, its excitements and opportunities, whereas my tastes seem to have locked into place fifty years ago and stayed there. But at other times, the wisdom that only comes with four extra decades of life experience is the thing that separates us. I am careful not to condescend. He is careful not to give way to incredulity at my ignorance of "now."

We veer away from any mother and son dynamic.

Unusually, I don't tire of Ralph's company and don't crave isolation. I feel as an addict might, wanting more of him, to grow closer. I realize I have nothing else in my life. He has a career, his mother. Given Margaret's washing her hands of me, I have only Judith, I suppose. Money too. But really, the only thing of importance is Ralph.

It's simple and complicated simultaneously. Simple because we're just two people with incredible chemistry, connecting quite profoundly. Complicated because of who we are to each other, our ages, my uncanny transformation. He must wonder how this can have happened to me. I wonder that myself. But rather than alienate him, the mystery draws him closer. *Magic Harriet.* It's magnetized me to him.

In the back of my mind, though, linger the questions. The memories of Margaret's comments on the journal and Dr. Phillips's words that day in the library. Angel's death. My gruesome visions of William and Tom. Margaret's vehement hatred of me the last time we spoke. The reminder, however insane, of possible supernatural involvement has me vibrating at a different frequency. I feel charged, potentially dangerous. The danger feels like a battery tastes. And while horrifying, it has a positive effect on our connection.

I'm terrified I'll wake one day and find myself returned to that old body, the diseased mind I hated so much, and I'll have to absorb the horror on Ralph's face as he sees me. He'd be disgusted, scraping me off him, mad with the shame of it.

But instead, so far, I awake each morning relieved I look more and not less youthful than the previous day. My fine lines are barely traceable now, my breasts lifted higher, my skin even smoother, more luminous. I look like the party-hostess Harriet back in the early eighties when we all wore too much makeup and off-the-shoulder Christian Dior. I see my own sparkle and know Ralph sees it too.

Despite his joyful energy, I see signs of wear on Ralph, dragging at the corners of his mouth and lining his eyes and forehead, dampening down his brilliance, fading him slightly. It's likely due to too much sex, or possibly the stress of poor Margaret. He's too considerate to talk about it, given the brutal fracture of our friendship.

I'm not the other woman now, though, I'm *the* woman. His center. I find myself wondering if things between Ralph and Lisa were ever this intense, this good. I doubt it. Could Margaret ever understand this? That I make him happy? Surely, that's what she wants for him?

Us not staying together seems like madness, an insult against nature. And an insult to dementia Harriet. She's out there somewhere, wanting all of this. This situation may be messy, but it's a rather beautiful tangle, I think. A meaningful muddle. Twisted, but spectacularly so.

We've been here for two full days, and Ralph will have to go home soon. I don't know what that means for me. I can't face the idea of returning to Marryat Manor, of being alone there. Here, my hallucinations have been kept at bay by love, by the intensity of us. I'm afraid to leave Ralph's side for fear of their return. I don't want to look into William's eyes again, be assaulted by their unnatural fury. I don't want to encounter the dead, the deterioration of the living, the dragging down of the staff. Being here has marked the beginning of my life's next chapter, and I'm unwilling to revisit the past.

"What do we do next, Ralph?" I ask. It's nearing midday, and he's distracted, his eyes drawn to the window as if taking in all the green, the patterns of the branches. We've both been worrying over Margaret, and Ralph has called the Manor several times to check on her condition. Bad, it seems. He wants to go to her but is afraid seeing him would increase her stress and exacerbate her illness. He must be pondering what to do. I've not seen him in this mode of worry before, and I find it endearing.

"Lunch, I guess?" he answers vaguely, then, "We could go out if you like. A pub?"

"Well, yes, that sounds lovely, but I meant what's next with us? Where do we go from here?"

Ralph looks at me, placing a hand to his temple before running it through his hair. His hairline has receded further back since we arrived at the inn. The thought of him aging physically hurts, and I feel the corners of my mouth pulled downwards, my eyebrow twitching in stress.

"Well, we need to sort that out," he agrees.

"Do you . . ." I start, not knowing how to phrase the question. "I mean, it's Christmas next week. Are you planning on spending it at . . . home?" I can't meet his eyes. Does he still think of his house with Lisa as his home? "I can't go back to Marryat Manor, you see, so if you're planning on going home, I need to find an alternative place to stay."

Ralph gasps, and I look up at him, alarmed.

"Harriet! Harriet, no." He withdraws from the window to sit next to me on the bed, clasping my hands in his. The hands I was so embarrassed of a couple of months ago—those unsightly arthritic claws, liver-spotted and wrinkled with protruding knuckles—are completely smooth again, my fingers long and elegant. "A pianist's hands" my mother used to say. Hands she'd be proud of. I experience an unexpected tremor of astonishment at the sight of them, and my idea that I'm in a dream—a coma—revisits me again. How could this be anything other than a dream?

"There's no way I'm going anywhere without you," Ralph continues, and my stomach turns over a couple of times. "We stay together. That's not up for debate."

A fresh wave of relief surges through me, and I hug Ralph tight.

"I love you, Harriet. And it's quite unlike anything I've ever felt. As though you're another part of me I never knew existed. There's no empty space in me now, you've filled it." Though he speaks with conviction, I can see he's embarrassed. He's not a wordsmith like his mother, and he's probably unused to such declarations.

"Oh, Ralph," I murmur appreciatively. "I love you too. It's remarkable, this chance we have. If there's anything that's ever been inevitable, or star-aligning, it's this." I'm aware I'm as inarticulate as Ralph, but he doesn't seem to notice. "This utterly bizarre condition that I have—what could it possibly be for if not to bring me to you?"

Ralph brushes my hair with his hand. The hotel phone rings. Though reluctant to interrupt this most significant conversation, he eventually picks up the handset. "Hello?"

I hear a muffled voice on the other end but can't make out the words.

Ralph's expression drops. "Okay." He sighs. "Yes, okay, we'll be right down."

"What is it?" I ask once he's hung up.

"Dr. Phillips is downstairs."

"What's he doing here? How did he find us?" I ask, distressed as I search for my shoes.

"The time my mobile wasn't working I used the hotel phone to call the Manor. He must have traced us back through the incoming number."

Dr. Phillips is perched in an armchair next to a large Christmas tree in the sitting room. He looks different out of his white coat. His country tweeds make him look more pallid and rather like a headmaster, underscoring the expression of disapproval he can't quite hide. His skin has a powdery texture I've never noticed before, like dried-out clay before it's been fired, and there's a new sagging at his jowls. The natural aging of a man of fifty, or the over-work of someone in his mid-forties.

I remind myself Ralph and I are grown adults and don't owe this man—this employee for whom I am a *client*—an explanation. Ralph places a protective arm around my waist as we approach Dr. Phillips, but although I appreciate the gesture, I step away. I am my own person, strong in body and will, and don't need protection. There's something sliding along the surface of Ralph's features, something I can't identify at first. Regret, or no . . . I think it's fear.

"Harriet." Dr. Phillips greets me grimly without standing as he usually might, manners apparently forgotten.

I sit in a slipper chair facing him and Ralph takes the one next to me. He's eyeing the tea-making area in the corner of the room, but he doesn't move, waiting to take my lead.

"Dr. Phillips. I am rather surprised you have the time to make the trip out to see us, given the state of many of your patients at the Manor." My tone is more cutting than I'd intended, but I'm pleased with the way it sounds. Haughtiness can be useful when holding one's own. "If you knew where we were, you could have just called."

"No, no. I need to see you in person. The timing of your departure was . . . *interesting*, Harriet. Given the unfortunate fate of poor Angel."

"What has that to do with me?" I ask, not appreciating his insinuation.

Ralph's confused look darts between the two of us.

"Quite," Dr. Phillips responds.

"No, really, what do you imagine his death might have to do with me?"

"Alyson said she was with you earlier in the day when you confronted Angel."

"I have a vague recollection of something to that effect." My response sounds evasive, though it's the full truth. My memories of that interaction remain elusive. The fact I don't know where he's going with this questioning makes me uneasy.

"And he was found dead in the very same spot."

Ralph makes a disbelieving, spluttering sound.

"Did Alyson say I attacked him?" I demand, outraged.

"No, but—"

"And was there any evidence of my involvement?"

There is a short silence. Dr. Phillips regards me coolly. "No. But in death, he had quite an expression of . . ."

"What?" I demand impatiently.

"Horror," he finishes.

The silence hangs in the air. Only the gentle twinkling of the Christmas tree lights indicate time is moving at all. Before I realize what I'm doing, I laugh—a rich, deep chortle, which tips into incredulity.

Ralph puffs out a single laugh, too, his body angled towards mine, a united force against this new absurdity.

"He died of fright, did he? This *drug addict?*" I say, continuing to laugh.

"There were no drugs in his system."

"So, you're accusing me of what? Scaring him to death? Well then, take me in!" I put my wrists together and raise them as though I'm offering to be cuffed. "The facts against me in this case are quite compelling!" I'm being dramatic. Excruciatingly so. Ralph chuckles again, the sound now forced and embarrassed on my behalf. I lean towards Dr. Phillips, serious now. "The fact that you're a medical professional is a joke. You should be struck off. You have no business being a physician. You have no business caring for the elderly."

As if in rebuke, an image of Angel with a grotesque, deathly expression flashes in my mind, and I recall the blackness I saw reflected in his eyes before I walked away. Terrifying, but obviously an imagined memory. Like my hallucinations.

Dr. Phillips coughs, the sound rattling through his chest, and he winces. Once recovered, he looks from me to Ralph. "I'm sorry, but your mother has passed away."

Something tears in me. Quick, ripping, brutal.

I turn to Ralph to see his face freeze, drop, then crumple.

"As you know, she's been barely conscious these past few days. She died this morning. I'm so sorry. Margaret was a wonderful woman," Dr. Phillips continues.

I pause my own pain, my own loss, holding the broken shards of myself together, and focus on Ralph, whose heart I know is breaking.

"And you, too, Harriet," Dr. Phillips adds. "I know she was your best friend."

My best friend. The other part of me. Dementia Harriet's rock. Her core.

Ralph searches my face, but I focus my concern back onto him.

His eyes blur, and he rubs the tears away with his thumbs, leaving them there, buried in his sockets, while he composes himself. I've seen men cry so few times in my life, I don't know quite what to do with it.

"She was very unwell," Ralph stammers finally. "Thank you for looking after her so well, Dr. Phillips."

Always a gentleman, my Ralph.

Dr. Phillips nods. We're quiet for a time in remembrance though our shock pervades the air.

"I'll have to make funeral arrangements," Ralph murmurs finally.

"Our staff can deal with most of it," Dr. Phillips tells him gently before looking at me uncertainly. He hesitates before adding, "There's another matter."

There isn't enough space in my mind for "another matter."

"A bill?" Ralph asks.

I would have assumed the same, though chasing payments really isn't the doctor's responsibility.

"No, no, not that I know of." Dr. Phillips holds up a hand. "It's a more delicate situation. Something quite alarming that needs urgent attention."

"To do with my mum?" Ralph asks, looking confused.

Dr. Phillips tilts his head to one side, looking at me carefully, making me dread what he'll say next. "In a way. It was what your mother was researching before she died."

I cover my face with my hands. "No!" Absolutely not. I will not have him bring up this nonsense again. Not now.

I make to stand, but Dr. Phillips leans forwards, blocking me. "Please, Harriet, we must talk about this."

"No! Margaret has just died!"

"Even more reason to discuss immediately."

Ralph's gaze is ping-ponging between us again, his expression bewildered. "What is this?"

"Nothing!" I bark.

"No, really, Harriet, I want to know. What was Mum researching and why is it so important?"

I'm Rottweiler-aggressive in the wake of his grief, but I can't bear Ralph hearing this diabolical gibberish and risk his believing it. But he's adamant, so I swivel to face him, my arms and legs crossed, ready to defend myself, preparing for more incredulity, more adamance. I pull those broken pieces of myself even more firmly together.

"I don't blame Harriet for not believing it. It's remarkable," Dr. Phillips says, more gently now.

"More than remarkable. Absurd." I'm too loud. Practically shouting, but I'm tingling with fury.

"Please tell me." Ralph's voice is quiet, resolute.

Dr. Phillips waits to see if I'm going to interrupt again, but I stay quiet, seething in my chair, so he says, "Harriet's condition."

Ralph chokes back a single sob, his hands clasped in front of his face as more tears escape. "It's bad, isn't it? Is Harriet going to die too?"

"That's not the immediate issue." Dr. Phillips doesn't deny my condition will lead to death, I notice. "We think—and please hear me out, Ralph—that Harriet has been, *is,* possessed by a daemon."

His delivery is matter of fact, like this is a regular diagnosis.

After a stunned silence, Ralph shakes his head, clearly doubtful, as any rational person would be.

"In early November, Margaret and Harriet held a séance, re-enacting an event that occurred over a hundred and twenty years ago," Dr. Phillips explains.

"The one to rejuvenate. I remember that," Ralph says. He's too interested, too willing to hear. Panic hurts my chest, somewhere around the heart, where the shards aren't fully meeting together.

"That's right. Only there were diary entries, from both Florence Marryat and her husband, showing there was a rather alarming consequence of the original séance. Florence was apparently taken over by a daemon, something I wouldn't believe were it not for reports from multiple sources that said everyone in the household died subsequently, including the husband. Anyone who came close to Florence aged. Rapidly. Some died within days. A woman miscarried. And all the time, Florence became younger. An exorcism was performed to—"

"Wait!" Ralph holds up a hand, his eyebrows raising practically to his hairline. "Are you telling me the same thing is happening to Harriet?"

"I'm afraid so." Dr. Phillips nods gravely. "It sounds utterly absurd in theory. I realize this. And it's not something that's been researched medically. But as a man of faith, given everything I've seen—everyone at Marryat Manor aging so dramatically in such a short space of time . . . We've lost fifteen residents in two weeks, Harriet."

I suck in a startled breath. *Fifteen.* "That's not . . . I mean . . . there were several different conditions. These people are elderly. It's winter. A virus. Nothing to do with me."

Still. Fifteen.

"But that's just it, Harriet, it's not just them. Not just the deaths. All the staff, everyone you've been around, have aged in the last few weeks. Dramatically. I've gathered before and after photos, in fact." He withdraws his phone from his pocket to show us, but I stop him.

"I don't want to see them," I say curtly.

"You can see how ridiculous this seems?" Ralph backs me up. I wonder if panic is jangling through him as it is me.

"But together with Harriet's dramatic and sudden youthfulness? Nobody ages backwards, Ralph. Nobody."

Nobody ages backwards. My persistent fears become doubly portentous.

"Look at the two of you," Dr. Phillips continues. "Ralph, you've aged a decade in a week. You look like you're almost sixty."

"Thanks very much!" Ralph exclaims, unconsciously reaching again to his hairline.

Dr. Phillips turns to me. "And Harriet, you look well under fifty, in your forties even. Although you're eighty-two."

Ralph sucks in a breath. Dementia Harriet—the same Harriet who was humiliated by Ralph's joking about not being a granny chaser with Alyson—buckles inside me.

Dr. Phillips appeals to both of us. "This is a problem, Harriet. You're going to kill more people. The more you're around others, the more they'll age. Ralph, if you stay with Harriet, you'll be dead within weeks, if not sooner."

"You haven't even investigated all the possible medical conditions I might have," I blurt. "You said yourself you hadn't been able to run more tests on me because of all the deaths at the Manor. Have you even considered the fact that I'm in a coma right now?"

I know I sound crazy, but I'm scrambling for any explanation at this point.

Dr. Phillips looks confused before he seems to understand. "You mean that this is all a hallucination inside your own head"—he motions between us—"and all that's happened is your imagination?" He shakes his head. "I can understand that it would be a more believable reality to you. More believable than possession. But the rest of us know we're here, Harriet."

He looks at Ralph, appealing for help.

Ralph scoffs. "I think *you* need to see a mental health professional, Dr. Phillips." He stands. "That you should have the audacity to come here, and moments after informing me of the death of my mother, you tell me the love of my life is what? A daemon? A vampire? And a murderer? Harriet's right, you should be struck off."

I've never seen Ralph so angry, his manners lost. I stand too.

"I've brought the books with me. Take them, please. Read them." Dr. Phillips points to the pile of old books on the table beside him I hadn't noticed before. I recognize the covers. "Take them." He picks them up and shoves them into my arms, so I have no choice but to take the damned things. "We need to talk about this, Harriet."

Dr. Phillips holds out a hand to stop us as we turn to leave, pleading, "Please! I know it's not your fault, you didn't intend for any of this to happen. But more people are going to die, Harriet! You're going to kill Ralph!"

"Leave us alone!" I spit back at him as we stomp back to our room.

17

As I continue to try and hold myself together, something squirms inside me, nudging through the gaps these pieces have made like a hernia. Some alien body, twisting itself up into a smirk. It's not me. It's . . . what? Madness?

In the periphery, I see figures in the trees. Hunched, pulse-deprived people I know aren't there. They will me to look at them. Too many people demanding me to see too many things.

Mayflower. Maypole. The words flower inside my head. Margaret words. Things I've said to her. Margaret. Things she laughed at. Margaret.

Robert Frost. Florence Marryat. The Blood of the Vampire.

It's impossible that she's gone, that she went so soon, blazed away by that fire gun of her own fury. I wonder if it's my guilt or my dementia causing the hallucinations this time, the people in the trees. Perhaps the disease never really went away, despite my younger appearance. Perhaps it's always lingering in the background of my mind, waiting to emerge and wreak havoc like a ghost in the attic.

I close my eyes and focus on the sound of the rain. Those obstinately un-festive, giant wet drops hitting the windowpane and sliding into already slush-sodden ground. When I open my eyes again, the darkness of the asphalt day and brightness of the light within our room has forced my reflection in the window. But it's not me, I realize. In my place is something withered, pained, and afraid.

Panicked, I race to the mirror, but I see only myself as I am now. My youthful, smooth face. A woman in her, what, early forties? Though ravished with grief.

Ralph finally emerges from the bathroom and starts packing his bag. I follow his lead.

"We've got to get out of here. Go where we can't be bothered." His tone is irate, his body tense. "I mean, how dare he?"

It might be the first time I've seen Ralph truly angry. It doesn't quite suit him. It's as though he's been overstretched into a different shape, wearing a different man's personality. Even with his outrage, however, I wonder if he gives Dr. Phillips's claim any credence. Is he stifling a layer of horror, or at least of trepidation, as I am?

I locate my bag and start folding my clothes into it, a combination of anxiety, sorrow, and apprehension knotting together inside me. "He's obviously ill, delusional. But, Ralph . . ."

I lay a hand on his arm.

He stops, too, and faces me. "Mum."

His expression crumples again as a child's might. I reach for him, and he buries his face in my shoulder, not sobbing, but clinging to me. I find myself caught between Harriet, his lover, and Harriet, his mother's beloved dementia-ridden best friend. Caught between roles, between generations.

"I'm sorry, Ralph. Your mother was a wonderful woman."

Such a paltry consolation. The kind of thing you'd say about an acquaintance, not your closest friend.

Margaret. Died in fury.

I close my eyes, an image of her face contorted in vitriol etching itself onto the insides of my eyelids. Please let this not be the way I will always think of her.

"Yes." Ralph pulls away from me. "But I'll have to think about that later. Oh, God, we need to get going. Go somewhere we won't be pestered by that lunatic! And you heard what he said about that Angel chap? He's trying to blame you for the man's murder!"

Angel. His terror. Blackness, reflected in his pupils. The absence of.

"Dr. Phillips probably murdered that man himself! He's probably responsible for all these deaths and blaming them on you. Who knows what he'll do next? Call the police, probably. We need to get out of here and away where we can't be found."

Through his tears, Ralph starts packing again, and I do the same. Why did I mention the coma hallucination to Dr. Phillips? He must think I'm of unsound mind. Maybe I am. But then, I think the same of him. Perhaps we're both insane and taking everyone down with us. My panic rises, edging on paranoia. Ralph will blame me. He'll come to believe what the doctor claims, that I'm some kind of daemon, that I'm killing everyone around me. He'll blame me for his mother's death.

Margaret. Dead.

I know she's there now, outside in the trees. When I hazard another glance out the window, I see many more figures gathered there now too. A collection of ghouls peering up at us. A recrimination of them. Is a "recrimination" the collective noun for ghosts?

Is a "glitter" the collective noun for fairies?

"I don't understand how Dr. Phillips can believe such things of me," I manage, overtaken with hammering despair. It tugs at my limbs, making me clumsy. I soften my tone. "Or, to be honest, how your mother believed it either. Quite frankly, it's unlike either of them to accept this supernatural nonsense, although Phillips is a Christian, of course." I'm thinking aloud, but I'm so tightly wound with stress I can't stop myself. "And I suppose with all the illnesses at the Manor, all the deaths, and my strange condition, he's under a great deal of strain. Still, someone like Dr. Phillips shouldn't be responsible for the health of the elderly."

"Absolutely not," Ralph agrees.

I feel a little sickened, shameful, as I scoop my dirty lingerie into my laundry bag. It seems indecent to do so in front of Ralph. *Don't show the boys your knickers.*

Our conversation is disjointed. I'm jittery, concussed and shaking after the sequence of blows Dr. Phillips dealt us. Keeping my line of sight so firmly away from the window I'm dizzied. But I still sense them out there, amongst the trees. All of them. Everyone who has died. It doesn't matter that I've escaped Marryat Manor. They're going to follow me wherever I go.

"Oh, Mum." Ralph's wail distracts me. He falls to the bed before curling into a fetal position.

I'd find this childlike collapse unbecoming on another man, but on Ralph all I see is heart.

Tentatively, unsure if he wants to be touched, but concluding he'll let me know if not, I join him on the bed and curve my body around the shape of his, sliding an arm over him, which he takes and squeezes gratefully. Holding him soothes me. I have him. If nothing else, I have Ralph. His love is unchanged. His huge, tender heart is mine.

Eventually, Ralph gathers himself, getting up slowly and washing his face before finishing the packing. He stops for a moment before folding me into his chest. "I'll miss this place," he murmurs into my hair. "The place we first made love. The place we fell in love."

Grief suffuses his words, dampening them with sadness.

"I know." I'm wretched with the loss, the stress, the anger, the fear of what's outside, of what's facing me. "Me too. But does it matter where we are?" I pull away slightly and look up into his pale blue eyes, now red-rimmed, as though they've been underlined, needing correction. "As long as we're together."

I'm not expecting a kiss, but then his mouth is on mine, transforming the moment from something fraught into something not sexual but profoundly connected, his tongue finding mine, breaking his way further into me. He stops as quickly as he started, cupping his hands a little too hard around my face, touching his forehead to mine, our noses a millimeter apart as he murmurs, "Thank god for you."

"Thank god for *you*," I repeat. The reality of the situation slowly permeates. His skin, breath, tears. Love and loss. Lust and pain. We are here. I know in my soul this isn't a dream. Dementia hasn't fashioned this bizarre situation from fragments of my desire and fear.

"I don't know what I would have done—hearing about Mum—without you."

My God, Margaret, why did you have to die? Why did our parting words have to be so damning? All that life, that wit, that intellect, dissolved.

"I don't want to be without you," he whimpers, a child again.

"You never will be," I reassure, smoothing my hands across his back, consoling.

We don't stop at a pub for lunch. Instead, we select prepared sandwiches and crisps from a petrol station shop and eat them in the car after Ralph fills the tank. A grubby and cheap thing to do, but it matches my mood. The squeaky plastic cheese and bread soggy with pickle is disgusting. I don't complain, just look out at the bleak drizzle and try not to cry. All this feels like a penance for some uncommitted misadventure.

Margaret. She still twinkled just a few weeks ago. She was so much healthier than I was then. My sorrow has now transformed into self-loathing. It should have been me, succumbing to the infection. I should be the one in the grave. Did our last altercation contribute to her rapid decline? Oh, God. What an excruciating thought. That I might have caused my best friend's demise. Shoved her towards her death somehow. Perhaps Dr. Phillips is right. Perhaps I am behind all this. Perhaps Margaret died terrified, like Angel.

Given her adamance of my possession, she probably feared for Ralph, too, and died with the sudden realization that—

No. I mentally shake myself. It's too ridiculous. Margaret died of a chest infection, her mind clouded, addled. I wish she'd understood the depth of our connection, that Ralph and I are in love, that our relationship isn't cheap or tawdry.

The combination of drizzle on the windshield, further blurring the greys of the motorway, and the warm air blasting from the heater pulls me, emotionally exhausted, into a half-sleep. And for the first time since before the séance, I dream.

This time, I'm not in the Manor, but outside on the grounds. People are looking for me, and they've brought dogs. Barking echoes over the gardens. It's raining there too. Hard, bruising. I'm only wearing my coffee-colored silk lingerie, which soaks in seconds, and I feel a hot flash of terror as I'm chased, the downpour impeding my progress as the wind attempts to blow me sideways. Unwisely, I run to the maze for shelter. But only two corners in I find a woman from my ghastly nightmares—now instantly recognizable as Florence Marryat from the portrait. Here, she's barely twenty, wearing a white nightgown of some sort, inappropriate. A Wilkie Collins *Woman in White* mirage. Her smile is both cruel and seductive.

"Join me, Harriet," she murmurs huskily, slightly wild as she lifts the skirt of her nightgown and masturbates. Even in the dream, I feel a scalding reproach. A sickening. Lust amidst decay.

"Join me," she pants. "I know you like it. They don't know what it's like to be us." Her fingers work faster, her gaze still focused on me. I don't know where to look, what to do. "They don't know that we . . . need . . . this."

Her head falls back, and her expression tips towards ecstasy as I wake with a jolt.

I'm in a car. It's raining. Ralph's driving. He either didn't notice I woke or that I slept at all. I check the sat nav. Forty-two minutes to our destination. I've only been asleep for maybe ten minutes. I adjust in my seat and recall the dream, shaking off a second shiver of shame.

The city of Brighton is usually a rather spectacular place. I've always loved it, even during its depressed years. The grand seafront with its wall of hotels and quirky piers. The antiques, art, and oddities you can discover when exploring the Lanes. The boutiques, the bakeries, and restaurants. Even the stony beach can be fun in the right frame of mind.

But though dressed for Christmas, bright lights strung from every place you can imagine, it's a scowl of a place in the rain. Sullen, as though disgruntled that we should dare to visit.

"I've found us a room at a little guest house in the area of Kemptown. Small, intimate," Ralph tells me as we turn off the motorway towards the city. His voice is flat, incapable of inflection.

I'm fractionally disappointed, having imagined a stay at one of the grander hotels on the seafront rather than an afterthought of a guest house further out. Something bolder, a greater distraction. A place to escape and feel alive again with Ralph. Although, given the reality of our shock, it could be more appropriate to fold ourselves away, to feel sore together.

"Sounds lovely," I say, surprised I can manage even a fraction of animation.

We're quiet for a moment as we look out at the gloom.

"It's supposed to clear up later," Ralph says, as if reading my mind.

"The weather doesn't matter." I place a hand over his as he changes gear. "We're together. That's what counts."

"Have you spent a lot of time in Brighton?" He continues to sound drained.

"William and I came here for weekends, but not for a long time." I smile a little, remembering that version of my husband. I always loved spending time with William, but it never felt like it does now with

Ralph. It never felt like we were holding hot coals between our bodies, sultry and ever-so-slightly dangerous. Lust and pain. I never valued my youth. I dare to wonder if Margaret's death will defeat us, bursting this buoyant, great bubble of love.

"Where did you stay?" Ralph asks, his tone filled more with exhaustion than lack of enthusiasm.

"Oh, I'm not sure I remember," I lie, not wanting him to feel bad about his choice of lodging. "Different places."

A prolonged silence ensues where I can practically hear the gears turning in his mind.

"What are you thinking about?" I ask the question I've always found pathetic and annoying in the mouths of others.

"Mum." His voice is solemn.

"I know." I rub my hand over his. I'm not known for my sympathy, but I've never felt it as genuinely as I do now. I hope Ralph feels the strength of my love.

"I expected she'd go at some point in the next few years, but it was so sudden, and we were on such strange terms."

I gulp, wretched. "My fault. I apologize."

"No!" Ralph turns his hand and laces his fingers through mine, squeezing them briefly before releasing me again and changing gears. "Never apologize, Harriet. There's nothing to apologize for. Mum would have got used to the idea. She would have forgotten her . . . strange notions."

Strange notions. Like my daemonic possession. My two sets of brain waves. My duality. My epilepsy. I cling to the possibility that my new disease changed me, transformed me. That I've emerged, a new Harriet, domineering over the weaker, older version of myself. Why didn't I just explain this to Margaret? She would have understood. And I'm still me, even in this new body, after all. I should have convinced her instead of letting my stupid pride be offended.

Then again, perhaps she wouldn't have listened. Margaret could be as stubborn as me. Stubbornness comes with age. We assume the right to use it once capability and dignity have tumbled away from us.

The guest house is as unremarkable as I'd expected. A tall townhouse jammed in between two others, with an awning stretched over a half-flight of steps to the door.

The inside is equally depressing, not because it's dirty or shabby but because it's so sparse, as though someone came along and shook all personality out of its corners and swept it away, the only decoration being several large framed black-and-white abstract photos.

Photos of anywhere for anyone.

"Phew," Ralph whispers. "I didn't have time to check it online, but this is nice." He nods approvingly at the achingly dull lobby before us. "Not doily."

Doily? Is that the word the young use to describe old-fashioned things these days? I think doilies can be rather nice. They help soften edges. I once crocheted one myself as a gift for my mother. Something we learned to do at school in those days.

Our room is equally soulless. A bed with a black, square, wooden headboard, plain white cotton sheets, a pale grey carpet, long drapes in another shade of grey, and more black and white photography so bland I wonder if it was selected specifically not to be viewed.

"This place looks like my own bedroom," Ralph comments, seeming relieved. I wonder what he made of my room at Marryat Manor. He likely assumed I hadn't selected its contents as I had. That they weren't my things.

Vacuumed of atmosphere, this room feels like a place ghosts would not bother to haunt. Too white-radiator, too polyester-cushioned to backdrop my hallucinations. A safe place to absorb grief's early poisons.

Ralph collapses onto the bed. I wonder if he wants time alone, and I quietly sit in the armchair in the corner of the room. He opens his eyes, regards me. Those eyes, usually so blue, have mottled into dirty grey in the gloom.

"What are you doing over there?" he asks, apparently confused.

"Well, I thought you might want a nap. If you like, I can leave you alone, go outside?"

"What, in the pouring rain? Don't be ridiculous. Come over here." His words are more assertive than he sounds, but I relax a fraction and join him on the bed where we curl together as we did before.

"You know she did this on purpose," he splutters as if trying to laugh.

"Who?"

"Mum."

"Why? What did she do?"

"Died on purpose, knowing her. Wanting to get in the way of things. Of us." He gathers me closer, whispering into my hair, "It's not going to happen. Through thick and thin, we stay together."

"Through thick and thin," I repeat—*in sickness and in health*—before he sinks into sleep, with me following him shortly after.

A second dream catches me as I lose consciousness. I'm in a dark contained space, lying straight and only able to move my arms a few inches in either direction.

"I don't belong here," a voice snarls from the darkness. I can't tell where it's coming from.

"Hello?" I call out.

"You put me here, Harriet," the rasp continues.

"Who are you?" Panicking, I jam my arms up and to the sides of the hard surface, trying to break out of whatever's containing me. Small pinpricks of light spear my eyeballs intermittently.

"Struggling makes it worse," the voice rasps, followed by a cruel cackle.

Now another sound. Something dropping above me. Gently.

Muffled. The sound sand might make if you dropped it on top of something hollow. Again. Again.

"Where am I?" I whimper into the darkness.

"Where you belong, Harriet. Where you've always belonged."

Creeping dread, the kind you rarely experience outside of dreams, tells me I'm lying inside a coffin. Dirt drops on top of it, meaning, therefore, I must be in a grave. A burial. But I can't tell if I'm dead or alive.

"Margaret!" I scream. "Is that you? We've got to get out of here!"

I slam my fists as hard as I can into the lid of the coffin, desperate to be heard by whoever is throwing dirt on it.

"Too late for that, slut!" Margaret squawks. "You've taken it too far. You've killed us all, Harriet. All of us. Even Ralph. *Sum quod eris.* You will be what I am."

I wake with a start, relieved.

Although it's dark, I know I'm not trapped in a coffin. The air is different, my sigh meeting no resistance from above. But something's there, leering at me from the gloom.

Ralph? No. Another hallucination. I'm still sleeping. I must be.

The pale figure moves closer, leaning over me, inspecting me. They're crooked, question mark shaped, bent over, wheezing. Elderly.

Margaret?

No. Not Margaret. She's dead. She died.

I want to move but can't. I'm paralyzed, my panic nailing me to the bed in horizontal crucifixion. Others join the first pale figure, their shapes squirming, slithering through the darkness, making a maggoty mess of my vision.

My dementia. Those other brain waves. I squeeze my eyes shut. But the ghostly figures persist, superimposing themselves onto my retinas. They're after me, attacking me, short-circuiting my nerves and suffocating the breath from me. *Sum quod eris.*

A sudden light. Movement. Substantial, human.

Ralph. He's sitting up in bed, the bedside lamp switched on.

Yes. A dream. A hallucination, I rationalize away, even as I struggle to catch my breath, to move my limbs. I glance to the side at the clock and see it's 9 p.m. I've slept almost a night's worth, but feel wretched with the torment of my nightmare, my waking terror. The awful dreams have returned, piled on top of my increasingly disturbing hallucinations, now that Margaret has died. A part of me has fallen to the floor at an angle and broken. Like that crucifix from the séance.

"Hi," Ralph murmurs, scratching his jaw, apparently not noticing my disconcertment. "We've slept the whole afternoon and evening. Our body clocks will be a mess." He squints at the time. "Not that it matters, I suppose. Why do we have to keep a schedule?" He sounds forlorn, his voice scratchy. He rubs his tear-crusted eyes. "I'm starving."

"Me too," I admit, finally managing to sit up shakily. The plastic cheese sandwich didn't sit well in my stomach, and I feel hollowed out, as though I'm a different person since learning of Margaret's death. Tormented, scabbed. The kind of person who stays in cheap hotels and eats plastic cheese and dreams of death. I don't know how to be this new Harriet, what to eat or say. How to have sex, or even if I should. It seems too impossibly indulgent.

"I'll go out and find us something." Ralph moves to the window. "The rain has stopped."

He is finally thinking rationally, pragmatically, while my own emotions are slip-sliding around me. Sleep has settled Ralph but rattled me, shaken me up, leaving my fear to boil over like an unwatched saucepan on the cooker.

"That's good at least," I respond finally, sounding level. I need to hold it together for Ralph. "I think I might have a quick shower while you're gone."

I stand, and he hugs me as he leaves.

"We'll go out tomorrow," Ralph promises. "Things will be better then. They'll look better in the morning."

His posture says otherwise, hunched and defeated. His outward appearance mirrors mine inside. But Ralph doesn't pretend to be robust, that he can cope. That's the difference between our generations.

I wasn't expecting the clawfoot tub. I loved mine back at Haywood Hall. Its presence feels like a proffering of comfort from my old house, and so I run myself a bath. The porcelain is cold on my back despite the warmth of the water, but I relax into it, training my thoughts on my house.

Would the new owners notice if I slipped into Haywood Hall while they were away, took a bath, and absconded to an unused part of the house to let myself exist there for a time? The thought of being back at the place I called home before my dementia set in is both comforting and painful. Everything would be more manageable if I still had Haywood Hall, the warmth of its fireplaces, its views, its gentle light and elegant rounded edges.

But with a sudden jolt of pain, I realize Ralph wouldn't like Haywood Hall. It would be too old-fashioned for him, too traditional. I always thought I'd be buried there, or in the village churchyard alongside William. But Judith will let Marryat Manor bury me on their grounds.

Near Margaret, I think sadly. Who hates me.

Lying in the tub, there's nothing to stare at other than my body. As I take in the sight of my nakedness, I try to imagine a daemon within me. Dark and shadowy, extracting life from everything around me, using it to plump my collagen, brighten my eyes, straighten my spine. Two distinct brain waves. Yet I know it's just me here. Two diseases in my mind, yes, two versions of myself, the old Harriet and the new, but no other presence. No other consciousness.

I don't feel darkness within. I don't feel taken over. A medical marvel, but still myself, nonetheless. I refuse to believe I'm responsible for the deaths at Marryat Manor. I've never hurt anyone in my life—not physically, at least—let alone killed anyone.

Ralph returns sooner than I expect and brings with him the smell of hot oil and vinegar. He knocks gently at the bathroom door. "Harriet?"

"It's okay, you can come in," I call.

In the old days, I'd bathe in front of William, but covered in bubbles, so only the most elegant parts of my body would emerge, glistening with the sheen of bath oil. Even after intimacy between us fizzled, I still wanted to dazzle him, hold his attention. Now, I'm less worried about being seen with my skin slightly pink from the heat, the natural folds at my stomach, my nipples emerging from the surface like twin periscopes from a submarine. But it still seems indecent, being so alive, so vital, given all the death around me. Like eating an ice cream in front of the hungry.

"My word!" Ralph exclaims, his features reanimating at the sight of me. "I wasn't expecting this."

I smile with forced playfulness. "What did you get? Chips?"

He nods and sits down next to the bath on the closed toilet lid, a heavy mass of paper in hand. Chips. Plastic cheese. Polyester sheets. Damp, cheap Harriet. He picks up a chip and lowers it into my mouth as a bird might feed its chick. It's been years since I've eaten chip shop chips, and longer still since they've been eaten directly out of the paper. The salt and vinegar are so sharp they sting my mouth. More penance. This feels obscene, eating chips in the bath. Pig-like. As if I'm a slab of ham being boiled in the bath, served with vinegar. I am jarred, not quite of my body, not feeling quite inside my skin.

"I don't think I've ever had a better view during dinner," Ralph declares.

"I should hope not." I laugh lightly, glad to see the sight of me has cheered him a bit.

"You're so beautiful." Ralph sets the chips on the floor near the door and washes his hands before kneeling beside the bath and trailing a hand into the water.

"What are you doing?" I squirm a little as he traces up my thigh.

"Oh, nothing," he murmurs, his fingers dancing up and between my legs, while his eyes travel down the length of my body, taking all of it in before fixing to my own, watching the effect he has on me. It feels so wrong. Intense pleasure over intense pain. Incongruent. Like a bee sting at a birthday party. Still, I know he needs this—the reassurance of our connection, that this is worth the pain of not having said goodbye to his mother—even if he's not ready to be touched.

I force myself to relax, to not feel obscene. *Showing the boys your knickers again, Harriet.* I close my eyes against the inappropriateness of the situation, shutting out the harsh fluorescence of the bathroom light, but my mind betrays me, showing me Florence Marryat's portrait, then her in the maze, her fingers moving between her legs as Ralph's move between mine.

We need this, Harriet.

18

Ralph falls into a deep sleep a little before sunrise once the rain ceases its off-key hammering. I've slipped in and out of consciousness, my wakefulness entangled with the elderly recriminations of my dreams. Margaret has pervaded them all, thronged with her deceased séance chums, jabbing, scratching, screaming their condemnations at me in what must have been Latin. Funny how your subconscious can dream in unknown languages.

Though I tumbled, warring, out of sleep, I feel totally awake now that the sky is fully light, as Ralph sleeps on. Our room is small, musty with breathed-out grief, and I'm suddenly claustrophobic. Sorrow has wedged itself firmly in the center of us, welding us together, but vibrating with a different timbre. If our love were the sound of cymbals before, it's a bass drum now. Huge and self-important, but also low, thumping, migraine-inducing.

I long to find a different beat, if only for a while. To walk a little more lightly, out in the world, bearing only the weight of my own loss and not Ralph's too. To live fully in my own skin, for it to be *mine*, before I give myself to Ralph again.

For so long, I've wanted to be able to go wherever and do as ever I please. As I leave the guest house, part of me thinks this is the time to fulfill this fantasy. To immerse myself with the shoppers, visit boutiques and salons and be pampered, be flattered, admired, adored even. But having escaped and been slapped down by sadness, the idea has lost its dazzle. Feeling part of the hubbub no longer entices. Instead, I'm sucked out towards the sea, alone and undistracted.

The sun has emerged after the rain, though damp still rests slickly over the city, making the light appear that it's trying too hard, as though smiling through a hangover of bad weather. Buoyancy feels inappropriate, and yet my feet feel light in my boots today, my body supple, and I'm almost tempted to join the scowling joggers as they run the boardwalk, squinting from the sun's rays bouncing off the sea, the pavement's puddles, car windscreens, and hotel awnings.

For a moment, as I walk, a fluttering catches my eye, blue against blue.

A butterfly? No. Not in December. Must be a trick of the light. A bit of fluff caught in my eye.

I blink rapidly to dislodge the culprit and find myself focusing on the pier's giant Christmas tree ahead. The pier is silent at this time in the morning, its lights unblinking, the Ferris wheel asleep. Judith always wanted me to bring her here, but I hated amusements, finding them loud, base, and chip-grease dirty.

I think of the chips Ralph fed me last night, of being fingered in the bath, and suddenly I'm ashamed of myself. Of that younger Harriet, depriving my child of her fun because of my own self-importance, my "station."

What had old Tom said? That I was a snob.

I don't know why I find myself drifting onto the pier. Perhaps to signal my departure from my old ways of being. The woman who said "no" to Judith, who hired others to bake for school events, who felt deserving of affairs but only with men of a certain class. I feel dislocated from her. I'm not my younger self even though I look like her, but neither am I old Harriet.

I'm something unnatural, uncanny. I shouldn't be as I am. Nobody should.

The wind is brisk today.

I buy scalding hot coffee in a paper cup and protect my hands by tucking them inside my coat sleeves and gripping the cup through the fabric. None of the other stands or rides are open yet on the pier. Ill-advised swags of Christmas lights swing wildly between sideshow stands. A small team of workers are cleaning the area—emptying bins, sweeping the deck—and a scowling woman in an elf costume is busy putting out queue dividers leading to Santa's temporary and gaudy grotto.

A strange sense pervades, being here. Something like déjà vu. Being in a place designed for enjoyment but at the wrong time. It's not meant for me now. Still, I stay. Margaret would have hated this place, too, but not for the same class-snobbishness reasons. I'm sure she would have perceived the pier as vacuous—as the reason why the poor didn't have money to spend on books. But I'm also sure she would have taken Ralph as a boy if he'd asked.

One of the sideshows opens as I pass. A young woman with bad skin draped in black and purple chiffon emerges from a wagon or caravan, carrying a sign with elaborately painted letters that she opens out and places on the ground. A mystic of some sort. Now *that* would have tickled Margaret. If she were with me, she'd insist on having our fortunes read.

Come on, Harriet. Don't be a spoilsport. It'll be a blast.

I glance at the caravan's sign—Mystic Willa's Fortunes—and freeze. The sign is decorated with butterflies spinning around the words. Blue butterflies.

It's a sign! My friendly version of imagined Margaret giggles beside me.

The woman notices my staring.

"I'm open." She sounds beleaguered, her voice groggy, possibly hungover, and not in the least mystical. Given my latest disasters with the hallucinations, I find her fakery a relief. It's no more real than the ghosts in the haunted house amusement ride.

The ghosts in the trees.

Go on, imagined Margaret urges, and I suddenly feel I owe her this—a small concession—to make her smile from beyond the grave.

"Okay," I agree, and the woman brightens fractionally as she beckons me into the wagon.

Inside, the place needs cleaning. Purple velvet decorated with tiny mirrors drapes the walls; a red tasseled lamp illuminates the interior. The air smells vaguely of sex, and I wonder if this woman is also a lady of the night. In the middle of the wagon is a tiny table with an ornate crystal ball at its center and two chairs at either end.

The woman takes one of the seats, and I take the other. With no preamble, she hovers her hands over the surface of the ball and closes her eyes in apparent concentration. After a short moment, she opens them again. "It's five quid."

I nod, fishing inside my purse to retrieve the note and placing it on the table next to the ball. She nods her satisfaction, then closes her eyes once more. It's interesting, watching a charlatan, expecting nothing other than a performance. Her brow puckers slightly, as though troubled.

She's quite convincing. I'm impressed.

"You poor soul," the woman starts. "What you thought you'd gained, but no, what you've lost . . ."

My breath catches. How could she know what I've lost?

"You thought you had it all again, but no." Her eyes are still closed, deep in concentration, seemingly held hostage by a thought or remembering her script. Still, her words hit far too close to home. I *did* think I had it all, that I'd received everything I wanted. Then Margaret—

"You lost your keys, and you can't get in anymore," she says finally, opening her eyes. For a stunned moment, I almost laugh. Does she mean I've literally lost my keys? Or metaphorically? Either way, it doesn't make any sense. I open my mouth to ask the question, but she interrupts.

"Each reading is five pounds."

I stifle a sigh and retrieve a second note. She resumes her position once more.

"You have a little one at home," she says, and I smile. Standard charlatan line. "She'll be harmed once she knows there's two of you."

My pulse stumbles. Two of me?

She opens her eyes again and leans into me, saying urgently, "Look out for the other woman."

A great, theatrical gust of wind bangs the unsecured wooden door open behind me, but the woman's eyes remain locked on mine, unwavering, unblinking. In their depths I see the dreaded blackness clouds swirling—that absence, that void—reflected back at me, same as with Angel.

"It's already there!" She screams—long and sustained and mounting in pitch and terror. The vibration in the air summons a hundred blue butterflies, swarming thick in the space between us.

"No!" I jump to my feet, knocking my chair backwards as I bat the butterflies out of my face. What is happening? Margaret? Is this her doing? Or William? The fluttering mass continues to attack, the wings moving hummingbird-fast, razor-sharp like a hundred pairs of scissors slicing into my skin, cutting into my sanity.

I spin towards the door, fumbling blindly because the butterflies are so thick now that I can't see, can't breathe, desperate to leave. The brokenness of the woman's scream hastens my own sense of violent, decapitating horror. All these tiny blue blades. As I finally reach the door I'm faced directly with Margaret. Not as she was, but as she is now. Acrid, skin rotting, putrid smelling, glowering at me, nose to

nose, with her black, beady eyes. I'd only witnessed this vitriolic version of Margaret once before, when she berated me from her death bed.

She's not there! She's dead. This is only a hallucination. The dementia again.

I close my eyes and want to take a deep breath, but I can't risk
breathing her in. I know she's not real—she can't be—so I push forwards, expecting the hallucination to evaporate as I move through it.
But instead, I meet with the resistance of her body. How can she have
a body? I open my eyes to find Margaret still there, her withered, decaying flesh falling off her bones and into my hands like slow-roasted
pork. I wail.

"Look at what you've done!" Margaret hisses, and I finally shove
past her and out the door.

Outside, the mystic's wails are muffled by the wind, the seagulls,
and the thick walls of the wagon.

It's not possible. A hallucination. But her flesh, rotting!

My palms are empty now, but I can still feel the slippery, vile wetness between my fingers, still smell the sickly sweet scent of death. Bile
surges hot in my throat, and I run to the edge of the pier before vom-
iting up coffee and stomach acid into the sea.

I stay there, by the railings, for some time, resting my forehead
on the frozen metal and watching the sea churn below. What a stupid
thing to do, going there, given these hallucinations. But how could
I feel Margaret if she was just an illusion? And why did the mystic
scream when she looked at me? What did she see?

Something trickles down my cheek, and I swipe it away, expecting
vomit, but instead find blood. I turn my hands over and find dozens of
tiny cuts covering the backs of them. The butterfly swarm, their razor
wings—were they real?

The air fuzzes with black dots, and the sound of the sea and the
wind muffles.

* * *

I come around moments later and find myself sitting on the pier. I blink hard several times until the tilted world corrects itself. I'm breathing heavily, shaking, my nerves frazzled. I must get away from this place. The woman is still screaming from inside the wagon and people are starting to notice. I remember the black cloud darkness swirling in her eyes and am fearful that she will suffer the same fate as Angel. That, impossible as it seems, I've done something to her. To Angel. What if I've killed them?

Angel didn't scream. It's different.

Maybe she's just a deranged woman. Or perhaps this is how she cuts all her sessions short.

Slowly, behind the cover of the stalls, I climb to my feet, scrambling over the thick power lines straddling the pier floor behind the rides and stands, making my way back towards the road without being seen. There, I turn onto the first quiet side street I find, relieved to come across a tea shop just opening that I can disappear into. The kind of place old Harriet would have favored with its antique teapots and chintzy tablecloths.

Too late, I remember the blood on my hands and cheek and dread the expected wary looks from the staff, but the friendly round waitress just smiles as I enter and tells me to take a seat. I receive a couple of casual glances from customers, but nobody seems concerned by my appearance. I glance down at my hands again and find them completely clean. Not a drop of red. Creamy white, unlined, un-liver-spotted, un-creped skin. They're shaking, but uncut.

I exhale, collapsing into the nearest available chair. What happened in that wagon wasn't real. Just another hallucination. Margaret, the butterflies, even the woman screaming, for all I know, weren't real.

"Hello, would you like some tea?" The waitress appears with her pad.

"Yes, a full pot please. And cake. And sandwiches. Sausage rolls. I'm really rather hungry."

The waitress smiles, delighted. "I'll do you a selection."

I thank her and she leaves. She seems so happy. This overly round lady, not particularly attractive, working in a tea shop. How can she be happy? Looking like that, with that life? But people are, I realize. There are many people happy with their lot and grateful for it. Why wasn't that me? Why did I think I deserved so much more attention? Why wasn't it ever enough in my youth? Why on earth did I think I needed it again?

A couple of elderly ladies sit together at the next table, a teapot and teacups between them, each with a slice of sensible-looking cake. They're chattering, tittering, lit with the joy of gentle conversation with a friend. I'd had that, too, not long ago, with Margaret.

I had friendship. Real, honest friendship. Why ever didn't I prize that as I should?

Then I think of Ralph. This second chance has given me Ralph, and I can't possibly regret him. Can't regret my freedom, being of the world again rather than swept up into a dusty corner to die, forgotten. I can't regret any of my choices or wish away the benefits of this unknown condition of mine.

Only . . . *the others.*

With all these hallucinations, this guilt, does some part of me believe Dr. Phillips is right? Am I responsible for all those deaths? It seems impossible, and yet I wonder how long these questions will plague me, this guilt, the gruesome visions.

Am I now destined to see the dead for the rest of my days?

After tea, I return the way I came to the seafront, past the pier and back towards Kemptown. In the distance, sirens wail before I see the flashing lights. Police, an ambulance. I don't look. I know they're going to the pier, to the mystic. I can't think about it anymore. It's too much.

***

"Harriet," Ralph puffs as I enter the room. He looks relieved propped up against the headboard on the bed, closing the lid of a laptop I didn't know he'd brought. "You were gone such a long time."

It's not a complaint as such. Rather, an explanation of the sigh.

Somebody may have died, I want to tell him but don't. In fact, I don't seem to be able to say anything. He gets up and folds me into a hug, inhaling the scent of my hair. I'm still in shock, slightly shivering with shame, when he kisses me. I worry I might taste of vomit, but he quells my fears, saying, "You taste of chocolate."

"I ate cake," I respond flatly.

"I phoned the Manor," he says, not seeming to notice my mood. "Mum's funeral is Friday."

Friday. Four days away.

Will that be it? Will we return for the funeral and then tip back into our old lives? That's impossible for me now. Even if I wanted to return, I wouldn't be welcome, not after what Dr. Phillips believes I'm responsible for.

"I—It's been a difficult morning." Ralph sighs again, his eyes lowered as he pulls away. I notice new lines at the corners of his eyes, his mouth, more deeply hollowed than usual.

"I'm sorry I wasn't here," I tell him automatically. *I was out scaring someone to death. I was tearing flesh off your mother's corpse, being knifed by hundreds of butterflies, I was throwing up over the pier's railings then eating cake, as if nothing had happened. And now I'm pretending to you that I'm not going mad.*

"Harriet." Ralph turns to me, his expression soft, his gaze adoring, his beloved face ever so slightly weakened, tufted with grief. "About Mum—I want you to know. Her death hasn't spoiled us. I'm still so in love with you. I want all of you."

I feel a little woozy as he leans forwards to kiss me. A gentle kiss, a gesture.

This is real. If nothing else, this is real. Our connection.

We draw apart and he slips his fingers into my hair. This is true.

This love. Making love. Suddenly I want to do the only thing I know is real. No, I don't *want* it, I *need* it, *need* him, desperately, urgently.

I push Ralph back towards the bed, and he unbuttons his shirt as I slip my shoes, tights, and underwear off before reaching over to unbutton his trousers. I kneel on the floor in front of him, and he groans, hardening in my mouth in moments. This is real. Ralph is real. This flesh—his flesh—is real. Not . . .

I refuse to think of Margaret when on my knees in front of Ralph, glancing up at him as I use my lips and tongue, catching his eye. His gaze feels dangerous now, somehow electric. He sees something in me as I watch him, something dark, and his expression changes, reflecting that same darkness.

Not him too!

I close my eyes and stand, forcing him onto his back before climbing on top of him and lowering myself down on his erection. He groans so loudly as he moves under me impatiently. I ride him—his flesh and blood realness inside me—lifting the skirt of my dress so he can see everything underneath, watching as I swallow him up. He looks up at my face, lustful, determined.

"This is real," I pant.

"This *is* real," he agrees as I continue to twist my hips up and down. *This is real. This!*

"I'm never going to have sex with anyone else ever again," he claims between groans. "It will never be this good with anyone else."

I stop moving and lean down and cover his mouth with mine. A deep, wet kiss, our tongues tangling, each owning the other. He bucks his hips to spur my movement again, and I comply, grinding down harder, moving faster until I sense the clenching of his abdomen, the convulsing, and I let go too.

"This is real!" I'm too loud for a guest house this size, too unwound, but I don't care. "Real!"

It feels like the most alive thing I can possibly experience.

19

I cling to Ralph in fear of what I'll see when I look in any other direction. I wish we could leave Brighton. I feel as though I've destroyed this place within twenty-four hours of arriving. Destroyed my happy memories along with the present.

Marryat Manor seems like a prison I was confined to a hundred years ago, in another lifetime, not my home as of a few days ago. It might have been a place I spent time as a child, visiting an elderly relative, bored, then released into the garden among the topiaries and butterflies. Someone else's gaol. An old woman's confinement.

But Friday is our destination. The point when we're required to shift, behave differently, face those we don't wish to face, acknowledge and mourn the absent.

Until then, Ralph and I will inch further inside each other's skin, massaging affirmation into each other's souls, finding life as grief gnaws at us. I remember it eating me when I lost William. I never grieved for either of my own parents to the same extent, their loss feeling like a release from some indefinable kind of entrapment. Judgement, expectation.

Ralph has gone grey quite rapidly before my eyes—his pallor, his hair, even his eyes have lost their brilliance, like the sea on a darkly overcast day. Sunken, as Gulliver might have done when, on his travels, he was fastened down by a thousand ropes of a thousand tiny, fearful people. Pulled at. Held.

And yet I love him all the same. I'm drawn to him regardless of his discoloring, his fading. Because inside me he reinflates, his inner flame burning hotter than ever, still looking at me with such desperate hunger it's impossible our union is anything other than intended by a higher entity, though neither of us believe in such a thing.

It feels important he's inside me alongside whatever else is there—the epilepsy, dementia Harriet, perhaps something more, I concede now. The thing Angel saw. Willa too.

I feel as though every time Ralph is inside me, he's countering any negativity, filling me with love and light, replenishing what may have been emptied by darkness. It's addictive, this medicine of Ralph. I find I want more and more of him as his strength so rapidly depletes.

My outward appearance continues to hold steady, as if it has reached its zenith of beauty and resplendence at age thirty-two, and that is where it will remain. My reflection in the mirror shines luminously as though contemptuous of the idea of death. Nothing sullies the perfect elegance of my features, the ripening of my body, warm and demanding attention, insensitive to Ralph's degradation. Physically, he's become a worn statue of the man I love rather than someone as alive and as feeling as I.

Let me be stone too. Let us match.

At least Ralph does not seem to notice my trembling. My subconscious has finally conceded to panic—too many dreams and hallucinations, blurring the edges of what is real.

William. Butterflies. Margaret's flesh.

I'm terrified of what will happen next. But my surface remains more lit than ever. I wonder how my appearance can counter my turmoil to this extent when Ralph's is the epitome of his.

I take another bath, unable to stand in the shower, hoping to wash away the fresh horror that invaded last night's sleep.

Me in my coffin, filled with flying knives. Nowhere to run or hide. Only entrapment.

I examine my hands again, shaking, quavering.

Without my accord, my right hand suddenly moves between my legs, flutters there. No. I don't want this. I don't want to touch myself. Alarmed, with a huge mental effort, I move it to rest on my thigh, but the hand goes right back again on its own, unnatural, lightning fast. This is not me! I'm not doing this! The fingers are moving again, touching, rubbing, thrusting. But I'm not aroused, and it's painful. Heart threatening to pound out of my chest, I struggle to breathe even as I catch sight of myself in the full-length mirror affixed to the back of the bathroom door.

I glimpse a face, not mine. A woman, I think. Dark haired. Margaret? Florence?

But as I try to study it more closely, it disappears, only returning when I slide my eyes away, laughing in my peripheral vision as my fingers now stab aggressively at my vagina of their own volition. Raped by my own body, as if it's reacting to my feelings of betrayal. As if it knows the shape of my regret and is punishing me for it. I know this at a deep, primordial level.

No! Please, I don't want this!

I struggle against my own extremities. Water flies out of the bath, flicking back in my face, as I slide in the tub, trying to escape.

"Harriet, it's Marryat Manor. They're on the television! A news report," Ralph calls through the door and finally my hand stops. It's mine again. The face has gone. The bathroom has straightened itself.

Was this another hallucination? Did I fall back asleep for a moment?

No. I examine my fingers and see blood. Real blood. Not the imagined kind from the pier. The water is tinged pink with it as well. I've injured myself, perhaps seriously.

Wait. Marryat Manor? On the news?

"What's happening?" I ask, my face hot with tears, flushed with adrenaline.

There's a pause. Did he hear the shiver in my breath? A surge of pain shoots its way through my uterus, menstruation making itself known. The cause of the blood, I realize. Not an injury.

"Come and see this," Ralph responds, his voice sounding strange. Hesitant, concerned.

"Be right there," I call through the door before getting out of the tub. Inside, I'm as shaky as Bambi learning to stand, but my body rises so easily, as though it's laughing at me. I towel down then wrap it around myself, entering the bedroom to see Ralph sitting on the bed in front of the television, transfixed.

"The Manor has been open as a residential home for the past nine years," the newscaster reads over footage of the grounds.

"What's going on?" I frown.

"Watch." Ralph points at the screen.

"It's one of the most exclusive residencies in the UK and claims exceptional care. This is the first time scandal has touched the independently owned business." More footage. What looks to be a sheet-covered corpse being loaded into an ambulance.

"Scandal? What's this about? Angel?"

Ralph gives me a confused look, not understanding.

"The man who died right before we left," I remind him.

"What? No! No, all the deaths."

All the deaths. A shot of another ambulance, another corpse.

"Twenty-five residents have died in the last two weeks," the newscaster continues. I splutter a cough. *Twenty-five?* Just the other day when Dr. Phillips was here, he'd said it was fifteen! Now another ten? A new shot shows a room of the Manor I don't recognize. A large low-ceilinged dark space with a row of coffins surrounded by people in dark suits, who I assume must be the undertakers.

"Where is that?" Those can't be the coffins for Marryat residents! Why would they show such a thing? Ice threads its way through my veins as I remember my dreams. Coffins.

"This is the basement of Marryat Manor," the BBC explains. "With mortuaries overrun after the traffic incident on the Hog's Back, the deceased are being kept here, given the low temperatures, ahead of funerals this week." He's referring to the accident on the road to Guildford we'd heard about on the radio on the way here. Black ice. A pileup. Awful. Mainly young people killed. Young people and parents of young children. "With burial grounds on-site, Marryat Manor will be conducting group funerals for the families, who will no doubt be asking a lot of questions about the sudden acceleration of deaths at the Manor."

Shots of the graveyard and the chapel merge onto the screen. I shiver at the sight of them. Coffins again. The camera passes over the row once more, each one containing a soul I have known. One must be Margaret.

"Batch funerals. And there'll be an investigation," I say, a quiver in my voice.

Without moving his eyes from the screen, Ralph covers my hand with his.

Then an older-version Imani appears on the screen, half-shivering in front of the building and wearing a black suit jacket that can't be hers—I've never seen her in anything like it. I gawp at her altered appearance. She's aged at least twenty years in just a few days.

"It's not just the unfortunate passing of so many residents," she tells the interviewer, her words far more carefully enunciated than usual. "Everyone here has rapidly aged in a matter of only a few weeks, and most are sick, including the staff." She sounds desperate, plaintive. "We passed an environmental health inspection. And residents all have very different illnesses and reasons for passing. The autopsies carried out so far show nothing alarming or untoward. Every resident has died of natural causes." She sounds as though she's about to cry, fighting to keep her characteristic control. "But they've all come at once. And it's very overwhelming."

"While the police have been contacted, it's unclear when or if an investigation will be started, despite multiple families increasing demands for one," the newsreader concludes.

Judith. I should call her. Let her know I'm okay. She'll be worried. I remember how ill she was last time I saw her. Oh, God, have I hurt my daughter too?

"I can't, Ralph. It's too horrible!" I bury my face against his shoulder, desperate for any explanation for these deaths that isn't my fault. "Do you remember Harold Shipman?"

Harold Shipman was a doctor who, over the course of many years, killed his elderly patients, until his eventual discovery, incarceration, and suicide. He was thought to have killed over two hundred and fifty people, making him the most prolific serial killer in Britain's history. A sickeningly evil man.

Ralph's expression shifts to disbelief. "No, Harriet. No. I can't believe it."

I straighten, considering the option more seriously. "Wouldn't the pieces fit?"

"Yes, but . . . not Dr. Phillips."

"They're all his patients—"

"But that doesn't explain the rapid aging of everyone at the home," Ralph cuts in. "All the staff, including him. And if it were true, somehow, then why wouldn't he kill you too?"

I concede the point with a sideways nod. Because I'm a medical marvel? Because I'm possessed by a daemon? No. I shake that ridiculousness away even as my mind returns to the unfamiliar face in the mirror, the hand I could not control in the tub.

"If Dr. Phillips is behind this, and he's doing something that *is* affecting staff, then he's doing it to himself too. You saw him on Sunday. He looks at least twenty years older. And then . . ." Ralph trails off, looking down.

"What?" I prompt.

"There's me."

"You?"

"Look at me, Harriet." He spreads his arms out, inviting an examination.

"You're beautiful," I say pathetically, but for once he doesn't smile at the compliment.

"I've changed a lot in the last week."

"Grief will do that." I can't bring myself to acknowledge what he's getting at.

He shakes his head. "Not this! I've lost half my hair. I'm entirely grey. None of my clothes fit. Luckily, parts of me still work." He looks down at his crotch. For a moment I think he's going to unbutton his trousers, but instead he retrieves his mobile phone from his pocket and swipes the screen a few times before turning it for me to see. "This is us, less than a week ago."

The image shows the two of us, lying in bed, my hair still threaded with grey and waving into old-fashioned curls, and Ralph, dark-haired, with a sprinkle of grey at his temples and barely any fine lines at the corners of his eyes. In the photo, I appear only a little older than him. Whereas now, we're separated by far more than a decade. He's right, he's aged ten, fifteen years in less than a week, while I've gone the opposite direction. The changes are stark, and I'm as alarmed by them as he obviously is.

I shake my head, desperate for another answer, for another explanation than the one all the evidence points to—Margaret's findings in the diaries and journal, Dr. Phillips's words, my own instincts, however reluctant. I don't want to believe it. I can't believe it. Because if it's true, then I'm the one killing people. I'm the evil.

"Okay, okay," I say, getting up to pace, needing to burn off my restless energy before I go insane. "I agree, there's a change. But perhaps he did something to you, too, Ralph, while you were at Marryat Manor? Or maybe he did something to both of us—*poisoned* us—when he came to see us at the hotel. But this new condition of mine somehow protects me from its effects."

It sounds like nonsense, a last-ditch effort of the guilty to provide an alternative explanation.

"So, you really believe Dr. Phillips is a serial killer?" Ralph asks dubiously.

I picture the man in his lab coat with his crucifix, his genuine, nerdish warmth, the overenthusiastic joking with Margaret, our conversation over the snowman. I sigh. "I . . . don't know. I just don't know how else to explain everything that's going on. And I don't understand why Dr. Phillips hasn't called in help from outside. This is a highly uncommon situation. And if it's not him behind it all, it could be someone else. Angel's death was unexplained." I regard Ralph. "That doesn't explain you, but—"

Nor does it explain the mystic at the pier.

I push on anyway, my questions becoming more desperate by the minute. "And as far as all this daemon nonsense your mother and Dr. Phillips talked about . . . I mean, if *I* were the problem, people wouldn't be continuing to age with me not there, would they?"

Ralph goes quiet for a moment before shrugging. "Well, we don't know how it works, how long someone needs to be exposed before the changes kick in. Perhaps once is enough to set off the aging cycle, then it continues after you're gone."

His words sting because his theory means he's thought about it.

My eyes prickle, and my head aches. "I don't know, it's all so absurd. Impossible."

"Though it would also explain why Phillips isn't asking for outside help."

"Why?"

"Well, firstly, no one would believe him. Secondly, even if they did, there's nothing they could do to stop it. And it would call his medical judgement, his competence, into question."

Throat thick, I slump down into a chair in the corner and cover my face with my hands. It can't be true. I simply can't be responsible for all this. Yes, I made mistakes in my past. I was selfish, self-centered, some would say downright bitchy and amoral. But a killer? A daemon? No. No. This cannot be happening. This cannot be real. I pinch my arms hard enough to bruise, hoping to wake myself up from this awful, unending nightmare.

"Hey, hey," Ralph says, rushing over to take my hands as he kneels beside me. His smile is kindness personified and my heart shatters. "It's not true, Harriet. Of course, it's not."

But now that the seed has germinated inside me, it refuses to die. I'm killing him. Killing this man that I love simply by being with him. "I don't want to hurt you anymore, Ralph."

My words sound scorched-dry, despondent, even to my own ears.

He looks at me carefully, as though he's realized something I haven't. An expression I've never seen on him before. "If, in the smallest chance, it *is* true, then I would gladly die for our time together. Even if it's only a week, it's the happiest of weeks. I would gladly sacrifice everything for you."

Ralph's words are both the purest declaration of love and the most wounding thing he could ever say to me. He's accepted the possibility of my being possessed by a daemon. But loves me all the same, even if it—even if *I*—kill him.

Dying for love.

It's something most of us claim we would do at some point in our lives. We'd die for a spouse, a child, even someone else's child. We usually say it in the context of saving another person, not spending a week with a lover.

Rarely do we get the opportunity to be love's foolhardy heroes.

20

I'm lost in a maze of coffins, stacked on top of each other to make high walls of black wood. An orderly, motionless forest with beveled edges. It's pitch black, the only light emerging from a wisp of a crescent moon hung apologetically above. Still, it catches on the brass handles so I can follow a path as I frantically search for a way out, or possibly a rescue. My legs feel wet as I run, and I realize I'm bleeding.

Soon, I notice labels on the coffins. Shipping labels. I make out the names but not the addresses and recognize some as residents of Marryat Manor. I scale the walls of coffins, my toes barely finding purchase on the handles, reading labels as I go, until finally, I find the one I seek. Margaret's. Hers is near the top of a stack at least twelve coffins high.

"Margaret?" I call. "Can you hear me? Do you need help?"

Nothing. Then I see the label of the coffin above. No! God, no!

"Ralph! Ralph!" I wail. "Are you in there?"

Desperately, I try to read his address only to see *Sum quod eris*.

My eye catches the coffin above—with my own name on it! Then these must be empty coffins. I'm not in there. I'm alive! Alive, but bleeding. Bleeding over my legs.

"Ralph! Ralph!" I continue to wail. "Are you there? You can't be dead!"

Then suddenly, as I'm bellowing directly at his coffin, I'm not standing, I'm lying down in blackness, my body hot, my legs wet. I hear muffled laughter echoing, a few jeering shouts. The kind of noises youths make on a night out as they traipse around with chips or kebabs.

Am I in a coffin now too?

No. I'm awake, I realize. I was dreaming. Dreaming as images from the news reports flash before my eyes. Batch funerals. Graveyards. The chapel. I sob, shiver. My legs are not wet now, just cold. I'd kicked the covers off in my sleep, sweating.

I take a few deep breaths, then turn in the bed to squint at Ralph's soft, sleeping shape, his body curled away from me, gently snoring. He's alive. The glowing face of the alarm clock beyond him suggests it's a little after midnight.

I haul myself from bed and go to the bathroom, drinking water and peering sleepily at my reflection, expecting to look abysmal. But no. My skin is still glowing and supple, my hair shining, the crossbow of my lips full, luscious even.

I wake up a little more as I brush my teeth, inspecting the white of my teeth, the whites of my eyes, the length of my eyelashes. Afterward, I lift my nightgown to inspect my breasts—high and round, the nipples pink and soft. This is what I wanted. But I find no pleasure in looking at myself now.

I'm disturbed by my youthfulness, knowing it's not natural. This body, this exterior, is not my own. While I hate admitting it, deep down inside I know the truth of my dreams, my hallucinations. I'm responsible for those coffins—all those lives withering into dust inside budget wooden shells. I did this. This body of mine, whatever it's housing. I am not new Harriet, I am the same old Harriet I always was, still confused, still victim of others' whims and commands. I'm just wrapped in a different skin now. Trapped. Not released, not freed. Hostage of a malevolent daemon hell-bent on destroying everything around me to survive.

Despite my distress, my face smiles back at me in the mirror. A jagged, sharp smile, made to maim and injure, not to please. My body acting of its own accord again. Betraying me with its cruelty. I can no longer trust myself. I wonder if I ever could.

I shuffle back to bed and curl myself around Ralph's body. He feels colder, heavy, defeated. I stroke his hair, feeling it tangle around my fingers, realizing the strands are falling out in my hands. Not just a little, but great clumps. Horrified, I take the hair into the bathroom and put it in the wastepaper basket. Did I do that? What will Ralph wake up to this morning?

Sleep evades me, my heart thumping with something close to panic. We're swapping years overnight.

Shouts on the street below continue through the early hours. Why do young people feel the need to make their presence known when they're out in the evenings? Do they think they're proving their existence, asserting their superiority for having the kind of life that allows them these freedoms at 2 a.m. on a Thursday? Miserably, I realize that's what I've been doing. Shouting, boastful of my freedoms. At the expense of . . .

I can barely wrap my head around what I've taken.

I wake to find Ralph sitting on the edge of the bed, looking at me. In the bright morning light, he's just a blurred silhouette at first.

"Ralph?" I yawn. "Are you okay?"

"I'm sorry, Harriet," he says gently, his head hung. He sounds almost ashamed.

"Why?" I ask, startled as I sit up to see him more closely. "What is it?"

He doesn't answer, waiting. He's quite different from yesterday. His hair is now a thin cuff of grey, like a squashed airplane pillow. His cheeks are hollow, and flesh has collected at his jowls. His posture curls forwards, as if he's embarrassed. His shoulders, once firm and strong, now slope as dramatically as an A-frame. He looks like a person whose air has been let out.

"Look at me!" he says, gesturing towards himself.

Remembering my own dejection at my very gradual decline at the end of what was objectively a full and happy life, my heart breaks for him. Ralph was so vital only a week ago. He's now been wiped of youth.

This shiny shell of mine did this. The daemon possessing my body, stealing my control.

It's attacking my Ralph. My poor, tender-hearted Ralph.

"Don't apologize to me," I demand, leaning forwards and resting my chin on his shoulder. "None of this is your fault. And I love you for you, Ralph. You're still everything to me. Still beautiful." I draw back and meet his gaze. "Still those wondrous eyes."

He gives me the smallest of grateful smiles.

"Still that lovely smile." I beam at him.

"But look at you!" he cries. "You're a literal goddess now. Not the kind of woman who should be with a man like me." A sob catches in his throat. Strange, this sensitivity on a man of his age. He's leap-frogged generations into a seventy-five-year-old's shoes, and they don't quite fit him.

My youthfulness doesn't fit me either. It's as though we've swapped clothes and look absurd.

"Listen to me," I say, holding his gaze with mine. "It's you and me. You and me! We're meant for each other, regardless of age, or how we look." I cling to this because if it isn't true, there's nothing else left.

"I'm going to die, Harriet."

"No." I stand and take his hands, drawing him to his feet in front of me.

"I am. I'm aging a decade a day, practically. I'm going to die." Tears race down his face, splashing onto his bare, sun-spotted arms.

"No. We're going to sort this out. We'll go to Dr. Phillips, get him to help us. He's read the same diaries and journals as your mother. He'll know what to do." My tone is certain, authoritative, absent of hesitance or apology, even though I have no idea if Dr. Phillips can help or not. Perhaps we're beyond help now.

"He doesn't know what to do." Ralph's voice has gone deep and gravelly, laced with despair.

"Then we'll find someone who does. There must be someone who knows what to do." We both know it's a lie, but Ralph seems grateful anyway. "Either way, we'll find a solution."

"God, I don't want to go back there." Ralph sniffs. "We have to, for Mum's funeral, obviously, but . . ."

"I know," I finish for him, and he nods. I'd rather be anywhere other than Marryat Manor too. I can't face what I've done, but I must. I must end this, once and for all. "But we must be there for your mother, and we must find a cure."

I'm not sure I ever really understood the word "sorrow" until now, seeing Ralph, so full of love but quite collapsed. I can't let this man go. I must find a way to save him, as I neglected to save Margaret.

"But today, we live for today," I tell him. "We're going to have today to ourselves. Tomorrow, we'll deal with it."

"Yes," Ralph says quietly. "Thank you, Harriet."

As we walk along the seafront, the wind whipping at my hair and the cold air wet and salty, I have a brief memory of William and myself at my age doing the same, laughing and chattering, linked arm in arm. Even just a few short years into our marriage, the early lustful excitement had dissipated, but friendship overtook it, and we focused on building our life together.

Ralph and I have no such promise. Our future is uncertain. We have only today.

He holds my hand, his grip a little weaker than usual, his expression reflective. "What will you do? If I die, what will you do then?"

"I'm not going to let that happen," I say adamantly.

"But if it does?" Ralph insists.

I pause, tipping my mind into places it doesn't want to go. "I don't know," I say truthfully. "I suppose there would still be a lot to sort out. More to understand. I should go back to the specialists at the hospital."

I imagine my dream from the night before again. A maze of coffins, my name on the label.

Honestly, if Ralph is dead, I do not want to live. But would the thing inside me let me die? I remember the cruel smile on my face in the mirror, the way my own hand raped me in the tub.

This evil inside me—it does not want to die. It wants to live, to thrive, by feeding on the lives of others. Is that what happened to Florence Marryat, turning her into a rabid, feral version of herself, sucking the energy from those around her until there was nothing left?

Vertigo engulfs me, and I clutch Ralph's arm to keep steady. He frowns down at me, looking concerned. Then I catch sight of the pier, the lit Ferris wheel moving lethargically, upbeat Christmas music bouncing, discordant, off the shallow grey waves. Did the mystic—Willa—die? Did this thing inside me frighten her to death as it did Angel? They both witnessed the daemon firsthand, that swirling darkness overtaking their gaze, their souls.

I can't think of them now. A few hours of normal. That's all I want.

"Let's get away from that ghastly pier, please," I tell Ralph.

He looks surprised. "You don't like it? I loved it as a child. Mum used to—"

"I've just got a bit of a headache," I say, pulling him away.

We visit a different tearoom and order tea and cakes. The normalcy of sitting down at a table in a warm, buttermilk-painted square room helps me recover a little, its homeliness soothing. It seems impossible for a daemon to exist in this world of poppyseed cake and cucumber sandwiches.

The waitress who takes our order is overly cheerful and talkative.

"Oh, isn't it nice? Taking your daughter out for a treat?" she asks Ralph. I freeze while he colors.

"Something like that," he offers, avoiding her eye with a fake smile.

"You feeling Christmassy yet? We've got mince pies and Christmas cake. I don't like Christmas cake myself, but I know the old folk like it." She looks at Ralph expectantly. She's barely younger than him in chronological years, and I can see he's struggling to calibrate.

"I think not today, thank you very much," I answer for him. If our situation weren't so horrifying, I'd make a joke, call him Daddy.

"I enjoyed this morning," I tell him instead once I've ordered for us and the waitress has gone, my voice artificial, upbeat. "The walk along the seafront."

It's a transparent move, drawing attention to our romantic connection to distract him from the waitress's insensitive mistake, and Ralph almost smiles, looking nearly grateful. He seems tired, washed out, even more so than a few hours ago when we woke. It occurs to me, given the rate of his aging, we might not be able to have intercourse again, that by the time I've stopped bleeding, he might be too old to manage. That brief part of life will be closed off again. I mourn the loss of it, but only momentarily. In the scheme of things, in the wake of the death I can't yet comprehend, it's meaningless.

We're surrounded by pairs of mainly women, smiling festively, chatting, laughing.

I imagine they're pausing their Christmas shopping by treating themselves or each other. I notice a couple of ladies in their fifties exchanging Christmas presents with elaborate shiny wrappings, opening them and laughing at whatever is inside. I think of the book I purchased for Margaret, the chocolates that were her favorite, and how much I was looking forward to giving them to her. She once gave me a knitted carrot and beetroot she'd found at a craft fair as a joke present, and how we both laughed at its obscurity.

I'm assaulted now by the emotion of missing her, my cheerful, intelligent, witty friend, so watchful and astute. The most painful part, though, is that at the time of her death, she despised me for loving her son.

I miss Judith, too, and the dreamy little girl she used to be. Has this thing inside me made her unwell? Dr. Phillips and the other staff and residents continued to age once away from me, and perhaps the same is true for my daughter. And what of poor Molly?

Everyone I love is crumbling away, leaving me with nothing. And it's all my fault.

Ralph declared he would be prepared to die for us to spend the little time he may have left together. He made his choice. But what about everyone else? Everyone around me? What if I'm making the other people in this tea shop ill right now? Do I remove myself from others to stop hurting them? Become a hermit? Even then, how could I be sure something about me wasn't continuing to make them age? Is there any way to stop the evil I've unleashed upon the world?

The sheet-covered corpses appear in my mind again, the maze of coffins. The number grows and grows until it takes over the Manor grounds . . . the nearby countryside . . . the world. Every moment I'm alive, another is added.

I try to shrug off my paranoia. This can't be happening. It *can't*. It's too fantastical. Dr. Phillips will have answers tomorrow, he'll know what to do. Otherwise, all is lost.

Ralph and I don't fit together anymore, our bouts of energy and surges of affection syncopated, missing each other. If our feelings were colors, they'd make an uncoordinated palette. Too soon, we're back in bed, my lithe limbs crosshatching his stiff and spent ones. I'm too aware of our physical differences and feel like a fraud because I am *not* a young woman. I am not this. This shell is *other*; it is evil.

I console myself by thinking it's the inside me Ralph loves, that he was still drawn to me when I looked much, much older. And I love him now for it. Our connection was apparent from the very beginning. My changed appearance simply allowed us an avenue to come together.

"I love you, Raucous Ralph," I whisper in his ear, emotions tangling up my words. "This last week has been the best of my life."

"Me too. I love you, Magic Harriet."

21

There are no news reporters at Marryat Manor when we arrive, but three hearses are parked outside. Each already contains a coffin, but I notice a second one is being loaded into one of the vehicles. They only need to travel a short distance, destined for the burial grounds at the back of the property next to the chapel. I wonder now if the reason the chapel and cemetery have always made me uncomfortable was because part of me knew something more horrific than my own burial was to come.

I swallow the bile bubbling up my throat. I don't want to be back at the Manor. This place, exactly as I remember, wet against a backdrop of iron clouds, seems so ominous. I know inside are more dying people. Sickness and necrosis and withering. Stiff. Rotting. Blackness.

"I wonder which one is Mum's," Ralph says as we park, his voice throttled with pain. We eliminate the smaller hearse with the lone coffin inside as I see a floral arrangement laid out with the word "Mum" resting on top of it. I helped Ralph choose Margaret's flowers and those are not them.

A cluster of people I've not seen before—family members or new residents, perhaps—watch from the entrance beneath a fairy-lit swag of greenery that already looks bedraggled, as though Christmas has passed by early. They're all wearing rather inappropriately trendy outdoor clothes and footwear more suited to young people.

"Is that you, Harriet?" one of them calls to me as we make our way inside. A voice I recognize. Scottish.

"Alyson?" I can't hide my shock at her appearance. She's significantly older now, in her late fifties maybe. She's aged in that unfortunate way where skin bags at the jowls and drags at the under-eye to give the impression of always being distraught. I realize that, given her rapid aging, she's unlikely to be able to have children. She's returning my look of surprise.

"You look so different, Harriet!" she splutters, scowling with obvious astonishment.

Other staff members are there as well. Imani, appearing even older now than she had on the news, her once-dark hair completely grey, her body heavy set and stooped. Another couple of orderlies, both aged two or three decades. I'm embarrassed, disconcerted even, given the reversal of my aging. I feel as though I'm living in a mansion among paupers, or every house in the village was flooded other than my own.

"I . . . I don't know . . . what to say." My words stumble over each other. "I-I'm . . . sorry."

Ralph takes my arm and moves me on. This isn't the time for such a conversation. It doesn't fit the scene, the mood. He's right. It seems disrespectful to discuss my part in all this death in front of the deceased.

I am wretched with grief, shame, and fear—no, complete abhorrence—over this situation. And slathered with an extra layer of misery induced by the frigid wind, the sleet, and charcoal, heavy-hanging sky.

Ralph woke having aged further still, crumbling, fading away. I'd expected it but still felt unprepared.

What he mistook for feathers having escaped his pillow was his remaining hair resting beneath his head. His skin now looks the same as mine before this nightmare started, like fabric when the elastic that holds the shape of a garment has disintegrated, leaving it useless and crumpled, obsolete. His bleary eyes are framed with a mass of lines and cupped with dark hollows, his teeth yellowed and slightly crooked.

He reminds me of my father in his late seventies, not portly but upholstered, soft and slightly curved forwards, as though he might topple at any point. Ralph's clothes barely fit him now, too tight across his middle, too sophisticated on his slightly wobbly, hesitant frame. He is unused to his new skin, and though unresentful, dragged down by the injustice of his predicament.

I got ready quickly this morning, taking no time to examine myself, avoiding makeup entirely. My reflection scares me—this shadow self that controls my body, that has entrapped me, possessed me.

And yet my appearance remains unchanged, locked in at optimum youth and beauty, despite all the ruination and decay around me. The *cause* of it all.

I wish I hadn't been recognized upon our arrival, that I'd pretended to be a younger relative who'd never visited Marryat Manor before. Ralph could have presented himself as Margaret's brother. But it's too late now, and—of course—Dr. Phillips would know the truth.

For the first time I wonder if I should have come at all. My being here can only do more damage—the murderer visiting the scene of the crime.

But where else am I to go? Especially if I want to stop this, once and for all.

Dr. Phillips will have the answers. We just need to find him. I wander into the drawing room, but nobody is there. The television room? Nobody. The dining room? Nobody. The air is still throughout the Manor, undisturbed, these once-vibrant spaces forgotten.

"Everyone must be getting ready for the funerals," I say, and Ralph murmurs his weary agreement.

There is movement from the stairs, and we emerge back out into the lobby to watch as Dr. Phillips supervises two orderlies carrying a sheet-wrapped cadaver down the stairs on a stretcher.

My revulsion is involuntary. The fact this thing inside me—this second set of brain waves—is responsible for this loss of life, sickens me. As does the somber indifference of the men transporting the body, a blandness born of having performed the same act many times recently. It looks easy for them now, their cargo light, the body wasted away to nothing but bones.

Dr. Phillips notices my discomfort and moves in beside me to say, "It's less shocking to those of us who see this several times a day." He's walking much more slowly now, using a cane for support, appearing maybe sixty or sixty-five. "I didn't think you'd return, Harriet."

"Well, Margaret . . ." I say, the words slipping out before I register that I'll say them. "And I need to speak with you about what to do."

Dr. Phillips glances at Ralph, then exhales audibly. He knows what I'm asking. "It will have to wait until later."

The unbearable knot of tension and dread inside me pulls tighter, ready to break.

"I don't think we have much time." I hate the pleading note to my voice but can't stop it. The anguish I've been holding like a tightly wound ball of wool is unraveling rapidly. It's the now-very-tangible confirmation of everything the news report showed about the state of this place. It's the hair on Ralph's pillow, the look of Alyson, the multiple hearses, the absence of residents. It's Angel and Willa, and butterflies, and my hand, my smile, possessed!

"You don't." Dr. Phillips looks at Ralph again. "He doesn't. But then, no one here does. I'm dealing with the last remaining survivors. Palliative care, you understand." There's a tightening to his mouth, a slight hardness to his gaze, as if he wants to be furious with me but lacks the energy. He withdraws as tears well in my eyes. Dr. Phillips is my last resort. If he won't help me, then . . .

"I'm sorry, this is all my fault," I offer feebly, quite unlike myself.

"I don't blame you, Harriet." Dr. Phillips clears his throat. "You are also a victim here. But you're right. We must deal with this. Come back after the funerals, and we'll talk."

Yes. The funerals. To say goodbye to poor Margaret, whom this thing inside me killed.

***

We take one of the many black umbrellas stored in the lobby's stands and watch the hearses leave before joining the stunted line of mourners behind them, bookended by the beleaguered remaining staff.

The walk to the chapel is short, but the path is ungainly and narrow, muddying easily. It's edged with gorse bushes that for some reason haven't been cut back and seem compelled to snag us as we make our way past them, little pinprick reminders to feel wounded, to be deserving of assault. The sleet whips us, and the tree limbs creak, giving in to the bullying wind.

"Ghastly weather," I comment to a fellow mourner walking with us, needing to break the silence and puncture the bleakness. I recognize her as the daughter of Irene, a resident who must be another of the five. Fortunately, she doesn't recognize me.

"It is," she agrees. "Ghastly day all around, really. Five funerals together? More deaths at the Manor, apparently. It's all very strange, but I hear it can happen like this sometimes. A bad flu season hits care homes quite badly."

I nod, grateful she hasn't noticed or at least commented on the other peculiarities afflicting the house.

"Who are you here for?" she asks.

"Margaret," I say. "And you?"

"Irene."

"I'm sorry for your loss."

"And I for yours."

She has a no-nonsense home-counties tenor to her voice and looks the country type, all Boxing Day shoots, gymkhanas, and pheasants.

I find her comforting. I had scores of friends like this lady once. Back when everyone wanted to be my friend. At the time, I didn't mind how closely these women watched me, copied everything I did. In fact, I rather liked it. I thought it underlined my significance, my importance. I know differently now. Imitation is not always the sincerest form of flattery. Sometimes it's just a desperate cry for attention, for relevance, for meaning.

"When our relatives become elderly, we expect their deaths, don't we?" the woman continues. "Abstractly, maybe, but not actually. We don't imagine having to bury them, or them ceasing to be here." Vacating the space. "It all seems too sudden, too soon. My mother was so healthy as an older person, so full of life." Irene was. I remember. "And her decline was so rapid, as though she was struck down, drained of life." She sees Ralph's pained expression, as do I, and she lays a hand on his arm. "Oh, I'm sorry. How thoughtless of me. Crass, even. I was just speaking aloud."

"It's okay, dear," I say reassuringly, though I'm shaking. She gives me a peculiar look, probably due to my use of the word "dear," rare in the mouth of the younger set.

Then she turns away and confides, "I feel a little guilty, actually. I didn't visit my mother as much as I should have done at the end. The truth is, visiting the Manor made me feel awfully unwell. Like I'd aged a year on every visit!"

I feel myself shrinking inwardly, crushed by my own culpability. I may as well have administered poison to the woman. To this and every other resident now residing in the grave. I'm doing it now, just being around these people. The thought winds me.

Ralph squeezes my hand with gentle reassurance.

He's not absolving me of responsibility. In fact, he accepted the truth before I did. No. He's reassuring me that he's here with me, that he loves me, regardless of what I inadvertently inflicted on others.

Facing the chapel, I see the truth. Clear. Final. As though I'm reading it on a page. It was there all along, if only I had looked.

Those recent dreams in which I'm lost in that confusion of a coffin maze . . . they were wrong. If only I'd looked in the other direction, behind the house towards the chapel, I might have seen it.

The dark stone building with its sharp dagger of a spire, probing the guts of the bulbous clouds above, whispers to me now. Telling me of the secret roiling beneath my skin. The evil sidling up to the worst parts of me but not yet touching my heart.

This darkness entered my body at the séance, I remember clearly now. I saw it from above. At first, I'd shunted it back into the depths of my consciousness, burying it under layers of more comforting things. But the daemon's been here all these weeks, squeezing the life from others, thriving as it injects months, years, decades into my veins. Stolen time. My youth and renewed visibility cost all these lives.

The neat little chapel looms, suddenly foreboding, gurgling its condemnation, rattling me with remorse. I want to scream at the thing that's overtaken me, at God, at whoever might be listening. *Take it back! Take it back, I don't want it.* I'd give up everything, even leave Ralph, if it meant saving him. Anything to turn back time and reinhabit old Harriet's dementia-ridden, arthritic bones.

Black spots invade my vision as we move closer to the chapel, my subconscious attempt to stamp out this excruciating realization. This stack of coffins, this fallen, dead flesh!

How could I have been so greedy? I didn't think I received enough attention the first time around? None of it was worth eating into the lives of everyone around me. How did this happen? How is it possible? This evil, evil thing inside me . . .

My head is spinning and throbbing simultaneously as I collapse into a pew. I squeeze my eyes shut, trying to push away the familiar images of the last time I felt like this. The church in Farnham. That first vision of William. I became dizzy as soon as I entered the churchyard, and the pain worsened as I approached the church. Is this the same thing? Is this—thing—inside me *protesting?*

I finally manage to open my eyes a fraction, grateful now the light is so dull outside. The diminutive stained-glass windows seem barely colored, and the chapel is deeply shadowed, lit only with candles, reminding me of the séance where all of this began. The remembrance drives fresh nails inside my skull. Ralph sits beside me, oblivious to my distress, which is both a relief and a worry. He looks too frail, even more so than when he woke this morning. Tears cloud his eyes, turning them into blurry shapes.

I killed his mother!

Darkness invades my peripheral vision again. Not just black dots this time but shapes—the corpses of the dead. Margaret, my William, screaming, *Why are you still alive?*

How can I possibly stay here, in this chapel, squashed and squeezed from every angle, assaulted, battered from within, pummeled from outside?

I must get out! And yet, I am compelled to stay, to support Ralph, to say goodbye to Margaret—my dear, dear friend, not the hideous corpse ghost.

"O Lord, open our lips," the priest begins. His eyes meet mine, and he speaks more loudly. "And our mouth shall proclaim your praise."

The small congregation, aside from Ralph and I, chant their assigned line before the priest continues. "Blessed are you, God of compassion and mercy, shepherd and protector of your grieving people, their beginning and their ending."

My neck feels stretched, my head pulled downwards.

Leave, the shadow shapes snarl in my ear.

"Lead us to a place of peace and refreshment; guide us to springs of life-giving water; wipe away the tears from our eyes and bring us to heaven . . ."

I can't possibly stay here. I'm going to die if I do!

Die then, the dark spirits screech in my brain.

I feel strangled, the pressure behind my temples becoming unbearable, as if the dead are inside my skull, pushing outwards. I'm going to explode.

"Where there is no more death, no more grief or crying or pain in your presence, Father, Son, and Holy Spirit."

"Blessed be God forever," the congregation chants again.

The words deliver a skull-shattering blast to my head.

"Christ yesterday and today, the beginning and the end, Alpha and Omega."

I fumble to my feet, managing to whisper to Ralph, "I have to go. I'm too unwell."

Concern crumples his deathly pale face, and he grasps the pew in front to steady himself as he rises too.

"No! Don't leave, Ralph," I say. "Stay and say goodbye to your mother."

Ralph complies but watches me worriedly as I practically run up the aisle, all eyes on me, questioning.

"All time belongs to him, and all ages," the priest concludes. "To him be glory and power, through every age and forever." I hear the congregation's final "amen" as the church doors close behind me, and I'm greeted by a thousand arrows of ice.

I hurry up the path away from the chapel, and with each step the pain abates, though my torment remains. My insides untwist, and the pressure in my skull fades to a gentle hum. I stop to catch my breath, recovering from the trauma of pain. I'm holding, not wearing, my coat and wrestle it onto my cold, wet arms. The umbrellas remain in the chapel.

I rush towards the Manor shivering, a stooped, wretched, pathetic thing. A golem. I ignore the churchyard with its crop of fresh graves and shiny marble headstones and shut out the sound of spades hitting earth. They're digging more holes. Preparing. It should have been me. Had I let myself unwind gracefully into the grave, there would only have been one. Not all these. Not this conveyer belt of cadavers.

How did I not loathe myself before now? Why didn't I see my conceit? My entitlement? The youthful mask I wear now is offensive. A slathered-on, cursed thing. Its cost has made it ugly, like wearing a wig from the shorn hair of children or a garment made from the skin of the dead.

I remember all the hours I spent here, wishing to be admired, seen, visible again. But it came at too high a price. The séance cost the hours, days, of the people around me. Those poor souls denied the years I had already lived and enjoyed. And Ralph. My Ralph. Our love cost him decades of his life. I could lose him soon, too, and the thought devastates me.

There must be a way out of this, I tell myself desperately, wet through and aching.

I deserve this pain, wheezing from the cold, wet air—a step towards penance, I think as I near the Manor again. Another exorcism, similar to the one performed on Florence Marryat as per her husband's journal? She died afterward, but I don't care anymore.

I must find a way to undo the damage.

22

As a child, I killed my pet rabbit by mistake.

I'd been dancing outside the long glass windows of my parents' sunroom and forgot we'd let her out to hop around the patch of lawn that bordered the gardens. I attempted a balletic leap, landing heavily, crushing her skull. She died instantly.

Something happened to my heart then. It felt as it does now. Malformed in my chest, threatening to stop pumping. The memory surfaces as I enter Marryat Manor amidst the sound of sobs echoing down the stairs. The kind of crying that comes with immense pain coupled with exhaustion, of giving way to the thing that's taking you. The weeping of the dying is the most excruciating sound I've ever heard. Pain contorts itself acrobatically around my body, and I accept its barbarism. I deserve it. I've caused so much of it.

"Dr. Phillips!" I call, my voice scratchy, cracked in a hundred places. "Dr. Phillips!"

From the hall, I look up the stairs. He could be anywhere, and I'm desperate to see him. After a minute, he emerges from a resident's room on the second floor and makes his way down to me wearily, his expression as leaden as the day outside.

"Harriet. You're wet," he observes, though without concern. I'm shaking with cold. Robotically, he takes my jacket, hangs it on the coat rack next to the door, then leads us to the living room where an aggressive fire is being maintained. It's pointless, given there's nobody here, the final residents busy upstairs dying. The roaring flames make me think of hell. Fire and brimstone. As though I'm hanging, snagged in the jaws of the underworld. My skin prickles from the sudden heat, or from fear, or desperation, or all three.

"Aren't you meant to be at the funeral?" he asks once we're seated. He looks a little afraid of me and registers how closely we're sitting. "I thought you wanted to support Ralph."

"It was too much. The chapel. Excruciating. I couldn't bear the torture." I look at him directly. "That time before, my last fit when I was in town . . ."

"Yes?"

"I think it was because I was at a church."

Sorrow, but lit with something warmer, crosses his features. A confirmation of his faith. For the first time, I envy his comfort from the divine. If I had believed, would I have been protected?

"You're right. About the . . . daemon." It may be the most difficult thing I've ever had to say. The thing inside hears and snarls, twisting my innards painfully. "You and Margaret were right about all of it." Hysteria swirls itself into anguish. "It's me causing all of this. I've hurt all these people, Dr. Phillips. But I didn't mean to!" The words squeak out of my dry throat, high and girlish.

"Oh, Harriet." By contrast, his is low, quiet, the voice of an old man. A father or grandfather even, attempting to console an irrational young woman. "I know you didn't mean to do all this. You and Margaret didn't know what you were dealing with having that séance. Even with what's recorded in those diaries and journals, it's hard to believe such a thing is real, that it could have such devastating consequences."

At another time, I may have been grateful for the consolation, the care and consideration, but the gravity of what's before me pushes me towards a precipice, dangling over the unknown. My fear is corporeal, not so much for myself now as for everyone else.

"Poor Ralph!" I wail. "You've seen what I've done to him!" Sobs wrack my body. I'm flailing, falling, unable to grab onto anything, unsure of what, if anything, can break my fall. Dr. Phillips remains still and silent, waiting until I'm able to continue. "Please, Dr. Phillips. You've got to help me!" I splutter, finally.

"Help you how?"

"Tell me what I need to do to stop hurting people. To get this thing out of me. An exorcism?" I look at him hopefully. He must have answers. "What about the mirror? That's where it resided before it entered me at the séance. Can't we put it back in there?"

I can't keep drawing the life from everyone around me. Soon I'll be the only one remaining who can bury the dead.

"Having reread the diaries again, I don't believe an exorcism and the mirror will work. The daemon was tricked once, but it knows better now. It will do anything, find anywhere, to live and feed. If the exorcism works, or you find some way to die, it will just find another host to live inside."

Host? I swallow hard against the vomit rising in my throat. Is that what I've been reduced to?

"But the church . . . I felt so unwell there. Like the daemon was in pain. That must have been a reaction to God, or belief, or something."

"It might," Dr. Phillips agrees. "But an exorcism will not cure you, Harriet. It will kill you. And once the daemon leaves your body, it will find a new person to inhabit and begin again."

I'm stunned into silence by the implication. That I'm doomed to walk the earth alone until the end of time. Abandoned. Unloved. Unseen. The irony isn't lost on me.

"What if I just went away, right now? Far, far away so this thing couldn't steal life anymore?"

"We still don't really know how it works," Dr. Phillips said. "So, there's no way to know how far away is enough to starve it." He folds his hands in his lap, staring down at them. "Besides, it's a bit too late for that, don't you think?"

"Too late?" My vision dissolves into tears again. Yes, it is too late.

For Margaret. For Ralph. How could I have extracted that beautiful man's life from him?

"I've come to think that your mere presence on earth is enough for the creature inside you to continue to feast, Harriet. You left Marryat Manor and yet we all continued to age. Ralph aged even more quickly than the rest of us due to his proximity to you, yes, but the aging has not stopped for the rest of us." He lowers his voice. "The staff . . . we might have been able to see Christmas had you not returned."

His bleak resignation destroys me, and I unspool. It's too much. I can't bear anymore. How I wish for a return of my old dementia, to be rid of the memory of what I've done. I would have gladly died on the day of the séance had I known what would happen. Hell, I would have sacrificed five, ten, twenty years, my whole life even, to have avoided afflicting all these people.

This time, Dr. Phillips moves closer and embraces me, leaning me into his shoulder where I sob, grateful but feeling worse simultaneously, as though I'm corroding him with my touch.

He holds me longer than I'd have thought wise, and then releases me and rises. "I must go tend to the residents, Harriet. See they're taken care of until the end." My tears dry up as he walks away.

I consider retreating to my room, finding comfort in my things. But upstairs, I'll be closer to the remaining residents, maybe worsening their pain, while being driven mad by their wails.

So, I stay in the empty living room instead, looking out the windows at the front of the house, watching the ice continue its assault on the landscape, waiting for Ralph's return from the burial. I watch two orderlies leave the house dressed in puffy black coats with fur-lined hoods, lifting the empty stretcher between them. They look like strange, modern undertakers. All day, they do this. Transport the dead. I think of the basement beneath me, the coffin maze, some filled, some waiting. Death upon death upon death.

Despite Dr. Phillips's statements to the contrary, there must be something I can do.

I think of Ralph only a little over a week ago, with his thick dark hair, clear blue eyes, his smile, his youth. The monster inside me has sucked all that out of him, stolen all those years. It was my greed that brought this on us. My need for recognition, for visibility. Losing my house gave me a false sense of losing everything, when in truth I still had so much left in my life. I had never really disappeared. The real Harriet was always there, seen, loved, and appreciated.

This daemon has destroyed all that. It's warped my behaviors, distorted my perspective. A parasite, it feeds off my goodness, darkens my motives, uses my needs to beguile me. I don't know where it ends and I begin. In trying to find Harriet again, I've let myself be consumed, eaten away.

There's movement outside as the men return with their stretcher, topped with another victim. Sleet has soaked the sheet, so it sticks to the body beneath, giving the impression of a sarcophagus. It must be someone from the funeral. Or a groundskeeper? I rush to the lobby to hold the front doors open for them.

"Thank you," the first man says as he backs through the door. His coat is soaked and slick, making him look almost oily. I dare to glance at the sheet-covered body as they pass, my shivers deepening to shakes again, perhaps from the cold wind through the open door or possibly creeping dread.

"What happened?" I ask the second man after closing the door behind him.

"He collapsed at the funeral." The man's voice is low, respectful. "Died instantly, apparently. Too late to save him."

It's difficult to speak. My throat feels constricted, though by what I'm not sure. As if the thing inside me knows something I don't. Does the daemon understand? *Do you, daemon?* My body trembles, my joints stiffening at the same time.

"The same with so many people around here," the first man agrees glumly. "Sudden cardiac arrest."

They shuffle into the hall with the stretcher, and I follow reluctantly, drawn by some strange need to stay near this body. It's obviously much heavier than the body I saw them move earlier.

"Do you know who it was?" I summon the courage to ask.

"Not a resident or a staff member this time. Old guy. I think he was mourning a relative. They were at the graveside."

"Oh, no." I clutch my chest, reaching out a hand blindly towards the wall to catch myself before I fall backwards. "No, no, no!"

"Ma'am?" The second man sounds as alarmed as I feel. "Everything okay?"

They set the stretcher down on the floor, then both men turn to look at me. Young, concerned, unaware their fate is now sealed. They don't know. They think we're of the same generation.

"I'm . . . not sure . . . I think he might be my . . ." My what? Boyfriend? Partner? Love of my life? "My partner."

The man's expression transforms into relief. "Oh, no, don't worry. He's a lot older than you."

"No, no." I hold out a hand, gasping, trying to steady my breath, which has become ragged. "My partner, he's been . . . unwell." *Don't let it be Ralph. Please don't let it be him.*

I don't know who my heart is pleading with. Anyone, anything that will listen.

"May I see him?" I ask finally. The men share an uncertain look. "Please. I need to know."

Both men shrug and one of them says tentatively, "If you're sure."

It might not be Ralph. It might be someone else. Ralph might still be alive.

The room holds its breath as the sodden sheet is drawn back to reveal a bald old man with a pallid face tinged with green, wearing a black woolen coat and an ill-fitting black shirt.

My Ralph. My poor, dead Ralph.

Someone is wailing nearby. It takes me a moment to realize it's me. The love of my life has died—*died!* I'm broken. Shattered. Not just because I've lost Ralph, but because the thing inside me did this.

I. Did. This!

I drop to my knees, keening and rocking unconsolably.

I knew this was coming, and that it had to come soon, but why the moment I was away from him? At his mother's funeral! I didn't get to say goodbye!

It's too unjust. Too unthinkable. I thought we'd have time left. I thought I'd be able to tell him I loved him again, hold him, tell him I was sorry. I needed him to know I was sorry, that I will find a way to stop this.

Now it's too late.

I push the sheet back further to hold his hand, so cold already. Not Ralph's hand. Not really. It's not him anymore, he's not there. But I can't bear to let him go. I must stay near him.

I howl and clutch at the skin near my throat. I want to tear this daemon out of me. Gouge it out, smother it, strangle it, smash it to pieces. My rage feels like the most powerful thing that could ever exist at this moment. It could kill anything. The injustice of having no way to undo this devastation!

"It has to die!" I screech. "Let this thing inside me die!"

"Harriet," a gentle voice emerges from behind me. Dr. Phillips places his hand on my shoulder.

"Look what I did!" I shriek, unable to catch my breath, not moving my eyes away from Ralph.

"I know. I know. You knew it was coming," Dr. Phillips says, as if the knowing was a comfort.

My rage is replaced with utter desolation as sobs take over again. "Not now! I didn't know it would be now! He died without me. I was waiting for him."

Dr. Phillips pulls me away from Ralph, forcing me to stand, holding me as my legs threaten to go out from under me. My body gives up. Everything gives up. He ushers me into a nearby chair, and as he does so, the men begin moving the stretcher away.

"Where are they taking him?" I ask, my voice catching and cracking midway.

"To the basement," Dr. Phillips answers. "With the others."

With all the other dead people. To be placed in a coffin that was waiting for him. Because he was always going to die. Because of me. Somewhere in the back of my mind I knew it. But I ignored it. The daemon could have blocked my realization. And I let it, because I didn't want it to be true, making me complicit in all of this.

"How can I have done this?"

"Stop this, Harriet." Dr. Phillips crouches in front of me, holding my hands. Another wail echoes from upstairs. He's needed by someone else. Another victim. I experience the same heart-stopping sensation as when I stepped on my pet rabbit.

My fault. Pain. Death. My fault.

"I thought it was you," I confess, closing my eyes for a moment, not wanting to witness more woundedness.

"Me?" Dr. Phillips asks. "What do you mean?"

"I thought you were like Harold Shipman. Killing everyone. Poison. Lethal doses of medication that couldn't be traced. I didn't really think you could do such a thing; I couldn't imagine it. But it seemed the most likely explanation."

When I open my eyes, Dr. Phillips looks sad, his lips compressing as he struggles to control his emotions. "It's a more likely explanation than a daemon, I suppose," he concedes generously. "More atrocious, doing this all on purpose, but yes, understandable."

My teeth are chattering. I'm very cold again. I hear the closing of the heavy basement door through the silence of the halls because there are so few people in this building. At least so few people still alive. I've hollowed it out.

Ralph! Oh, my Ralph. I'm so sorry.

"We'll have his funeral tomorrow," Dr. Phillips says as he straightens.

I notice that his remaining hair has fallen out since this morning. "Until then . . ."

"I'll try to stay away from everyone," I confirm, and he nods.

The library is cold and dark. Nobody maintains the fire here anymore, and I don't bother with the lights. I don't deserve lights.

I curl into one of the leather armchairs, my knees drawn into my chest, and give in to devastation. It pounds its fists into my eye sockets, jostles endless tears from me, brutalizes me, battering me down and down until it feels as though I'm going to meld into the leather of the chair, become part of it.

When my body is finally drained of all moisture and my tears and sobs cease, I stay there, unable to move, listening to the relentless sleet hammer the leaded windows. The guilty room is full of moving shadows, but they no longer scare me. There's nothing to be afraid of anymore. I don't care what happens to me.

This place—this rotten, evil Manor—is to blame for all of this. Malodorous secrets absorbed into the walls where they mutated, watchful, looking for a way out. Searching for an impure, needy soul and finding me. Jubilant when discovering my conscience's frailty. How the daemon must have laughed, watching me, as I reveled in what I thought was new freedom.

It was what they wanted—Marryat Manor, this daemon. I gave them exactly what they wanted. And worse, I enjoyed it. At least until it was too late. Now my life has toppled over, disaster dragging behind without letting go.

And still, despite all that's happened, everything this evil has wrought, I live. *I* live. Continuing to accelerate the aging of everyone around me. Pushing them towards death. Pushing and pushing.

Never going over the edge myself.

23

Terror's hangover drags me into an awkward, painful sleep.

I dream I'm dying. The cause is indiscernible, but I'm torn away from my body, finally free from the daemon's murderous cruelty. I'm spinning away from my flesh, from the damaged world behind, trying to keep my eyes open, looking for Ralph. It's the only time I've dreamt of ascending, though naturally, I've dreamt of falling.

The leather chair I wake in feels like a carbon prison. Too real, too much of the world. I've slept at an awkward angle and feel as though all my muscles on one side have been gathered in a single stitch. Now I must pull them apart painfully, breaking the thread. My throat is sore, sinuses stuffed, head pounding. I deserve this, far worse than this, but I resent it nonetheless because it reminds me of my traitorous physicality. While I am flesh, and the vessel for this daemon, I am inflicting pain on others. The knowledge is excruciating. It bangs on my bones, a venomous sting on my brain.

I must end this. I have no business being so selfishly alive. Every breath I take feels like a travesty, a further betrayal of Ralph.

The library presents no obvious opportunity to end my life unless I attempt suicide by a thousand papercuts. Time, I learned too late, is something not to be played with. It costs lives.

The fireplace is cold, but there must be matches nearby. I could set myself on fire but would likely spread the flames in the process, so others perish too. Groggy, I wander into the hall and to a downstairs bathroom. It's decorated with yellow wallpaper with tiny white flowers. Cheerful and twee to distract the elderly from death. I almost find it funny. The fact that I should be looking at it. That I'm emptying my bowels. That this is my life at this moment when Ralph is dead. Life itself is absurd. How stupid we all are, going about papering walls with little flowers so we can think nice thoughts while we shit.

As I wash my hands, I catch sight of my reflection in the little mirror over the sink. I am pale with shock and grief but recognize the woman looking vacantly back at me.

I hate her. *Hate* her. She has no place here. No right to live.

For the first time, I long for my old age, my gnarled arthritic knuckles, my stoop. I want to travel backwards, revisit the elderly, mid-stage dementia Harriet, the justly aged version of me. I want to tell her that it's okay, that she is still seen, still important. Tell her to rest and enjoy the beauty around her, feel privileged at having the time to appreciate it. One doesn't have to be the center of attention to be noticed and worthy, to have an impact. Looking down at the sink, something occurs to me, and I insert the old plug in the drain, letting the basin fill with warm water. Without taking a deep breath, I plunge my face into it.

Don't move, I tell myself. *Stay here. Breathe in water if you breathe at all.*

My lungs burn as I grip the sides of the sink. I've counted to twenty-five and crave oxygen. I grip tighter, willing myself to drown. I want to die. *Long* to die. I must, there's no other way forwards. And yet my body, the thing inside me, won't allow it. The daemon yanks my face up, out of the water, demanding a full breath of bathroom air.

I cry as the water soaks my collar. I don't think anyone in the history of the world has wanted to kill themselves more than I do in this moment, but I can't.

It's the daemon, the thing inside me keeping me alive so it can thrive, eating the lives of everyone around us.

There must be a way it will let me die. I must find a way to kill it.

I make my way upstairs, holding my breath to block out the acrid-sweet stench of decay. On the way, Florence Marryat stares out at me from her neat frame, delighted with herself as I was once too.

I continue up more of those immaculately polished stairs—past my room, past all the rooms—until I reach the hatch for the stairs to the attic, the roof. I was shown it only once, back when I first arrived at the Manor, was told it was only for emergencies.

This is the worst kind of emergency.

I climb into the attic, which is neatly organized with plastic crates filled with things like blankets, tablecloths, and party plates. Things for the celebrations no one here will ever have again. I don't pause for long before I locate the steps to the roof, then the door at the top of them. It opens easily, and I'm assaulted by freezing rain, drenching me in seconds. Still, I walk out into the angry blackness, the only light coming from the doorway behind me. From this part of the roof, I see the chapel, its colored story-telling windows lit by the candles within. Though I can't see it, the churchyard is there, too, nearly full. Ralph's grave will have been dug by now, open for him, waiting. I wonder if Dr. Phillips will know to place me there, too, or if I'll have a grave of my own.

In the end, I don't need to summon the courage to jump from the roof. The tiles are slick with ice, and my feet fly out from under me as I attempt to navigate the slope. I land heavily on my side then slip down the bumpy tiles, moving faster as I near the edge, like the world's speediest toboggan. This is it. This is how I die. My relief gathers as speed increases. My ankle catches the guttering, slowing me slightly. I register the crunching pain of it briefly before tipping off the side of the Manor like an icicle. A blast of air, then my body strikes the ground, such warm release in the impact.

When I open my eyes, I think I must be dead. No one could survive such a fall. Is this the great beyond? Consciousness after death? From the same perspective as their physical body?

Then icy pellets of rain batter my face, sink into my hair, chilling my scalp. I slowly, carefully test my limbs, wondering if I'm paralyzed, but no. I can stand easily. Move around fine. I am utterly unharmed. Not even bruised. I've landed on the side of the building where, ironically, Angel died. I look up towards the top of the Manor. Four high-ceilinged stories tower over me.

Impossible.

Yet, this thing is keeping me from death, its thirst for life bigger than my own determination to end it. The daemon inside.

Slowly, I make my way around the side of the building and in through the front entrance. I am wet, cold, covered with mud. My heart is broken, my soul torn apart, but jarringly, I have never felt more alive, as if the daemon is fueling me. Its energy prickling my every nerve ending and making my heart race so powerfully it feels as though it will fly right out of my chest. An inner heat, an inner fire, building, growing furnace strong.

I don't want it but don't know how to rid myself of it either.

The grandfather clock in the hall tells me it's 6 p.m., but there are no comforting aromas of cooking food wafting from the kitchen, few sounds at all, other than the sleet being persuaded into rain and battering the windows, and gentle shuffling from upstairs, closing doors. Then, husky murmurs and heavier tread on the landing above. The orderlies with their stretcher.

My heart sinks lower. I can't bear to see another sheeted victim. Not now.

Somehow, I know I will find Dr. Phillips in his office, though he's spent most of the day out tending to his patients. He's there, dozing in his chair, his exhaustion indifferent to the glare of the bright overhead fluorescent light. He's an old man now. A wave of tenderness floods me as I catch him in this rare, human moment of vulnerability. This man has dedicated his life to his patients, to making them comfortable, caring for their emotional states in addition to the physical. He lives to serve, both God and his fellow man, and he will perish before his time, like everyone else around him, through no fault of his own. All because of me.

He wakes with a start as I enter, and again, there's that flicker of fear when he first sees me. What's left of my heart collapses in on itself. I am a monster. Then he covers it quickly, his features falling into resignation. This might be more heartbreaking to me than his fear.

He is a man who knows he will die soon, and he knows exactly why.

"Still here, Harriet?" He sounds disappointed. I realize too late he wishes I'd left, that everyone would have been safer, lived a little bit longer if I had. Why hadn't I? I could have taken Ralph's car, driven out to the middle of a wood somewhere and disappeared.

Dr. Phillips sighs, coughing as he does so, then squints at me. "What happened to you, Harriet? You look as if you've gone twenty rounds with a tornado."

I glance down at myself and see that I'm a mess. Just because my body was fine after the fall doesn't mean the same for my clothes. My dress is ripped, one sleeve hanging off my arm forlornly. My stockings have huge runs and holes in them. One of the heels on my expensive shoes has broken off, and my hair on one side is matted to my head, a wet, tangled mess. I shrug, my appearance the least of my concerns.

"Well, I suppose it's better you're here, and not out there where other people can be affected, given that our fates are sealed." Dr. Phillips gives a short, strangled laugh, shaking his head at me. "Tried to end it all, did you?" He motions at my torn and muddy clothes, my dripping wet hair. "I suppose that's shaved a few more hours off each of our lives."

"I'm sorry," I stammer wretchedly.

"As I said before"—his speech is labored, slow—"you weren't to know."

I glance around the office, wondering what he might keep here that could kill me. "I need your help."

His stare is weary, his eyes rheumy. He removes his glasses and rubs them. "My help with what?"

"Killing myself," I tell him, and the room holds its breath. No space is ready for that kind of statement, no matter who it's from. "The longer I stay alive the more I hurt people, and it must stop. Please, Dr. Phillips. Help me." I'm crying, my voice wavering. A young woman attempting bravery. "I've tried. Drowning myself. Jumping off the roof. It's impossible."

He shakes his head, obviously expecting this conversation. "Your reflexes wouldn't have allowed the drowning," he says dismissively. "But the roof? You remained unharmed."

It's not a question.

"Completely. Not a bruise, not a scratch. I'm just a bit wet." I throw my hands up in exasperation. "Whatever's inside me is preventing my death. I'll show you. Do you have a knife? Or a medical instrument of some sort? Something sharp?"

Dr. Phillips regards me carefully for a moment, considering, then unlocks a small cabinet to the side of his desk and retrieves a long-bladed scalpel. He hands it to me, handle first. I take a deep breath, then drive the blade into the vein at my wrist, breaking the skin painfully, dragging the blade upwards into a long, dark-red split in my forearm. The agony deepens for a fraction of a moment, and I almost relish it. Dr. Phillips gasps and steps forwards, his instinct to heal urging him to clasp my wrist and staunch the flow of blood, but he stops himself as the blood slows to a trickle and the wound begins to heal itself before our eyes. In moments, the gash is gone, my body resolutely refusing the wound. Jointly, we stare at my wrist.

"My word!" Dr. Phillips exclaims. "I've never seen anything like it. It's—"

"Unholy. Inhuman. Please, you must help me, doctor."

He looks bewildered, lost as he holds out his hands. "I don't know what to do!"

"How can this happen? How?" I collapse, my mind desperately

scampering to stabilize. More tears well, and I give way to them, as broken as a person can be. Dr. Phillips is also crying, defeated as well. I've taken away his ability to heal and comfort. Removed his purpose out from under his feet.

"I'm sorry." His voice is as small as a little boy's. "There is nothing I can do, Harriet. Nothing to help you die. It's hopeless. As you've just demonstrated, you'll heal."

"So, then what? I just go on forever? Killing everyone I come into contact with?

Dr. Phillips shakes his head, his cheeks damp with tears. "I have no answers. None. Not one."

My eyes fall on the crucifix behind him. A stab of pain between the eyes.

"You could pray?" I've never made such a suggestion in my life before.

He only shrugs. "You think I haven't prayed for you already, Harriet? Every day. All the time. I pray for my patients constantly. I pray that you'll find a way through, that you'll be rid of this evil. It does no good." He coughs, a painful-sounding, phlegm-filled thing. It weakens him. "Whatever possessed you is too strong. Or it is His will to let it thrive. Whatever the reason, I . . . don't think it's in my power to stop it. It's beyond me." He looks at me sadly. "And it's beyond you too."

Some God, I think. This daemon's existence is irrefutable. This supernatural evil must therefore prove the existence of an opposite— something purely good. But not all-powerful, it seems. Omnipotence, omniscience, all good, outside of time. How can a God be all these things? How can this God not have stopped me?

But my mind again returns to Florence Marryat. They trapped the daemon outside of her, forcing it to lay dormant for over a century in the mirror. There must be a way to do that again.

God or no God.

I think about the chapel, the church in town, how every time I'm on hallowed ground the daemon reacts, hating it. The crucifix right here in the office. "It doesn't like sacred things. Perhaps we could trap it on hallowed ground, keep it from escaping. Then while it is weakened, I can kill myself and it will neither be able to heal me nor escape into another victim. It will finally be over, the daemon trapped inside my dead body."

Dr. Phillips stares at me for a long moment, considering the proposition. Finally, he leans back, arms crossed, looking thoughtful. "Maybe."

The solution is suddenly so clear. "You can bury me there on hallowed ground. The daemon will be trapped there, unable to escape." I look around the office again, my gaze landing on the locked medicine cabinet against the wall. "You can give me something—something to knock me out so I won't know what's happening—and strong enough to kill me a few hours later. I'm buried with Ralph in sacred ground, the pills kill me while the daemon is weakened, and it's then trapped."

After a deep breath, Dr. Phillips uncrosses his arms and leans forwards. "Are you sure, Harriet?"

"I'm sure," I say vehemently. "After all the destruction I've caused, I deserve to die. And I'll be with my beloved, or his body at least. It's all I've ever wanted."

Time ticks by slowly as I wait for his answer. In all honestly, now that I've found my solution, I'll go through with it anyway, with or without his help. He must sense this because he finally relents with a nod. "Come see me in the morning, before the burial."

24

I spend the night in the library, searching out evidence that my solution is the right one.

The rain has finally stopped, and the chilled moon regards me thoughtfully through the window, wondering what I'm made of. I'm sitting at a table, ignoring my shivers, the stack of spiritualism books I've ignored for so long in a haphazard mess in front of me.

These are the same books Margaret tried to push on me. The same Dr. Phillips insisted I read at the hotel. I am an obstinate person. Contrary and willful. Had I not refused them, I would have discovered the truth so much earlier and lives would have been saved.

Over the last few hours, fueled by resolve and adrenaline, I've trudged through the dreaded tomes—each as heavy and foreboding as a tombstone—forcing myself to concentrate. I hate these books, with their malodorous conceit, their vicious truths. I despise that spiritualism exists, that it has enticed this evil into the world. Spiritualism opened a door to let evil feed on weaknesses—on my need for control, and perceived loss of autonomy—things I didn't even notice were overtaking me, probably because they're so accepted in our modern world that thrives on pandering to the young and ignoring the old. Spiritualism, and the door it opened, has claimed lives, smashing through the Manor like a hurricane, pulling my friends, my lover, into the earth.

Now I must finish it. I must deny its authority in this world, I must cripple it, starve it.

"The darkness may not cross the hallowed grounds. It may not live where God loves."

There. The phrase appears to illuminate on the page. Two little sentences buried in the oldest of the spiritualist books. I found no answers in the diaries, only the desperate scampering of others trying and failing to rid this realm of monstrosity. But this new discovery proves I must be right. A small hope.

Despite my telling Dr. Phillips I wish to be buried with Ralph, I still long for William in this moment. His steady wisdom and comfort. Closing my eyes, I try to feel his presence, that blue butterfly of reassurance, not the ghoulish William, here to instruct in hate. But neither version of him visits me now that my decision is made. Now that I've realized what I've become, I no longer need hallucinations to lead me to the truth. Maybe they were old dementia Harriet trying to break through to me the whole time.

Burial. I'll be buried on the hallowed ground, trapping the daemon in the graveyard. This thing in me won't survive it. It won't escape me, won't be able to keep me alive, and won't survive my death. I'll be released from it at last. Perhaps I'll descend with it, wherever it falls.

The thought of lying in a coffin beside Ralph's corpse is terrifying. The fear is visceral, taking hold of my body, shaking it, churning my stomach painfully over and over as though my intestines were a pit of angry snakes writhing and lashing, trying to escape my body. But my mind remains clear. I'm resolute. There is no other choice, and this is an answer. Finally! An *answer*. Something I can do to stop all this suffering, and so much death. Rows of it. A churchyard full of it.

Time has run out.

The funeral is scheduled for tomorrow morning. The next on the conveyer belt. There are others who died today whose funerals will come after his. Judith flits into my mind, and I consider why I've not thought of her before now. I have attempted suicide multiple times today, yet I barely considered my daughter or granddaughter. I love my Judith, despite in some way feeling that her having sold my house and moved me into Marryat Manor was the root of all of this. My stupid, selfish decisions all came from that heartless act. But I don't blame my daughter. I can't. The elderly are removed from their homes every day and don't behave as I have. They don't take those risks. They don't ignore painful truths.

I am exhausted with emotion. I can bear no more. No more guilt. I can't underline another separation from someone I love.

Early the next morning, I go to Dr. Phillips's office, knowing he will still be there, on call, ready to help a patient in need.

I find him as I did before, sleeping in his chair. The fluorescent overhead light is off, but a glow emerges from the screensaver on his computer. Green, moving bubbles. Generic, non-personal. It casts a deathly glow over his face, and I wonder for a moment if he has died too. Maybe the time he's spent in my proximity has hastened his demise. The strain of caring for so many dying patients squeezing his aging heart into cardiac arrest.

To die alone in his office. A sad but fitting end.

Dr. Phillips wakes with a start, and his eyes immediately bolt onto mine.

"Harriet." He scrapes out my name, rasps a cough, then leans forwards, cradling his head in his hands. "What time is it?"

"It's early. I'm sorry to wake you." I haven't spoken for several hours and have barely drunk anything since yesterday, so my voice cracks too.

"Am I needed somewhere?" he asks seriously, ignoring his obviously crippling exhaustion.

"No. But I came for the drugs we talked about last night."

He nods and stands slowly, exhausted, unlocking his medicine cabinet to withdraw a small orange bottle. He hands it to me. "They're strong, Harriet. They will do the trick."

"Good."

He looks at me carefully. "Are you sure you want to do this?"

"Absolutely," I say. As I leave, I tell him, "Thank you, for everything, Dr. Phillips."

"Take care, Harriet," he calls after me. "Be kind to yourself."

Although I've never visited the basement before, it's as I expected. Low-ceilinged and musty, rustling with mice at its edges. I dry swallow a couple of pills, then look around. Old boxes and sheeted crates occupy a corner of the space, and the rest is dominated by coffins. Lined up, side by side, like blackened hospital beds in a ward. All shiny wood, ebony or mahogany, with brass handles. Identical to William's coffin. Identical to the ones in my dreams.

Some are open, some closed. I expected engraved brass plaques on each, but of course, there hasn't been time for engraving. Instead, each closed casket is topped with a folded card with the name of its inhabitant handwritten on it. They remind me of the place settings at the dinner parties I used to host. I insisted on writing the names myself. Black, looping script. Quite unlike these blue-Biro-inked ones, scratched out in block capital letters.

It feels oddly indecent that Ralph's coffin should not be the last closed casket in line. That there have been more deaths since his feels offensive. Other bodies overshadowing the enormity of him having been pushed from this life. And yet, I know these other poor souls are here because of me too.

My body is heavy, and I'm very cold. The pills Dr. Phillips gave me are beginning to work.

Am I ready? I could wait longer. Stay here. Think. But although I'm down in the basement, I'm still in the building, still extracting life from those living upstairs, and my minutes deny them hours, days. While I'm out in the world I'm giving the daemon a chance to escape my body, to continue its rampage elsewhere. It's time.

I take a shaky breath in, then let it out and swallow the remaining pills in the bottle before tossing it aside. Something moves in my peripheral vision, and I turn fast, startled, only to see my reflection in the big antique mirror from the séance, scabbed with its grotesque gargoyle decoration. I look pale and shaken, a glitchy hologram of a person. So young.

It occurs to me to smash it. I want to. But it's futile. It's only an object, after all, a victim, really, as I have been. We've both housed evil, kept it safe. I pay no attention to the unknowable shadows passing over the mirror's surface as the earth seems to drop from below my feet, as though my life has fallen out of me.

The pills. They're taking hold so quickly. As I droop, willing my legs to move towards Ralph's coffin, I feel increasing relief with every dragging step. Forwards to Ralph's body. Forwards to Ralph, and to the end of this madness.

Finally, I open the lid of the coffin. Ralph's old-man body lies there, cushioned by the dark-red, vampiric satin nobody will ever see again. Only me, now. Achingly, I hook my foot into the bottom of the coffin between Ralph's shoes, then pull myself up with the little energy I have left. Moving is so difficult as I'm hauled towards unconsciousness.

I fall onto Ralph with a thud, his body stiff and unyielding as a stone. But he's still my Ralph. His clothes still smell of his aftershave, his skin of soap. Was it only yesterday morning that we left the guest house in Brighton? It seems so long ago. Time continues to play its contemptuous game.

"I'm sorry," I whisper, my voice limp, barely holding on. "This is the only way. I can make it stop. Finally. And we'll be together."

It takes great effort to stretch my arm up and pull down the lid of the coffin. A simple action, like the turning on of a bedside lamp.

I take comfort in the fact it's the last movement my body will ever have to make. But the daemon inside me bubbles. I feel its energy, as though it's excited. Then the blackness folds in, becomes larger, taking me away into a half-dream, a manic scrambling of consciousness, flicking through the pages of my life. Margaret. Ralph. The maze. The mirror. Florence Marryat's portrait. Her diary. Dr. Phillips. Pills. A coffin. A body. The mirror. Two bodies. The mirror.

My eyes open to pitch blackness. Where am I? I strain to see, but there isn't even the faintest hint of light. I'm lying on my stomach atop a cold, knobbly rock, my frame crooked and bent around its contours. I roll onto my side and reach out with one hand, hitting a smooth, unyielding surface. I struggle to free my other hand, which had been pinned at my side. Trying to make sense of it, I grope and push, but the silky walls don't budge.

A low grumble, almost imperceptible, begins to reverberate, as consciousness slowly asserts itself. And then a flutter of anxiety grips me. A fleeting, panicked thought takes shape but remains just out of reach.

William?

The sound grows louder, like a motor, a chainsaw.

Margaret?

Still louder, and I realize it's the sound of pure terror, of every whipping and tearing, smashing and pummeling—of every trauma, every painful death—combined.

I lift my head and immediately bang it on the low ceiling. A groan escapes my lips, the only sound aside from that infernal rumbling.

All of a sudden, my memories flood in and I realize where I am. What this cramped space is. What it means.

Not a rock. A body. Ralph's body. My beloved Ralph. Dead. Like I'm supposed to be. Like the daemon is supposed to be.

"No!" A scream explodes from me, raking my throat. "Help! Help me!" I pound my fists, but the walls around me are solid, unrelenting. "Somebody! William!"

Panic gripping every inch of me, I rip at the silky lining above me, then scratch at the wood beneath it. I scratch and hit and claw until my fingernails are raw, until blood drips down onto my face.

I try to roll on my back but there isn't enough space. The rock beneath me offers no slack. The rock. Ralph. My beloved Ralph, dead, beneath me.

The rumbling grows closer and closer until it transforms into a deep, low, raspy whisper that fills the cramped space:

"*Sum quod eris.*" I am as you will be.

The daemon lives on, as do I, buried beneath the earth, entombed with my dead lover.

We are both trapped in this box.

And we always will be.

Other books by
DANI LAMIA

Scavenger Hunt
Winner of the First Horizon Award for best debut novel and short-listed for the Grand Prize for the Eric Hoffer Award, *Scavenger Hunt* is the story of an extremely wealthy family feuding over the estate of their recently deceased father. The siblings are sent on a scavenger hunt with the family fortune as the prize. But things turn deadly as long-buried secrets are revealed and it becomes clear that only the winner will survive.

The Raven
In a world where dreams and reality overlap, a dream-world stalker begins killing the tormentors of a bullied high school girl. But when she tries to stop the deadly attacks on her behalf, the Raven sets his terrifying sights on her. Silver Medal winner of the IBPA Benjamin Franklin Award for Horror.

666 Gable Way
When a young woman who has always suppressed her disturbing psychic powers finds herself faced with a hostile witches' coven, she must embrace her power in order to save her life. A finalist for the Eric Hoffer Award for Horror.

Stay up to date
Follow Dani on Amazon

https://www.amazon.com/author/danilamia